To Him That Hath
A Novel Of The West Of Today

by

Ralph Connor

Double 9
BOOKS

To Him That Hath
A Novel Of The West Of Today
by Ralph Connor

ISBN: 978-93-65789-70-6

Published by

DOUBLE 9 BOOKS

2/13-B, Ansari Road
Daryaganj, New Delhi – 110002
info@double9books.com
www.double9books.com
Tel. 011-40042856

This book is under public domain

ABOUT THE AUTHOR

Charles William Gordon, CMG, commonly known as Ralph Connor, was a Canadian novelist who used the Connor pen name while simultaneously serving as a church leader, first in the Presbyterian and later in the United Church of Canada. Gordon was born in Glengarry County, Canada West. He was the son of Rev. Daniel and Mary Robertson Gordon. His father was a Free Church of Scotland missionary in Upper Canada. While at Knox College, Gordon was impressed by Superintendent Robertson's presentation on the issues in the West, which led him to pursue his summer mission work there and, eventually, to dedicate his life working for reform and mission in Western Canada. Gordon felt called to become one of these missionaries, establishing not only churches, but also Christian social and moral change in Western Canada. To that purpose, Gordon completed his theological schooling in Edinburgh, Scotland, where he was strengthened in his resolve to introduce the church to Western Canada. During the 1870s and 1880s, theological attitudes in Scotland shifted toward liberalism. Gordon was very interested in the endeavor to harmonize ancient Christian doctrine with modern achievements such as science and evolution. He became a powerful advocate for Western social change and church unity.

CONTENTS

CHAPTER I
THE GAME

"Forty-Love."

"Game! and Set. Six to two."

A ripple of cheers ran round the court, followed by a buzz of excited conversation.

The young men smiled at each other and at their friends on the side lines and proceeded to change courts for the next set, pausing for refreshments on the way.

"Much too lazy, Captain Jack. I am quite out of patience with you," cried a young girl whose brown eyes were dancing with mock indignation.

Captain Jack turned with a slightly bored look on his thin dark face.

"Too lazy, Frances?" drawled he. "I believe you. But think of the temperature."

"You have humiliated me dreadfully," she said severely.

"Humiliated you? You shock me. But how, pray?" Captain Jack's eyes opened wide.

"You, a Canadian, and our best player—at least, you used to be—to allow yourself to be beaten by a—a—" she glanced at his opponent with a defiant smile—"a foreigner."

"Oh! I say, Miss Frances," exclaimed that young man.

"A foreigner?" exclaimed Captain Jack. "Better not let Adrien hear you." He turned toward a tall fair girl standing near.

"What's that?" said the girl. "Did I hear aright?"

"Well, he's not a Canadian, I mean," said Frances, sticking to her guns. "Besides, I can't stand Adrien crowing over me. She is already far too English, don-che-know. You have given her one more occasion for triumph over us Colonials."

"Ah, this is serious," said Captain Jack. "But really it is too hot you know for—what shall I say?—International complications."

"Jack, you are plain lazy," said Frances. "You know you are. You don't deserve to win, but if you really would put your back into it—"

"Oh, come, Frances. Why! You don't know that my cousin played for his College at Oxford. And that is saying something," said Adrien.

"There you are, Jack! That's the sort of thing I have to live with," said Frances. "She thinks that settles everything."

"Well, doesn't it rather?" smiled Adrien.

"Oh, Jack, if you have any regard for your country, not to say my unworthy self, won't you humble her?" implored Frances. "If you would only buck up!"

"He will need to, eh, Adrien?" said a young fellow standing near, slowly sipping his drink.

"I think so. Indeed, I am quite sure of it," coolly replied the girl addressed. "But I really think it is quite useless."

"Ha! Ha! Cheer up, Jack," laughed the young man, Stillwell by name.

"Really, old chap, I feel I must beat you this set," said Captain Jack to the young Englishman. "My country's credit as well as my own is at stake, you see."

"Both are fairly assured, I should say," said the Englishman.

"Not to-day," said Stillwell, with a suspicion of a polite sneer in his voice. "My money says so."

"Canada vs. the Old Country!" cried a voice from the company.

"Now, Jack, Jack, remember," implored Frances.

"You have no mercy, Miss Frances, I see," said the Englishman, looking straight into her eyes.

"Absolutely none," she replied, smiling saucily at him.

"Vae victis, eh, old chap?" said Sidney, as they sauntered off together to their respective courts. "By the way, who is that Stillwell chap?" he asked in a low voice of Captain Jack as they moved away from the others. "Of any particular importance?"

"I think you've got him all right," replied Jack carelessly. The Englishman nodded.

"He somehow gets my goat," said Jack. The Englishman looked mystified.

"Rubs me the wrong way, you know."

"Oh, very good, very good. I must remember that."

"He rather fancies his own game, too," said Jack, "and he has come on the last year or two. In more ways than one," he added as an afterthought.

As they faced each other on the court it was Stillwell's voice that rang out:

"Now then, England!"

"Canada!" cried a girl's voice that was easily recognised as that of Frances Amory.

"Thumbs down, eh, Maitland?" said the Englishman, waving a hand toward his charming enemy.

Whatever the cause, whether from the spur supplied by the young lady who had constituted herself his champion or from the sting from the man for whom for reasons sufficient for himself he had only feelings of hostility and dislike, the game put up by Captain Jack was of quite a different brand from that he had previously furnished. From the first service he took the offensive and throughout played brilliant, aggressive, even smashing tennis, so much so that his opponent appeared to be almost outclassed and at the close the figures of the first set were exactly reversed, standing six to two in Captain Jack's favour.

The warmth of the cheers that followed attested the popularity of the win.

"My word, old chap, that is top-hole tennis," said the Englishman, warmly congratulating him.

"Luck, old boy, brilliant luck!" said Captain Jack. "Couldn't do it again for a bet."

"You must do it just once more," said Frances, coming to meet the players. "Oh, you dear old thing. Come and be refreshed. Here is the longest, coolest thing in drinks this Club affords. And one for you, too," she added, turning to the Englishman. "You played a great game."

"Did I not? I was at the top of my form," said the Englishman gallantly. "But all in vain, as you see."

"Now for the final," cried Frances eagerly.

"Dear lady," said Captain Jack, affecting supreme exhaustion, "as you are mighty, be merciful! Let it suffice that we appear to have given you an exposition of fairly respectable tennis. I am quite done."

"A great win, Jack," said Adrien, offering her hand in congratulation.

"All flukes count, eh, Maitland?" laughed Stillwell, unable in spite of his laugh to keep the bite out of his voice.

"Fluke?" exclaimed the Englishman in a slow drawling voice. "I call it ripping good tennis, if I am a judge."

A murmur of approval ran through the company, crowding about with congratulations to both players.

"Oh, of course, of course," said Stillwell, noting the criticism of his unsportsmanlike remark. "What I mean is, Maitland is clearly out of condition. If he were not I wouldn't mind taking him on myself," he added with another laugh.

"Now, do you mean?" said Captain Jack lazily.

"We will wait till the match is played out," said Stillwell with easy confidence. "Some other day, when you are in shape, eh?" he added, smiling at Maitland.

"Now if you like, or after the match, or any old time," said Captain Jack, looking at Stillwell with hard grey, unsmiling eyes. "I understand you have come up on your game during the war."

Stillwell's face burned a furious red at the little laugh that went round among Captain Jack's friends.

"Frankly, I have had enough for to-day," said the Englishman to Jack.

"All right, old chap, if you don't really mind. Though I feel you would certainly take the odd set."

"Not a bit of it, by Jove. I am quite satisfied to let it go at that. We will have another go some time."

"Any time that suits you—to-morrow, eh?"

"To-morrow be it," said the Englishman.

"Now, then, Stillwell," said Captain Jack, with a curt nod at him. "Whenever you are ready."

"Oh, come, Maitland. I was only joshing, you know. You don't want to play with me to-day," said Stillwell, not relishing the look on Maitland's face. "We can have a set any time."

"No!" said Maitland shortly. "It's now or never."

"Oh, all right," said Stillwell, with an uneasy laugh, going into the Club house for his racquet.

The proposed match had brought a new atmosphere into the Club house, an atmosphere of contest with all the fun left out.

"I don't like this at all," said a man with iron grey hair and deeply tanned face.

"One can't well object, Russell," said a younger man, evidently a friend of Stillwell's. "Maitland brought it on, and I hope he gets mighty well trimmed. He is altogether too high and mighty these days."

"Oh, I don't agree with you at all," broke in Frances, in a voice coldly proper. "You heard what Mr. Stillwell said?"

"Well, not exactly."

"Ah, I might have guessed you had not," answered the young lady, turning away.

Edwards looked foolishly round upon the circle of men who stood grinning at him.

"Now will you be good?" said a youngster who had led the laugh at Edwards' expense.

"What the devil are you laughing at, Menzies?" he asked hotly.

"Why, don't you see the joke?" enquired Menzies innocently. "Well, carry on! You will to-morrow."

Edwards growled out an oath and took himself off.

Meantime the match was making furious progress, with the fury, it must be confessed, confined to one side only of the net. Captain Jack was playing a driving, ruthless game, snatching and employing without mercy every advantage that he could legitimately claim. He delivered his service with deadly precision, following up at the net with a smashing return, which left his opponent helpless. His aggressive tactics gave his opponent almost no opportunity to score, and he kept the pace going at the height of his speed. The onlookers were divided in their sentiments. Stillwell had a strong following of his own who expressed their feelings by their silence at Jack's brilliant strokes and their loud approval of Stillwell's good work when he gave them opportunity, while many of Maitland's friends deprecated his tactics and more especially his spirit.

At whirlwind pace Captain Jack made the first three games a "love" score, leaving his opponent dazed, bewildered with his smashing play and blind with rage at his contemptuous bearing.

"I think I must go home, Frances," said Adrien to her friend, her face pale, her head carried high.

Frances seized her by the arm and drew her to one side.

"Adrien, you must not go! You simply must not!" she said in a low tense voice. "It will be misunderstood, and—"

"I am going, Frances," said her friend in a cold, clear voice. "I have had enough tennis for this afternoon. Where is Sidney? Ah, there he is across the court. No! Let me go, Frances!"

"You simply must not go like that in the middle of a game, Adrien. Wait at least till this game is over," said her friend, clutching hard at her arm.

"Very well. Let us go to Sidney," said Adrien.

Together they made their way round the court almost wholly unobserved, so intent was the crowd upon the struggle going on before them. As the game finished Adrien laid her hand upon her cousin's arm.

"Haven't you had enough of this?" she said. Her voice carried clear across the court.

"What d'ye say? By Jove, no!" said her cousin in a joyous voice. "This is the most cheering thing I've seen for many moons, Adrien. Eh, what? Oh, I beg pardon, are you seedy?" he added glancing at her. "Oh, certainly, I'll come at once."

"Not at all. Don't think of it. I have a call to make on my way home. Please don't come."

"But, Adrien, I say, this will be over now in a few minutes. Can't you really wait?"

"No, I am not in the least interested in this—this kind of tennis," she said in a bored voice.

Her tone, pitched rather higher than usual, carried to the ears of the players who were changing ends at the moment. Both of the men glanced at her. Stillwell's face showed swift gratitude. On Jack's face the shadow darkened but except for a slight straightening of the line of his lips he gave no sign.

"You are quite sure you don't care?" said Sidney. "You don't want me? This really is great, you know."

"Not for worlds would I drag you away," said Adrien in a cool, clear voice. "Frances will keep you company." She turned to her friend. "Look after him, Frances," she said. "Good-bye. Dinner at seven to-night, you know."

"Right-o!" said Sidney, raising his hat in farewell. "By Jove, I wouldn't miss this for millions," he continued, making room for Frances beside him. "Your young friend is really somewhat violent in his style, eh, what?"

"There are times when violence is the only possible thing," replied Frances grimly.

"By the way, who is the victim? I mean, what is he exactly?"

"Mr. Stillwell? Oh, he is the son of his father, the biggest merchant in Blackwater. Oh, lovely! Beautiful return! Jack is simply away above his form! And something of a merchant and financier on his own account, to be quite fair. Making money fast and using it wisely. But I'm not going to talk about him. You see a lot of him about the Rectory, don't you?"

"Well, something," replied Sidney. "I can't quite understand the situation, I confess. To be quite frank, I don't cotton much to him. A bit sweetish, eh, what?"

"Yes, at the Rectory doubtless. I would hardly attribute to him a sweet disposition. Oh, quit talking about him. He had flat feet in the war, I think it was. Jack's twin brother was killed, you know—and mine—well, you know how mine is."

A swift vision of a bright-faced, cheery-voiced soldier, feeling his way around a darkened room in the Amory home, leaped to Sidney's mind and overwhelmed him with pity and self-reproach.

"Dear Miss Frances, will you forgive me? I hadn't quite got on to the thing. I understand the game better now."

"Now, I don't want to poison your mind. I shouldn't have said that—about the flat feet, I mean. He goes to the Rectory, you know. I want to be fair—"

"Please don't worry. We know all about that sort at home," said Sidney, touching her hand for a moment. "My word, that was a hot one! The flat-footed Johnnie is obviously bewildered. The last game was sheer massacre, eh, what?"

If Maitland was not in form there was no sign of it in his work on the court. There was little of courtesy, less of fun and nothing at all of mercy in his play. From first to last and without reprieve he drove his game ruthlessly to a finish. So terrific, so resistless were his attacks, so coldly relentless the spirit he showed, ignoring utterly all attempts at friendly exchange of courtesy, that the unhappy and enraged Stillwell, becoming utterly demoralized, lost his nerve, lost his control and hopelessly lost every chance he ever possessed of winning a single game of the set which closed with the score six to nothing.

At the conclusion of the set Stillwell, with no pretense of explanation or apology, left the courts to his enemy who stood waiting his appearance in a silence so oppressive that it seemed to rest like a pall upon the side lines. So overwhelming was Stillwell's defeat, so humiliating his exhibition of total collapse of morale that the company received the result with but slight manifestation of feeling. Without any show of sympathy even his friends slipped away, as if unwilling to add to his humiliation by their commiseration. On the other side, the congratulations offered Maitland were for the most part lacking in the spontaneity that is supposed to be proper to such a smashing victory. Some of his friends seemed to feel as if they had been called upon to witness an unworthy thing. Not so, however, with either Frances Amory or Sidney Templeton. Both greeted Captain Jack with enthusiasm and warmth, openly and freely rejoicing in his victory.

"By Jove, Maitland, that was tremendous, appalling, eh, what?"

"I meant it to be so," said Maitland grimly, "else I should not have played with him."

"It was coming to him," said Frances. "I am simply completely delighted."

"Can I give you a lift home, Frances?" said Maitland. "Let us get away. You, too, Templeton," he added to Sidney, who was lingering near the young lady in obvious unwillingness to leave her side.

"Oh, thanks! Sure you have room?" he said. "All right. You know my cousin left me in your care."

"Oh, indeed! Well, come along then, since our hero is so good. Really, I am uplifted to quite an unusual height of glorious exultation."

"Don't rub it in, Frank," said Jack gloomily. "I made an ass of myself, I know quite well."

"What rot, Jack. Every one of your friends was tickled to death."

"Adrien, for instance, eh?" said Jack with a bitter little laugh, taking his place at the wheel.

"Oh, Adrien!" replied Frances. "Well, you know Adrien! She is—just Adrien."

As he turned into the street there was a sound of rushing feet.

"Hello, Captain Jack! Oh, Captain Jack! Wait for me! You have room, haven't you?"

A whirlwind of flashing legs and windblown masses of gold-red hair, which realised itself into a young girl of about sixteen, bore down on the car. It was Adrien's younger sister, Patricia, and at once her pride and her terror.

"Why, Patsy, where on earth did you come from? Of course! Get in! Glad to have you, old chap."

"Oh, Captain Jack, what a game! What a wonderful game! And Rupert has been playing all summer and awfully well! And you have hardly played a game! I was awfully pleased—"

"Were you? I'm not sure that I was," replied Captain Jack.

"Well, you WERE savage, you know. You looked as if you were in a fight."

"Did I? That was very rotten of me, wasn't it?"

"Oh, I don't know exactly. But it was a wonderful game. Of course, one doesn't play tennis like a fight, I suppose."

"No! You are quite right, Pat," replied Captain Jack. "You see, I'm afraid I lost my temper a bit, which is horribly bad form I know, and—well, I wanted to fight rather than play, and of course one couldn't fight on the tennis court in the presence of a lot of ladies, you see."

"Well, I'm glad you didn't fight, Captain Jack. You have had enough of fighting, haven't you? And Rupert is really very nice, you know. He has a wonderful car and he lets me drive it, and he always brings a box of chocolates every time he comes."

"He must be perfectly lovely," said Captain Jack, with a grin at her.

The girl laughed a laugh of such infectious jollity that Captain Jack was forced to join with her.

"That's one for you, Captain Jack," she cried. "I know I am a pig where chocs are concerned, and I do love to drive a car. But, really, Rupert is quite nice. He is so funny. He makes Mamma laugh. Though he does tease me a lot."

Captain Jack drove on in silence for some moments.

"I was glad to see you playing though to-day, Captain Jack."

"Where were you? I didn't see you anywhere."

"Not likely!" She glanced behind her at the others in the back seat. She need not have given them a thought, they were too deeply engrossed to heed her. "Do you know where I was? In the crutch of the big elm—you know!"

"Don't I!" said Captain Jack. "A splendid seat, but—"

"Wouldn't Adrien be shocked?" said the girl, with a deliciously mischievous twinkle in her eye. "Or, at least, she would pretend to be.

Adrien thinks she must train me down a bit, you know. She says I have most awful manners. She wants Mamma to send me over to England to her school. But I don't want to go, you bet. Besides, I don't think Dad can afford it so they can't send me. Anyway, I could have good manners if I wanted to. I could act just like Adrien if I wanted to—I mean, for a while. But that was a real game. I felt sorry for Rupert, a little. You see, he didn't seem to know what to do or how to begin. And you looked so terrible! Now in the game with Cousin Sidney you were so different, and you played so awfully well, too, but differently. Somehow, it was just like gentlemen playing, you know—"

"You have hit it, Patsy,—a regular bull!" said Captain Jack.

"Oh, I don't mean—" began the girl in confusion, rare with her.

"Yes, you do, Pat. Stick to your guns."

"Well, I will. The first game everybody loved to watch. The second game—somehow it made me wish Rupert had been a Hun. I'd have loved it then."

"By Jove, Patsy, you're right on the target. You've scored again."

"Oh, I'm not saying just what I want—but I hope you know what I mean."

"Your meaning hits me right in the eye. And you are quite right. The tennis court is no place for a fight, eh? And, after all, Rupert Stillwell is no Hun."

"But you haven't been playing this summer at all, Captain Jack," said the girl, changing the subject. "Why not?" The girl's tone was quite severe. "And you don't do a lot of things you used to do, and you don't go to places, and you are different." The blue eyes earnestly searched his face.

"Am I different?" he asked slowly. "Well, everybody is different. And then, you know, I am busy. A business man has his hours and he must stick to them."

"Oh, I don't believe you a bit. You don't need to be down at the mills all the time. Look at Rupert. He doesn't need to be at his father's office."

"Apparently not."

"He gets off whenever he wants to."

"Looks like it."

"And why can't you?"

"Well, you see, I am not Rupert," said Captain Jack, grinning at her.

"Now you are horrible. Why don't you do as you used to do? You know you could if you wanted to."

"Yes, I suppose, if I wanted to," said Captain Jack, suddenly grave.

"You don't want to," said the girl, quick to catch his mood.

"Well, you know, Patsy dear, things are different, and I suppose I am too. I don't care much for a lot of things."

"You just look as if you didn't care for anything or anybody sometimes, Captain Jack," said Patricia quietly. Then after a few moments she burst forth: "Oh, don't you remember your hockey team? Oh! oh! oh! I used to sit and just hold my heart from jumping. It nearly used to choke me when you would tear down the ice with the puck."

"That was long ago, Pat dear. I guess I was—ah—very young then, eh?"

"Yes, I know," nodded the girl. "I feel the same way—I was just a kid then."

"Ah, yes," said Captain Jack, with never a smile. "You were just—let's see—twelve, was it?"

"Yes, twelve. And I felt just a kid."

"And now?" Captain Jack's voice was quite grave.

"Now? Well, I am not exactly a kid. At least, not the same kind of kid. And, as you say, a lot of things are different. I think I know how you feel. I was like that, too—after—after—Herbert—" The girl paused, with her lips quivering. "It was all different—so different. Everything we used to do, I didn't feel like doing. And I suppose that's the way with you, Captain Jack, with Andy—and then your Mother, too." She leaned close to him and put her hand timidly on his arm.

Captain Jack, sitting up very straight and looking very grave, felt the thrill of the timid touch run through his very heart. A rush of warm, tender emotion such as he had not allowed himself for many months suddenly surprised him, filling his eyes and choking his throat. Since his return from the war he had without knowledge been yearning for just such an understanding touch as this child with her womanly instinct had given him. He withdrew one hand from the wheel and took the warm clinging fingers tight in his and waited in silence till he was sure of himself. He drove some blocks before he was quite master of his voice. Then, releasing the fingers, he turned his face toward the girl.

"You are a real pal, aren't you, Patsy old girl?" he said with a very bright smile at her.

"I want to be! Oh, I would love to be!" she said, with a swift intake of breath. "And after a while you will be just as you were before you went away."

"Hardly, I fear, Patsy."

"Well, not the same, but different from what you are now. No, I don't mean that a bit, Captain Jack. But perhaps you know—I do want to see you on the ice again. Oh, it would be wonderful! Of course, the old team wouldn't be there—Herbert and Phil and Andy. Why! You are the only one left! And Rupert." She added the name doubtfully. "It WOULD be different! oh, so different! Oh! I don't wonder you don't care, Captain Jack. I won't wonder—" There was a little choke in the young voice. "I see it now—"

"I think you understand, Patsy, and you are a little brick," said Captain Jack in a low, hurried tone. "And I am going to try. Anyway, whatever happens, we will be pals."

The girl caught his arm tight in her clasped hands and in a low voice she said, "Always and always, Captain Jack, and evermore." And till they drew up at the Rectory door no more was said.

Maitland drove homeward through the mellow autumn evening with a warmer, kindlier glow in his heart than he had known through all the dreary weeks that had followed his return from the war. For the war had wrought desolation for him in a home once rich in the things that make life worth while, by taking from it his mother, whose rare soul qualities had won and held through her life the love, the passionate, adoring love of her sons, and his twin brother, the comrade, chum, friend of all his days, with whose life his own had grown into a complete and ideal unity, deprived of whom his life was left like a body from whose raw and quivering flesh one-half had been torn away.

The war had left his life otherwise bruised and maimed in ways known only to himself.

Returning thus from his soul-devastating experience of war to find his life desolate and maimed in all that gave it value, he made the appalling discovery that he was left almost alone of all whom he had known and loved in past days. For of his close friends none were left as before. For the most part they were lying on one or other of the five battle fronts of the war. Others had found service in other spheres. Only one was still in his home town, poor old Phil Amory, Frances' brother, half-blind in his darkened room, but to bring anything of his own heart burden to that brave soul seemed sacrilege or worse. True enough, he was passing through the new and thrilling experience of making acquaintance with his father. But old Grant Maitland was a hard man to know, and they were too much alike in their reserve and in their poverty of self-expression to make mutual acquaintance anything but a slow and in some ways a painful process.

Hence in Maitland's heart there was an almost extravagant gratitude toward this young generous-hearted girl whose touch had thrilled his heart and whose voice with its passionate note of loyal and understanding comradeship still sang like music in his soul, "Always and always, Captain Jack, and evermore."

"By Jove, I have got to find some way of playing up to that," he said aloud, as he turned from the gravelled driveway into the street. And in the months that followed he was to find that the search to which he then committed himself was to call for the utmost of the powers of soul which were his.

CHAPTER II
THE COST OF SACRIFICE

Perrotte was by all odds the best all-round man in the planing mill, and for the simple reason that for fifteen years he had followed the lumber from the raw wood through the various machines till he knew woods and machines and their ways as no other in the mill unless it was old Grant Maitland himself. Fifteen years ago Perrotte had drifted down from the woods, beating his way on a lumber train, having left his winter's pay behind him at the verge of civilisation, with old Joe Barbeau and Joe's "chucker out." It was the "chucker out" that dragged him out of the "snake room" and, all unwitting, had given him a flying start toward a better life. Perrotte came to Maitland when the season's work was at its height and every saw and planer were roaring night and day.

"Want a job?" Maitland had shouted over the tearing saw at him. "What can you do?"

"(H)axe-man me," growled Perrotte, looking up at him, half wistful, half sullen.

"See that slab? Grab it, pile it yonder. The boards, slide over the shoot." For these were still primitive days for labor-saving devices, and men were still the cheapest thing about a mill.

Perrotte grabbed the slab, heaved it down to its pile of waste, the next board he slid into the shoot, and so continued till noon found him pale and staggering.

"What's the matter with you?" said Maitland.

"Notting—me bon," said Perrotte, and, clutching at the door jamb, hung there gasping.

Maitland's keen blue eyes searched his face. "Huh! When did you last eat? Come! No lying!"

"Two day," said Perrotte, fighting for breath and nerve.

"Here, boy," shouted Maitland to a chore lad slouching by, "jump for that cook house and fetch a cup of coffee, and be quick."

The boss' tone injected energy into the gawky lad. In three minutes Perrotte was seated on a pile of slabs, drinking a cup of coffee; in five minutes more he stood up, ready for "(h)anny man, (h)anny ting." But Maitland took him to the cook.

"Fill this man up," he said, "and then show him where to sleep. And, Perrotte, to-morrow morning at seven you be at the tail of the saw."

"Oui, by gar! Perrotte be dere. And you got one good man TOO-day, for sure."

That was fifteen years ago, and, barring certain "jubilations," Perrotte made good his prophecy. He brought up from the Ottawa his Irish wife, a clever woman with her tongue but a housekeeper that scandalised her thrifty, tidy, French-Canadian mother-in-law, and his two children, a boy and a girl. Under the supervision of his boss he made for his family a home and for himself an assured place in the Blackwater Mills. His children fell into the hands of a teacher with a true vocation for his great work and a passion for young life. Under his hand the youth of the rapidly growing mill village were saved from the sordid and soul-debasing influences of their environment, were led out of the muddy streets and can-strewn back yards to those far heights where dwell the high gods of poesy and romance. From the master, too, they learned to know their own wonderful woods out of which the near-by farms had been hewn. Many a home, too, owed its bookshelf to Alex Day's unobtrusive suggestions.

The Perrotte children were prepared for High School by the master's quiet but determined persistence. To the father he held up the utilitarian advantages of an education.

"Your boy is quick—why should not Tony be a master of men some day? Give him a chance to climb."

"Oui, by gar! Antoine he's smart lee'le feller. I mak him steek on his book, you mak him one big boss on some mill."

To the mother the master spoke of social advantages. The empty-headed Irish woman who had all the quick wit and cleverness of tongue characteristic of her race was determined that her girl Annette should learn to be as stylish as "them that tho't themselves her betters." So the children were kept at school by their fondly ambitious parents, and the master did the rest.

At the Public School, that greatest of all democratic institutions, the Perrotte children met the town youth of their own age, giving and taking on equal terms, sharing common privileges and advantages and growing into a community solidarity all their own, which in later years brought its own harvest of mingling joy and bitterness, but which on the whole made for sound manhood and womanhood.

With the girl Annette one effect of the Public School and its influences, educational and social, was to reveal to her the depth of the educational and social pit from which she had been taken. Her High School training might have fitted her for the teaching profession and completed her social emancipation but for her vain and thriftless mother, who, socially ambitious for herself but more for her handsome, clever children, found herself increasingly embarrassed for funds. She lacked the means with which to suitably adorn herself and her children for the station in life to which she aspired and for which good clothes were the prime equipment and to "eddicate" Tony as he deserved. Hence when Annette had completed her second year at the High School her mother withdrew her from the school and its associations and found her a place in the new Fancy Box Factory, where girls could obtain "an illigant and refoined job with good pay as well."

This change in Annette's outlook brought wrathful disappointment to the head master, Alex Day, who had taken a very special pride in Annette's brilliant school career and who had outlined for her a University course. To Annette herself the ending of her school days was a bitter grief, the bitterness of which would have been greatly intensified had she been able to measure the magnitude of the change to be wrought in her life by her mother's foolish vanity and unwise preference of her son's to her daughter's future.

The determining factor in Annette's submission to her mother's will was consideration for her brother and his career. For while for her father she cherished an affectionate pride and for her mother an amused and protective pity, her great passion was for her brother—her handsome, vivacious, audacious and mercurial brother, Tony. With him she counted it only joy to share her all too meagre wages whenever he found himself in financial straits. And a not infrequent situation this was with Tony, who, while he seemed to have inherited from his mother the vivacity, quick wit and general empty-headedness, from his father got nothing of the thrift and patient endurance of grinding toil characteristic of the French-Canadian habitant. But he did get from his father a capacity for the knowing and handling of machinery, which amounted almost to genius. Of the father's steadiness under the grind of daily work which had made him the head mechanic in the Mill, Tony possessed not a tittle. What he could get easily he got, and getting this fancied himself richly endowed, knowing not how slight and superficial is the equipment for life's stern fight that comes without sweat of brain and body. His cleverness deceived first himself and then his family, who united in believing him to be destined for high place and great things. Only two of those who had to do with him in his boyhood weighed him in the balance of truth. One was his Public School master, who labored with incessant and painful care to awaken in him some glimmer of the need of preparation for that bitter fight to which every man is appointed. The other was Grant Maitland, whose knowledge of men and of life, gained at cost of desperate conflict, made the youth's soul an open book to him. Recognising the boy's aptitude, he had in holiday seasons set Tony behind the machines in his planing mill, determined for his father's sake to make of him a mechanical engineer. To Tony each new machine was a toy to be played with; in a week or two he had mastered it and grown weary of it. Thenceforth he slacked at his work and became a demoralizing influence in his department, a source of anxiety to his steady-going father, a plague to his employer, till the holiday time was done.

"Were you my son, my lad, I'd soon settle you," Grant Maitland would say, when the boy was ready to go back to his school. "You will make a mess of your life unless you can learn to stick at your job. The roads are full of clever tramps, remember that, my boy."

But Tony only smiled his brilliant smile at him, as he took his pay envelope, which burned a hole in his pocket till he had done with it. When the next holiday came round Tony would present himself for a job with Jack Maitland to plead for him. For to Tony Jack was as king, to whom he gave passionate loyalty without stint or measure. And thus for his son Jack's sake, Jack's father took Tony on again, resolved to make another effort to make something out of him.

The bond between the two boys was hard to analyse. In games at Public and High School Jack was always Captain and Tony his right-hand man, held to his place and his training partly by his admiring devotion to his Captain but more by a wholesome dread of the inexorable disciplinary measures which slackness or trifling with the rules of the game would inevitably bring him. Jack Maitland was the one being in Tony's world who could put lasting fear into his soul or steadiness into his practice. But even Jack at times failed.

Then when both were eighteen they went to the War, Jack as an Officer, Tony as a Non-Commissioned Officer in the same Battalion, Jack hating the bloody business but resolute to play this great game of duty as he played all games for all that was in him, Tony aglow at first with the movement and glitter and later mad with the lust for deadly daring that was native to his Keltic Gallic soul. They returned with their respective decorations of D. S.

O. and Military Medal and each with the stamp of war cut deep upon him, in keeping with the quality of his soul.

The return to peace was to them, as to the thousands of their comrades to whom it was given to return, a shock almost as great as had been the adventure of war. In a single day while still amid the scenes and with all the paraphernalia of war about them an unreal and bewildering silence had fallen on them. Like men in the unearthly realities of a dream they moved through their routine duties, waiting for the orders that would bring that well-known, sickening, savage tightening of their courage and send them, laden like beasts of burden, up once more to that hell of blood and mud, of nerve-shattering shell, of blinding glare and ear-bursting roar of gun fire, and, worse than all, to the place where, crouching in the farcical deceptive shelter of the sandbagged trench, their fingers gripping into the steel of their rifle hands, they would wait for the zero hour. But as the weeks passed and the orders failed to come they passed from that bewildering and subconscious anxious waiting, to an experience of wildly exultant, hysterical abandonment. They were done with all that long horror and terror; they were never to go back into it again; they were going back home; the New Day had dawned; war was no more, nor ever would be again. Back to home, to waiting hearts, to shining eyes, to welcoming arms, to peace, they were going.

Thereafter, when some weeks of peace had passed and the drums of peace had fallen quiet and the rushing, crowding, hurrahing people had melted away, and the streets and roads were filled again with men and women bent on business, with engagements to keep, the returned men found themselves with dazed, listless mind waiting for orders from someone, somewhere, or for the next movie show to open. But they were unwilling to take on the humdrum of making a living, and were in most cases incapable of initiating a congenial method of employing their powers, their new-found, splendid, glorious powers, by means of which they had saved an empire and a world. They had become common men again, they in whose souls but a few weeks ago had flamed the glory and splendour of a divine heroism!

Small wonder that some of these men, tingling with the consciousness of powers of which these busy, engaged people of the streets and shops knew nothing, turned with disdain from the petty, paltry, many of them non-manly tasks that men pursued solely that they might live. Live! For these last terrible, great and glorious fifty months they had schooled themselves to the notion that the main business of life was not to live. There had been for them a thing to do infinitely more worth while than to live. Indeed, had they been determined at all costs to live, then they had become to themselves, to their comrades, and indeed to all the world, the most despicable of all living things, deserving and winning the infinite contempt of all true men.

While the "gratuity money" lasted life went merrily enough, but when the last cheque had been cashed, and the grim reality that rations had ceased and Q. M. Stores were not longer available thrust itself vividly into the face of the demobilised veteran, and when after experiencing in job hunting varying degrees of humiliation the same veteran made the startling and painful discovery that for his wares of heroic self-immolation, of dogged endurance done up in khaki, there was no demand in the bloodless but none the less strenuous conflict of living; and that other discovery, more disconcerting, that he was not the man he had been in pre-war days and thought himself still to be, but quite another, then he was ready for one of two alternatives, to surrender to the inevitable dictum that after all life was really not worth a fight, more particularly if it could be sustained without one, or, to fling his hat into the Bolshevist ring, ready for the old thing, war—war against the enemies of civilisation and his own enemies, against those who possessed things which he very much desired but which for some inexplicable cause he was prevented from obtaining.

The former class, to a greater or less degree, Jack Maitland represented; the latter, Tony Perrotte. From their war experience they were now knit together in bonds that ran into life issues. Together they had faced war's ultimate horror, together they had emerged with imperishable memories of sheer heroic manhood mutually revealed in hours of desperate need.

At Jack's request Tony had been given the position of a Junior Foreman in one of the planing mill departments, with the promise of advancement.

"You can have anything you are fit for, Tony, in any of the mills. I feel that I owe you, that we both owe you more than we can pay by any position we can offer," was Grant Maitland's word.

"Mr. Maitland, neither you nor Jack owes me anything. Jack has paid, and more than once, all he owed me. But," with a rueful smile, "don't expect too much from me in this job. I can't see myself making it go."

"Give it a big try. Do your best. I ask no more," said Mr. Maitland.

"My best? That's a hard thing. Give me a bayonet and set some Huns before me, and I'll do my best. This is different somehow."

"Different, yet the same. The same qualities make for success. You have the brains and with your gift for machinery—Well, try it. You and Jack here will make this go between you, as you made the other go."

The door closed on the young man.

"Will he make good, Jack?" said the father, anxiously.

"Will any of us make good?"

"You will, Jack, I know. You can stick."

"Yes, I can stick, I suppose, but, after all—well, we'll have a go at it, anyway. But, like Tony, I feel like saying, 'Don't expect too much.'"

"Only your best, Jack, that's all. Take three months, six months, a year, and get hold of the office end of the business. You have brains enough. I want a General Manager right now, Wickes is hardly up to it. He knows the books and he knows the works but he knows nothing else. He doesn't know men nor markets. He is an office man pure and simple, and he's old, too old. The fact is, Jack, I have to be my own Manager inside and outside. My foremen are good, loyal, reliable fellows, but they only know their orders. I want someone to stand beside me. The plant has been doubled in capacity during the war. We did a lot of war work—aeroplane parts. We got the spruce in the raw and worked it up, good work, too, if I do say it myself. No better was done."

"I know something about that, Dad. I had a day with Badgley in Toronto. I know something about it, and I know where the money went, too, Dad."

"The money? Of course, I couldn't take the money—how could I with my boys at the war, and other men's boys?"

"Rather not. My God, Dad, if I thought—! But what's the use talking? They know in London all about the Ambulance Equipment and the Machine Gun Battery, and the Hospital. Do you know why Caramus took a job in the Permanent Force in England? It was either that or blowing out his brains. He could not face his father, a war millionaire. My God, how could he?"

The boy was walking about his room with face white and lips quivering.

"Caramus was in charge of that Machine Gun Section that held the line and let us get back. Every man wiped out, and Caramus carried back smashed to small pieces—and his father making a million out of munitions! My God! My God!"

A silence fell in the room for a minute.

"Poor old Caramus! I saw him in the City a month ago," said the father. "I pitied the poor wretch. He was alone in the Club, not a soul would speak to him. He has got his hell."

"He deserves it—all of it, and all who like him have got fat on blood money. Do you know, Dad, when I see those men going about in the open and no one kicking them I get fairly sick. I don't wonder at some of the boys seeing red. You mark my words, we are going to have bad times in this country before long."

"I am afraid of it, boy. Things look ugly. Even in our own works I feel a bad spirit about. There are some newcomers from the old country whom I can't say I admire much. They grouch and they won't work. Our production is lower than ever in our history and our labor cost is more than twice what it was in 1914."

"Well, Dad, give them a little time to settle down. I have no more use for a slacker than I have for a war millionaire."

"We can't stand much of that thing. Financially we are in fairly good shape. We broke even with our aeroplane work. But we have a big stock of spruce on hand—high-priced stuff, too—and a heavy, very heavy overhead. We shall weather it all right. I don't mind the wages, but we must have production. And that's why I want you with me."

"You must not depend on me for much use for some time at least. I know a little about handling men but about machinery I know nothing."

"Never fear, boy, you've got the machine instinct in you. I remember your holiday work in the mill, you see. But your place is in the office. Wickes will show you the ropes, and you will make good, I know. And I just want to say that you don't know how glad I am to have you come in with me, Jack. If your brother had come back he would have taken hold, he was cut out for the job, but—"

"Poor old Andy! He had your genius for the business. I wish he had been the one to get back!"

"We had not the choosing, Jack, and if he had come we should have felt the same about you. God knows what He is doing, and we can only do our best."

"Well, Dad," said Jack, rising and standing near his father's chair, "as I said before, I'll make a go at it, but don't count too much on me."

"I am counting a lot on you. You are all I have now." The father's voice ended in a husky whisper. The boy swallowed the rising lump in his throat but could find no more words to go on with. But in his heart there was the resolve that he would make an honest try to do for his father's sake what he would not for his own.

But before a month had gone he was heartily sick of the office. It was indoors, and the petty fussing with trivial details irked him. Accuracy was a sine qua non of successful office work, and accuracy is either a thing of natural gift or is the result of long and painful discipline, and neither by nature nor by discipline had Jack come into the possession of this prime qualification for a successful office man. His ledger wellnigh brought tears to old Wickes' eyes and added a heavy load to his day's work. Not that old Wickes grudged the extra burden, much less made any complaint; rather did he count it joy to be able to cover from other eyes than his own the errors that were inevitably to be found in Jack's daily work.

Had it seemed worth while, Jack would have disciplined himself to accuracy. But what was the end of it all? A larger plant with more machines to buy and more men to work them and to be overseen and to be paid, a few more figures in a Bank Book—what else? Jack's tastes were simple. He despised the ostentation of wealth in the accumulation of mere things. He had only pity for the plunger and for the loose liver contempt. Why should he tie himself to a desk, a well appointed desk it is true, but still a desk, in a four-walled room, a much finer room than his father had ever known, but a room which became to him a cage. Why? Of course, there was his father—and Jack wearily turned to his correspondence basket, sick of the sight of paper and letter heads and cost forms and production reports. For his father's sake, who had only him, he would carry on. And carry on he did, doggedly, wearily, bored to death, but sticking it. The reports from the works were often ominous. Things were not going well. There was an undercurrent of unrest among the men.

"I don't wonder at it," said Jack to old Wickes one day, when the bookkeeper set before him the week's pay sheet and production sheet, side by side. "After all, why should the poor devils work for us?"

"For us, sir?" said the shocked Wickes. "For themselves, surely. What would they do for a living if there was no work?"

"That's just it, Wickes. They get a living—is it worth while?"

"But, sir," gasped the old man, "they must live, and—"

"Why must they?"

"Because they want to! Wait till you see 'em sick, sir. My word! They do make haste for the Doctor."

"I fancy they do, Wickes. But all the same, I don't wonder that they grouch a bit."

"'Tis not the grumbling, sir, I deplore," said Wickes, "if they would only work, or let the machines work. That's the trouble, sir. Why, sir, when I came to your father, sir, we never looked at the clock, we kept our minds on the work."

"How long ago, Wickes?"

"Thirty-one years, sir, come next Michaelmas. And glad I was to get the job, too. You see, sir, I had just come to the country, and with the missus and a couple of kids—"

"Thirty-one years! Great Caesar! And you've worked at this desk for thirty-one years! And what have you got out of it?"

"Well, sir, not what you might call a terrible lot. I hadn't the eddication for much, as you might say—but—well, there's my little home, and we've lived happy there, the missus and me, and the kids—at least, till the war came." The old man paused abruptly.

"You're right, Wickes, by Jove," exclaimed Jack, starting from his seat and gripping the old man's hand. "You have made a lot out of it—and you gave as fine a boy as ever stepped in uniform to your country. We were all proud of Stephen, every man of us."

"I know that, sir, and he often wrote the wife about you, sir, which we don't forget, sir. Of course, it's hard on her and the boys—just coming up to be somethin' at the school."

"By the way, Wickes, how are they doing? Two of them, aren't there? Let's see—there's Steve, he's the eldest—"

"No, sir, he's the youngest, sir. Robert is the eldest—fourteen, and quite clever at his books. Pity he's got to quit just now."

"Quit? Not a bit of it. We must see to that. And little Steve—how is the back?"

"He's twelve. The back hurts a lot, but he is happy enough, if you give him a pencil. They're all with us now."

"Ah, well, well. I think you have made something out of it after all, Wickes. And we must see about Robert."

Thirty-one years at the desk! And to show for it a home for his wife and himself, a daughter in a home of her own, a son dead for his country, leaving behind him a wife and two lads to carry the name—was it worth while? Yes, by Jove, it was worth it all to be able to give a man like Stephen Wickes to his country. For Stephen Wickes was a fine stalwart lad, a good soldier, steady as a rock, with a patient, cheery courage that nothing could daunt or break. But for a man's self was it worth while?

Jack had no thought of wife and family. There was Adrien. She had been a great pal before the war, but since his return she had seemed different. Everyone seemed different. The war had left many gaps, former pals had formed other ties, many had gone from the town. Even Adrien had drifted away from the old currents of life. She seemed to have taken up with young Stillwell, whom Jack couldn't abide. Stillwell had been turned down by the Recruiting Officer during the war—flat feet, or something. True, he had done great service in Red Cross, Patriotic Fund, Victory Loan work, and that sort of thing, and apparently stood high in the Community. His father had doubled the size of his store and had been a great force in all public war work. He had spared neither himself nor his son. The elder Stillwell, high up in the Provincial Political world, saw to it that his son was on all the big Provincial War Committees. Rupert had all the shrewd foresight and business ability of his father, which was saying a good deal. He began to assume the role of a promising young capitalist. The sources of his income no one knew—fortunate investments, people said. And his Hudson Six stood at the Rectory gate every day. Well, not even for Adrien would Jack have changed places with Rupert Stillwell. For Jack Maitland held the extreme and, in certain circles, unpopular creed that the citizen who came richer out of a war which had left his country submerged in debt, and which had drained away its best blood and left it poorer in its manhood by well-nigh seventy thousand of its noblest youth left upon the battlefields of the various war fronts and by the hundreds of thousands who would go through life a burden to themselves and to those to whom they should have been a support—that citizen was accursed. If Adrien chose to be a friend of such a man, by that choice she classified herself as impossible of friendship for Jack. It had hurt a bit. But what was one hurt more or less to one whom the war had left numb in heart and bereft of ambition? He was not going to pity himself. He was lucky indeed to have his body and nerve still sound and whole, but they need not expect him to show any great keenness in the chase for a few more thousands that would only rank him among those for whom the war had not done so badly. Meantime, for his father's sake, who, thank God, had given his best, his heart's best and the best of his brain and of his splendid business genius to his country, he would carry on, with no other reward than that of service rendered.

CHAPTER III
THE HEATHEN QUEST

They stood together by the open fire in the study, Jack and his father, alike in many ways yet producing effects very different. The younger man had the physical makeup of the older, though of a slighter mould. They had the same high, proud look of conscious strength, of cool fearlessness that nothing could fluster. But the soul that looked out of the grey eyes of the son was quite another from that which looked out of the deep blue eyes of the father—yet, after all, the difference may not have been in essence but only that the older man's soul had learned in life's experience to look out only through a veil.

The soul of the youth was eager, adventurous, still believing, yet with a certain questioning and a touch of weariness, a result of the aftermath of peace following three years of war. There was still, however, the outlooking for far horizons, the outreaching imagination, the Heaven given expectation of the Infinite. In the older man's eye dwelt chiefly reserve. The veil was always there except when he found it wise and useful to draw it aside. If ever the inner light flamed forth it was when the man so chose. Self-mastery, shrewdness, power, knowledge, lay in the dark blue eyes, and all at the soul's command.

But to-night as the father's eyes rested upon his son who stood gazing into and through the blazing fire there were to be seen only pride and wistful love. But as the son turned his eyes toward his father the veil fell and the eyes that answered were quiet, shrewd, keen and chiefly kind.

The talk had passed beyond the commonplace of the day's doings. They were among the big things, the fateful thing—Life and Its Worth, Work and Its Wages, Creative Industry and Its Product, Capital and Its Price, Man and His Rights.

They were frank with each other. The war had done that for them. For ever since the night when his eighteen-year-old boy had walked into his den and said, "Father, I am eighteen," and stood looking into his eyes and waiting for the word that came straight and unhesitating, "I know, boy, you are my son and you must go, for I cannot," ever since that night, which seemed now to belong to another age, these two had faced each other as men. Now they were talking about the young man's life work.

"Frankly, I don't like it, Dad," said the son.

"Easy to see that, Jack."

"I'm really sorry. I'm afraid anyone can see it. But somehow I can't put much pep into it."

"Why?" asked the father, with curt abruptness.

"Why? Well, I hardly know. Somehow it hardly seems worth while. It is not the grind of the office, though that is considerable. I could stick that, but, after all, what's the use?"

"What would you rather do, Jack?" enquired his father patiently, as if talking to a child. "You tried for the medical profession, you know, and—"

"I know, I know, you are quite right about it. You may think it pure laziness. Maybe it is, but I hardly think so. Perhaps I went back to lectures too soon after the war. I was hardly fit, I guess, and the whole thing, the inside life, the infernal grind of lectures, the idiotic serious mummery of the youngsters, those blessed kids who should have been spanked by their mothers—the whole thing sickened me in three months. If I had waited perhaps I might have done better at the thing. I don't know—hard to tell." The boy paused, looking into the fire.

"It was my fault, boy," said the father hastily. "I ought to have figured the thing out differently. But, you see, I had no knowledge of what you had gone through and of its effect upon you. I know better now. I thought that the harder you went into the work the better it would be for you. I made a mistake."

"Well, you couldn't tell, Dad. How could you? But everything was so different when I came back. Mere kids were carrying on where we had been, and doing it well, too, by Jove, and we didn't seem to be needed."

"Needed, boy?" The father's voice was thick.

"Yes, but I didn't see that then. Selfish, I fear. Then, you know, home was not the same—"

The older man choked back a groan and leaned hard against the mantel.

"I know, Dad, I can see now I was selfish—"

"Selfish? Don't say that, my lad. Selfish? After all you had gone through? No, I shall never apply that word to you, but you—you don't seem to realise—" The father hesitated a few moments, then, as if taking a plunge:

"You don't realise just how big a thing—how big an investment there is in that business down there—." His hand swept toward the window through which could be seen the lights of that part of the town which clustered about the various mills and factories of which he was owner.

"I know there is a lot, Dad, but how much I don't know."

"There's $250,000 in plant alone, boy, but there's more than money, a lot more than money—" Then, after a pause, as if to himself, "A lot more than money—there's brain sweat and heart agony and prayers and tears—and, yes, life, boy, your mother's life and mine. We worked and saved and prayed and planned—"

He stepped quickly toward the window, drew aside the curtain and pointed to a dark mass of headland beyond the twinkling lights.

"You see the Bluff there. Fifty years ago I stood with my father on that Bluff and watched the logs come down the river to the sawmill—his sawmill, into which he had put his total capital, five hundred dollars. I remember well his words, 'My son, if you live out your life you will see on that flat a town where thousands of men and women will find homes and, please God, happiness.' Your mother and I watched that town grow for forty years, and we tried to make people happy—at least, if they were not it was no fault of hers. Of course, other hands have been at the work since then, but her hands and mine more than any other, and more than all others together were in it, and her heart, too, was in it all."

The boy turned from the window and sat down heavily in a deep armchair, his hands covering his face. His heart was still sick with the ache that had smitten it that day in front of Amiens when the Colonel, his father's friend, had sent for him and read him the wire which had brought the terrible message of his mother's death. The long months of days and nights heavy with watching, toiling, praying, agonising, for her twin sons, and for the many boys who had gone out from the little town wore out her none too robust strength. Then, the sniper's bullet that had pierced the heart of her boy seemed to reach to her heart as well. After that, the home that once had been to its dwellers the most completely heart-satisfying spot in all the world became a place of dread, of haunting ghosts, of acutely poignant memories. They used the house for sleeping in and for eating in, but there was no living in it longer. To them it was a tomb, though neither would acknowledge it and each bore with it for the other's sake.

"Honestly, Dad, I wish I could make it go, for your sake—"

"For my sake, boy? Why, I have all of it I care for. Not for my sake. But what else can we do but stick it?"

"I suppose so—but for Heaven's sake give me something worth a man's doing. If I could tackle a job such as you and"—the boy winced—"you and mother took on I believe I'd try it. But that office! Any fool could sit in my place and carry on. It is like the job they used to give to the crocks or the slackers at the base to do. Give me a man's job."

The father's keen blue eyes looked his son over.

"A man's job?" he said, with a grim smile, realising as his son did not how much of a man's job it was. "Suppose you learn this one as I did?"

"What do you mean, Dad, exactly? How did you begin?"

"I? At the tail of the saw."

"All right, I'm game."

"Boy, you are right—I believe in my soul you are right. You did a man's job 'out there' and you have it in you to do a man's job again."

The son shrugged his shoulders. Next morning at seven they were down at the planing mill where men were doing men's work. He was at a man's job, at the tail of a saw, and drawing a man's pay, rubbing shoulders with men on equal terms, as he had in the trenches. And for the first time since Armistice Day, if not happy or satisfied, he was content to carry on.

CHAPTER IV
ANNETTE

Sam Wigglesworth had finished with school, which is not quite the same as saying that he had finished his education. A number of causes had combined to bring this event to pass. First, Sam was beyond the age of compulsory attendance at the Public School, the School Register recording him as sixteen years old. Then, Sam's educational career had been anything but brilliant. Indeed, it might fairly be described as dull. All his life he had been behind his class, the biggest boy in his class, which fact might have been to Sam a constant cause of humiliation had he not held as of the slightest moment merely academic achievements. One unpleasant effect which this fact had upon Sam's moral quality was that it tended to make him a bully. He was physically the superior of all in his class, and this superiority he exerted for what he deemed the discipline of younger and weaker boys, who excelled him in intellectual attainment.

Furthermore, Sam, while quite ready to enforce the code of discipline which he considered suitable to the smaller and weaker boys in his class, resented and resisted the attempts of constituted authority to enforce discipline in his own case, with the result that Sam's educational career was, after much long suffering, abruptly terminated by the action of the long-suffering head, Alex Day.

"With great regret I must report," his letter to the School Board ran, "that in the case of Samuel Wigglesworth I have somehow failed to inculcate the elementary principles of obedience to school regulations and of adherence to truth in speech. I am free to acknowledge," went on the letter, "that the defect may be in myself as much as in the boy, but having failed in winning him to obedience and truth-telling, I feel that while I remain master of the school I must decline to allow the influence of this youth to continue in the school. A whole-hearted penitence for his many offences and an earnest purpose to reform would induce me to give him a further trial. In the absence of either penitence or purpose to reform I must regretfully advise expulsion."

Joyfully the School Board, who had for months urged upon the reluctant head this action, acquiesced in the course suggested, and Samuel was forthwith expelled, to his own unmitigated relief but to his father's red and raging indignation at what he termed the "(h)ignorant persecution of their betters by these (h)insolent Colonials," for "'is son 'ad 'ad the advantages of schools of the 'ighest standin' in (H)England."

Being expelled from school Sam forthwith was brought by his father to the office of the mills, where he himself was employed. There he introduced his son to the notice of Mr. Grant Maitland, with request for employment.

The old man looked the boy over.

"What has he been doing?"

"Nothin'. 'E's just left school."

"High School?"

"Naw. Public School." Wigglesworth Sr.'s tone indicated no exalted opinion of the Public School.

"Public School! What grade, eh?"

"Grade? I dinnaw. Wot grade, Samuel? Come, speak (h)up, cawn't yeh?"

"Uh?" Sam's mental faculties had been occupied in observing the activities and guessing the probable fate of a lumber-jack gaily decked in scarlet sash and blue overalls, who was the central figure upon a flaming calendar tacked up behind Mr. Maitland's desk, setting forth the commercial advantages of trading with the Departmental Stores of Stillwell & Son.

"Wot grade in school, the boss is (h)askin'," said his father sharply.

"Grade?" enquired Sam, returning to the commonplace of the moment.

"Yes, what grade in the Public School were you in when you left?" The blue eyes of the boss was "borin' 'oles" through Sam and the voice pierced like a "bleedin' gimblet," as Wigglesworth, Sr., reported to his spouse that afternoon.

Sam hesitated a bare second. "Fourth grade it was," he said with sullen reluctance.

"'Adn't no chance, Samuel 'adn't. Been a delicate child ever since 'is mother stopped suckin' 'im," explained the father with a sympathetic shake of his head.

The cold blue eye appraised the boy's hulking mass.

"'E don't look it," continued Mr. Wigglesworth, noting the keen glance, "but 'e's never been (h)able to bide steady at the school. (H)It's 'is brain, sir."

"His—ah—brain?" Again the blue eyes appraised the boy, this time scanning critically his face for indication of undue brain activity.

"'Is brain, sir," earnestly reiterated the sympathetic parent. "'Watch that (h)infant's brain,' sez the Doctor to the missus when she put 'im on the bottle. And you know, we 'ave real doctors in (H)England, sir. 'Watch 'is brain,' sez 'e, and, my word, the care 'is ma 'as took of that boy's brain is wunnerful, is fair beautiful, sir." Mr. Wigglesworth's voice grew tremulous at the remembrance of that maternal solicitude.

"And was that why he left school?" enquired the boss.

"Well, sir, not (h)exackly," said Mr. Wigglesworth, momentarily taken aback, "though w'en I comes to think on it that must a been at the bottom of it. You see, w'en Samuel went at 'is books of a night 'e'd no more than begin at a sum an' 'e'd say to 'is ma, 'My brain's a-whirlin', ma', just like that, and 'is ma would 'ave to pull 'is book away, just drag it away, you might say. Oh, 'e's 'ad a 'ard time, 'as Samuel." At this point the boss received a distinct shock, for, as his eyes were resting upon Samuel's face meditatively while he listened somewhat apathetically, it must be confessed, to the father's moving tale, the eye of the boy remote from the father closed in a slow but significant wink.

The boss sat up, galvanised into alert attention. "Eh? What?" he exclaimed.

"Yes, sir, 'e's caused 'is ma many a (h)anxious hour, 'as Samuel." Again the eye closed in a slow and solemn wink. "And we thought, 'is ma and me, that we would like to get Samuel into some easy job—"

"An easy job, eh?"

"Yes, sir. Something in the office, 'ere."

"But his brain, you say, would not let him study his books."

"Oh, it was them sums, sir, an' the Jography and the 'Istory an' the Composition, an', an'—wot else, Samuel? You see, these 'ere schools ain't a bit like the schools at 'ome, sir. They're so confusing with their subjecks. Wot I say is, why not stick to real (h)eddication, without the fiddle faddles?"

"So you want an easy job for your son, eh?" enquired Mr. Maitland.

"Boy," he said sharply to Samuel, whose eyes had again become fixed upon the gay and daring lumber-jack. Samuel recalled himself with visible effort. "Why did you leave school? The truth, mind." The "borin'" eyes were at their work.

"Fired!" said Sam promptly.

Mr. Wigglesworth began a sputtering explanation.

"That will do, Wigglesworth," said Mr. Maitland, holding up his hand. "Sam, you come and see me tomorrow here at eight. Do you understand?"

Sam nodded. After they had departed there came through the closed office door the sound of Mr. Wigglesworth's voice lifted in violent declamation, but from Sam no answering sound could be heard.

The school suffered no noticeable loss in the intellectual quality of its activities by the removal of the whirling brain and incidentally its physical integument of Samuel Wigglesworth. To the smaller boys the absence of Sam brought unbounded joy, more especially during the hours of recess from study and on their homeward way from school after dismissal.

More than any other, little Steve Wickes rejoiced in Sam's departure from school. Owing to some mysterious arrangement of Sam's brain cells he seemed to possess an abnormal interest in observing the sufferings of any animal. The squirming of an unfortunate fly upon a pin fascinated him, the sight of a wretched dog driven mad with terror rushing frantically down a street, with a tin can dangling to its tail, convulsed him with shrieking delight. The more highly organised the suffering animal, the keener was Sam's joy. A child, for instance, flying in a paroxysm of fear from Sam's hideously contorted face furnished acute satisfaction. It fell naturally enough that little Steve Wickes, the timid, shrinking, humpbacked son of the dead soldier, Stephen Wickes, afforded Sam many opportunities of rare pleasure. It was Sam that coined and, with the aid of his sycophantic following never wanting to a bully, fastened to the child the nickname of "Humpy Wicksy," working thereby writhing agony in the lad's highly sensitive soul. But Sam did not stay his hand at the infliction of merely mental anguish. It was one of his favorite forms of sport to seize the child by the collar and breeches and, swinging him high over head, hold him there in an anguish of suspense, awaiting the threatened drop. It is to be confessed that Sam was not entirely without provocation at the hands of little Steve, for the lad had a truly uncanny cunning hidden in his pencil, by means of which Sam was held up in caricature to the surreptitious joy of his schoolmates. Sam's departure from school deprived him of the full opportunity he formerly enjoyed of indulging himself in his favourite sport. On this account he took the more eager advantage of any opportunity that offered still to gratify his taste in this direction.

Sauntering sullenly homeward from his interview with the boss and with his temper rasped to a raw edge by his father's wrathful comments upon his "dommed waggin' tongue," he welcomed with quite unusual eagerness the opportunity for indulging himself in his pastime of baiting Humpy Wicksy whom he overtook on his way home from school during the noon intermission.

"Hello, Humpy," he roared at the lad.

Like a frightened rabbit Steve scurried down a lane, Sam whooping after him.

"Come back, you little beast. Do you hear me? I'll learn you to come when you're called," he shouted, catching the terrified lad and heaving him aloft in his usual double-handed grip.

"Let me down, you! Leave me alone now," shrieked the boy, squirming, scratching, biting like an infuriated cat.

"Bite, would you?" said Sam, flinging the boy down. "Now then," catching him by the legs and turning him over on his stomach, "we'll make a wheelbarrow of you. Gee up, Buck! Want a ride, boys?" he shouted to his admiring gallery of toadies. "All aboard!"

While the unhappy Steve, shrieking prayers and curses, was struggling vainly to extricate himself from the hands gripping his ankles, Annette Perrotte, stepping smartly along the street on her way from the box factory, came past the entrance to the lane. By her side strode a broad-shouldered, upstanding youth. Arrested by Steve's outcries and curses she paused.

"What are those boys at, I wonder?" she said. "There's that big lout of a Wigglesworth boy. He's up to no good, I bet you."

"Oh, a kids' row of some kind or ither, a doot," said the youth. "Come along."

"He's hurting someone," said Annette, starting down the lane. "What? I believe it's that poor child, Steve Wickes." Like a wrathful fury she dashed in upon Sam and his company of tormentors and, knocking the little ones right and left, she sprang upon Sam with a fierce cry.

"You great brute!" She seized him by his thatch of thick red hair and with one mighty swing she hurled him clear of Steve and dashed him head on against the lane fence. Sheer surprise held Sam silent for a few seconds, but as he felt the trickle of warm blood run down his face and saw it red upon his hand, his surprise gave place to terror.

"Ouw! Ouw!" he bellowed. "I'm killed, I'm dying. Ouw! Ouw!"

"I hope so," said Annette, holding Steve in her arms and seeking to quiet his sobbing. But as she saw the streaming blood her face paled.

"For the love of Mike, Mack, see if he's hurt," she said in a low voice to her companion.

"Not he! He's makin' too much noise," said the young man. "Here, you young bull, wait till I see what's wrang wi' ye," he continued, stooping over Sam.

"Get away from me, I tell you. Ouw! Ouw! I'm dying, and they'll hang her. Ouw! Ouw! I'm killed, and I'm just glad I am, for she'll be hung to death." Here Sam broke into a vigorous stream of profanity.

"Ay, he's improvin' A doot," said Mack. "Let us be going."

"'Ello! Wot's (h)up?" cried a voice. It was Mr. Wigglesworth on his way home from the mill. "Why, bless my living lights, if it bean't Samuel. Who's been a beatin' of you, Sammy?" His eye swept the crowd. "'Ave you been at my lad?" he asked, stepping toward the young man, whom Annette named Mack.

"Aw, steady up, man. There's naethin' much wrang wi' the lad—a wee scratch on the heid frae fa'in' against the fence yonder."

"Who 'it 'im, I say?" shouted Mr. Wigglesworth. "Was it you?" he added, squaring up to the young man.

"No, it wasn't, Mr. Wigglesworth. It was me." Mr. Wigglesworth turned on Annette who, now that Sam's bellowing had much abated with the appearance of his father upon the scene, had somewhat regained her nerve.

"You?" gasped Mr. Wigglesworth. "You? My Samuel? It's a lie," he cried.

"Hey, mon, guairrd y're tongue a bit," said Mack. "Mind ye're speakin' to a leddy."

"A lidy! A lidy!" Mr. Wigglesworth's voice was eloquent of scorn.

"Aye, a leddy!" said Mack. "An' mind what ye say aboot her tae. Mind y're manners, man."

"My manners, hey? An' 'oo may you be, to learn me manners, you bloomin' (h)ignorant Scotch (h)ass. You give me (h)any of your (h)imperance an' I'll knock y're bloomin' block (h)off, I will." And Mr. Wigglesworth, throwing himself into the approved pugilistic attitude, began dancing about the young Scot.

"Hoot, mon, awa' hame wi' ye. Tak' yon young tyke wi' ye an' gie him a bit wash, he's needin' it," said Mack, smiling pleasantly at the excited and belligerent Mr. Wigglesworth.

At this point Captain Jack, slowly motoring by the lane mouth, turned his machine to the curb and leaped out.

"What's the row here?" he asked, making his way through the considerable crowd that had gathered. "What's the trouble, Wigglesworth?"

"They're knockin' my boy abaht, so they be," exclaimed Mr. Wigglesworth. "But," with growing and righteous wrath, "they'll find (h)out that, wotsomever they do to a kid, w'en they come (h)up agin Joe Wigglesworth they've struck somethin' 'ard—'ard, d'ye 'ear? 'Ard!" And Mr. Wigglesworth made a pass at the young Scot.

"Hold on, Wigglesworth," said Captain Jack quietly, catching his arm. "Were you beating up this kid?" he asked, turning to the young man.

"Nae buddie's beatin' up the lad," said Mack quietly.

"It was me," said the girl, turning a defiant face to Captain Jack.

"You? Why! great Scot! Blest if it isn't Annette."

"Yes, it's me," said the girl, her face a flame of colour.

"By Jove, you've grown up, haven't you? And it was you that—"

"Yes, that big brute was abusing Steve here."

"What? Little Steve Wickes?"

"He was, and I pitched him into the fence. He hit his head and cut it, I guess. I didn't mean—"

"Served him right enough, too, I fancy," said Captain Jack.

"I'll 'ave the law on the lot o' ye, I will. I'm a poor workin' man, but I've got my rights, an' if there's a justice in this Gawd forsaken country I'll 'ave protection for my family." And Mr. Wigglesworth, working up a fury, backed off down the lane.

"Don't fear, Wigglesworth, you'll get all the justice you want. Perhaps Sam will tell us—Hello! Where is Sam?"

But Sam had vanished. He had no mind for an investigation in the presence of Captain Jack.

"Well, well, he can't be much injured, I guess. Meantime, can I give you a lift, Annette?"

"No, thank you," said the girl, the colour in her cheeks matching the crimson ribbon at her throat. "I'm just going home. It's only a little way. I don't—"

"The young leddy is with me, sir," said the young Scotchman quietly.

"Oh, she is, eh?" said Captain Jack, looking him over. "Ah, well, then— Good-bye, Annette, for the present." He held out his hand. "We must renew our old acquaintance, eh?"

"Thank you, sir," said the girl.

"'Sir?' Rot! You aren't going to 'sir' me, Annette, after all the fun and the fights we had in the old days. Not much. We're going to be good chums again, eh? What do you say?"

"I don't know," said Annette, flashing a swift glance into Captain Jack's admiring eyes. "It depends on—"

"On me?"

"I didn't say so." Her head went up a bit.

"On you?"

"I didn't say so."

"Well, let it go. But we will be pals again, Annette, I vow. Good-bye." Captain Jack lifted his hat and moved away.

As he reached his car he ran up against young Rupert Stillwell.

"Deucedly pretty Annette has grown, eh?" said Stillwell.

"Annette's all right," said Jack, rather brusquely, entering his car.

"Working in your box factory, I understand, eh?"

"Don't really know," said Jack carelessly. "Probably."

The crowd had meantime faded away with Captain Jack's going.

"Did na know the Captain was a friend of yours, Annette," said Mack, falling into step beside her.

"No—yes—I don't know. We went to Public School together before the war. I was a kid then." Her manner was abstracted and her eyes were far away. Mack walked gloomily by her on one side, little Steve on the other.

"Huh! He's no your sort, A doot," he said sullenly.

"What do you say?" cried Annette, returning from her abstraction. "What do you mean, 'my sort'?" Her head went high and her eyes flashed.

"He would na look at ye, for ony guid."

"He did look at me though," replied Annette, tossing her head.

"No for ony guid!" repeated Mack, stubbornly.

Annette stopped in her tracks, a burning red on her cheeks and a dangerous light in her black eyes.

"Mr. McNish, that's your road," she said, pointing over his shoulder.

"A'll tak it tae," said McNish, wheeling on his heel, "an' ye can hae your Captain for me."

With never a look at him Annette took her way home.

"Good-bye, Steve," she said, stooping and kissing the boy. "This is your corner."

"Annette," he said, with a quick, shy look up into her face, "I like Captain Jack, don't you?"

"No," she said hurriedly. "I mean yes, of course."

"And I like you too," said the boy, with an adoring look in his deep eyes, "better'n anyone in the world."

"Do you, Steve? I'm glad." Again she stooped swiftly and kissed him. "Now run home."

She hurried home, passed into her room without a word to anyone. Slowly she removed her hat, then turning to her glass she gazed at her flushed face for a few moments. A little smile curved her lips. "He did look at me anyway," she whispered to the face that looked out at her, "he did, he did," she repeated. Then swiftly she covered her eyes. When she looked again she saw a face white and drawn. "He would na look at ye." The words smote her with a chill. Drearily she turned away and went out.

CHAPTER V
THE RECTORY

The Rectory was one of the very oldest of the more substantial of Blackwater's dwellings. Built of grey limestone from the local quarries, its solid square mass relieved by its quaint dormer windows was softened from its primal ugliness by the Boston ivy that had clambered to the eaves and lay draped about the windows like a soft green mantle. Built in the early days, it stood with the little church, a gem of Gothic architecture, within spacious grounds bought when land was cheap. Behind the house stood the stable, built also of grey limestone, and at one side a cherry and apple orchard formed a charming background to the grey buildings with their crowding shrubbery and gardens. A gravelled winding drive led from the street through towering elms, a picturesque remnant from the original forest, to the front door and round the house to the stable yard behind. From the driveway a gravelled footpath led through the shrubbery and flower garden by a wicket gate to the Church. When first built the Rectory stood in dignified seclusion on the edge of the village, but the prosperity of the growing town demanding space for its inhabitants had driven its streets far beyond the Rectory demesne on every side, till now it stood, a green oasis of sheltered loveliness, amid a crowding mass of modern brick dwellings, comfortable enough but arid of beauty and suggestive only of the utilitarian demands of a busy manufacturing town.

For nearly a quarter of a century the Rev. Herbert Aveling Templeton, D.D., LL.D., for whom the Rectory had been built, had ministered in holy things to the Parish of St. Alban's and had exercised a guiding and paternal care over the social and religious well-being of the community. The younger son of one of England's noble families, educated in an English Public School and University, he represented, in the life of this new, thriving, bustling town, the traditions and manners of an English gentleman of the Old School. Still in his early sixties, he carried his years with all the vigour of a man twenty years his junior. As he daily took his morning walk for his mail, stepping with the brisk pace of one whose poise the years had not been able to disturb, yet with the stately bearing consistent with the dignity attaching to his position and office, men's eyes followed the tall, handsome, white-haired, well set up gentleman always with admiration and, where knowledge was intimate, with reverence and affection. Before the recent rapid growth of the town consequent upon the establishment of various manufacturing industries attracted thither by the unique railroad facilities, the Rector's walk was something in the nature of public perambulatory reception. For he knew them all, and for all had a word of greeting, of enquiry, of cheer, of admonition, so that by the time he had returned to his home he might have been said to have conducted a pastoral visitation of a considerable proportion of his flock. Even yet, with the changes that had taken place, his walk to the Post Office was punctuated with greetings and salutations from his fellow-citizens in whose hearts his twenty-five years of devotion to their well-being, spiritual and physical, had made for him an enduring place.

The lady of the Rectory, though some twenty years his junior, yet, by reason of delicate health due largely to the double burden of household cares and parish duties, appeared to be quite of equal age. Gentle in spirit, frail in body, there seemed to be in her soul something of the quality of tempered steel, yet withal a strain of worldly wisdom mingled with a strange ignorance of the affairs of modern life. Her life revolved around one centre, her adored husband, a centre enlarged as time went on to include her only son and her two daughters. All others and all else in her world were of interest solely as they might be more or less closely related to these, the members of her family. The town and the town folk she knew solely as her husband's parish. There were other people and other communions, no doubt, but being beyond the pale they could hardly be supposed to matter, or, at any rate, she could not be supposed to regard them with more than the interest and spasmodic concern which she felt it her duty to bestow upon those unfortunate dwellers in partibus infidelium.

Regarding the Public School of the town with aversion because of its woefully democratic character, she was weaned from her hostility to that institution when her son's name was entered upon its roll. Her eldest daughter, indeed, she sent as a girl of fourteen to an exclusive English school, the expense of which was borne by her husband's eldest brother, Sir Arthur Templeton, for she held the opinion that while for a boy the Public School was an excellent institution with a girl it was quite different. Hence, while her eldest daughter went "Home" for her education, her boy went to the Blackwater Public and High Schools, which institutions became henceforth invested with the highest qualifications as centres of education. Her boy's friends were her friends, and to them her house was open at all hours of day or night. Indeed, it became the governing idea in her domestic policy that her house should be the rallying centre for everything that was related in any degree to her children's life. Hence, she quietly but effectively limited the circle of the children's friends to those who were able and were willing to make the Rectory their social centre. She saw to it that for Herbert's intimate boy friends the big play room at the top of the house, once a bare and empty room and later the large and comfortable family living room, became the place of meeting for all their social and athletic club activities. With unsleeping vigilance she stood on guard against anything that might break that circle of her heart's devotion. The circle might be, indeed must be enlarged, as for instance to take in the Maitland boys, Herbert's closest chums. She was wise enough to see the wisdom of that, but nothing on earth would she allow to filch from her a single unit of the priceless treasures of her heart.

To this law of her life she made one glorious, one splendid exception. When her country called, she, after weeks of silent, fierce, lonely, agonised struggle gave up her boy and sent him with voiceless, tearless pride to the War.

But, when the boy's Colonel wrote in terms of affectionate pride of her boy's glorious passing, with new and strange adaptability her heart circle was extended to include her boy's comrades in war and those who like herself had sent them forth. Thenceforth every khaki covered lad was to her a son, and every soldier's mother a friend.

As her own immediate home circle grew smaller, the intensity of her devotion increased. Her two daughters became her absorbing concern. With the modern notion that a girl might make for herself a career in life she had no sympathy whatever. To see them happily married and in homes of their own became the absorbing ambition of her life. To this end she administered her social activities, with this purpose in view she encouraged or discouraged her daughters' friendships with men. With the worldly wisdom of which she had her own share she came to the conclusion that ineligible men friends, that is, men friends unable to give her daughters a proper setting in the social world, were to be effectively eliminated. That the men of her daughters' choosing should be gentlemen in breeding went without saying, but that they should be sufficiently endowed with wealth to support a proper social position was equally essential.

That Jack Maitland had somehow dropped out of the intimate circle of friends who had in pre-war days made the Rectory their headquarters was to her a more bitter disappointment than she cared to acknowledge even to herself. Her son and the two Maitland boys had been inseparable in their school and college days, and with the two young men her daughters had been associated in the very closest terms of comradeship. But somehow

Captain Jack Maitland after the first months succeeding his return from the war had drawn apart. Disappointed, perplexed, hurt, she vainly had striven to restore the old footing between the young man and her daughters. Young Maitland had taken up his medical studies for a few months at his old University in Toronto and so had been out of touch with the social life of his home town. Then after he had "chucked" his course as impossible he had at his father's earnest wish taken up work at the mills, at first in the office, later in the manufacturing department. There was something queer in Jack's attitude toward his old life and its associations, and after her first failures in attempting to restore the old relationship her eldest daughter's pride and then her own forbade further efforts.

Adrien, her eldest daughter, had always been a difficult child, and her stay in England and later her experience in war work in France where for three years she had given rare service in hospital work had somehow made her even more inaccessible to her mother. And now the situation had been rendered more distressing by her determination "to find something to do." She was firm in her resolve that she had no intention of patiently waiting in her home, ostensibly busying herself with social duties but in reality "waiting if not actually angling for a man." She bluntly informed her scandalised parent that "when she wanted a man more than a career it would be far less humiliating to frankly go out and get him than to practise alluring poses in the hopes that he might deign to bestow upon her his lordly regard." Her mother wisely forebore to argue. Indeed, she had long since learned that in argumentative powers she was hopelessly outclassed by her intellectual daughter. She could only express her shocked disappointment at such intentions and quietly plan to circumvent them.

As to Patricia, her younger daughter, she dismissed all concern. She was only a child as yet, wise beyond her years, but too thoroughly immature to cause any anxiety for some years to come. Meantime she had at first tolerated and then gently encouraged the eager and obvious anxiety of Rupert Stillwell to make a footing for himself in the Rectory family. At the outbreak of the war her antipathy to young Stillwell as a slacker had been violent. He had not joined up with the first band of ardent young souls who had so eagerly pointed the path to duty and to glory. But, when it had been made clear to the public mind that young Stillwell had been pronounced physically unfit for service and was therefore prevented from taking his place in that Canadian line which though it might wear thin at times had never broken, Mrs. Templeton relieved him in her mind of the damning count of being a slacker. Later, becoming impressed with the enthusiasm of the young man's devotion to various forms of patriotic war service at home, she finally, though it must be confessed with something of an effort, had granted him a place within the circle of her home. Furthermore, Rupert Stillwell had done extremely well in all his business enterprises and had come to be recognised as one of the coming young men of the district, indeed of the Province, with sure prospects of advancement in public estimation. Hence, the frequency with which Stillwell's big Hudson Six could be seen parked on the gravelled drive before the Rectory front door. In addition to this, Rupert and his Hudson Six were found to be most useful. He had abundance of free time and he was charmingly ready with his offers of service. Any hour of the day the car, driven by himself or his chauffeur, was at the disposal of any member of the Rectory family, a courtesy of which Mrs. Templeton was not unwilling to avail herself though never with any loss of dignity but always with appearance of bestowing rather than of receiving a favour. As to the young ladies, Adrien rarely allowed herself the delight of a motor ride in Rupert Stillwell's luxurious car. On the other hand, had her mother not intervened, Patricia would have indulged without scruple her passion for joy-riding. The car she adored, Rupert Stillwell she regarded simply as a means to the indulgence of her adoration. He was a jolly companion, a cleverly humourous talker, and an unfailing purveyor of bon-bons. Hence he was to Patricia an ever welcome guest at the Rectory, and the warmth of Patricia's welcome went a long way to establish his position of intimacy in the family.

It was not to be supposed, however, that that young lady's gracious and indeed eager acceptance of the manifold courtesies of the young gentleman in question burdened her in the very slightest with any sense of obligation to anything but the most cavalier treatment of him, should occasion demand. She was unhesitatingly frank and ready with criticism and challenge of his opinions, indeed he appeared to possess a fatal facility for championing her special aversions and antagonising her enthusiasms. Of the latter her most avowed example was Captain Jack, as she loved to call him. A word of criticism of Captain Jack, her hero, her knight, sans peur et sans reproche and her loyal soul was aflame with passionate resentment.

It so fell on an occasion when young Stillwell was a dinner guest at the Rectory.

"Do you know, Patricia," and Rupert Stillwell looked across the dinner table teasingly into Patricia's face, "your Captain Jack was rather mixed up in a nice little row to-day?"

"I heard all about it, Rupert, and Captain Jack did just what I would have expected him to do." Patricia's unsmiling eyes looked steadily into the young man's smiling face.

"Rescued a charming young damsel, eh? By the way, that Perrotte girl has turned out uncommonly good looking," continued Rupert, addressing the elder sister.

"Rescuing a poor little ill-treated boy from the hands of a brutal bully and the bully's brutal father—" Patricia's voice was coolly belligerent.

"My dear Patricia!" The mother's voice was deprecatingly pacific.

"It is simply true, Mother, and Rupert knows it quite well too, or—"

"Patricia!" Her father's quiet voice arrested his daughter's flow of speech.

"But, Father, everyone—"

"Patricia!" The voice was just as quiet but with a slightly increased distinctness in enunciation, and glancing swiftly at her father's face Patricia recognised that the limits of her speech had been reached, unless she preferred to change the subject.

"Yes, Annette has grown very pretty, indeed," said Adrien, taking up the conversation, "and is really a very nice girl, indeed. She sings beautifully. She is the leading soprano in her church choir, I believe."

"Captain Jack Maitland appeared to think her quite charming," said Rupert, making eyes at Patricia. Patricia's lips tightened and her eyes gleamed a bit.

"They were in school together, I think, were they not, Mamma?" said Adrien, flushing slightly.

"Of course they were, and so was Rupert, too—" said Patricia with impatient scorn, "and so would you if you hadn't been sent to England," she added to her sister.

"No doubt of it," said Rupert with a smile, "but you see she was fortunate enough to be sent to England."

"Blackwater is good enough for me," said Patricia, a certain stubborn hostility in her tone.

"I have always thought the Blackwater High School an excellent institution," said her mother quickly, "especially for boys."

"Yes, indeed, for boys," replied Stillwell, "but for young ladies—well, there is something in an English school, you know, that you can't get in any High School here in Canada."

"Rot!" ejaculated Patricia.

"My dear Patricia!" The mother was quite shocked.

"Pardon me, Mother, but you know we have a perfectly splendid High School here. Father has often said so."

Her mother sighed. "Yes, for boys. But for girls, I feel with Rupert that you get something in English schools that—" She hesitated, looking uncertainly at her elder daughter.

"Yes, and perhaps lose something, Mamma," said Adrien quietly. "I mean," she added hastily, "you lose touch with a lot of things and people, friends. Now, for instance, you remember when we were all children, boys and girls together, at the Public School, Annette was one of the cleverest and best of the lot of us, I used to be fond of her—and the others. Now—"

"But you can't help growing up," said Rupert, "and—well, democracy is all right and that sort of thing, but you must drift into your class you know. There's Annette, for instance. She is a factory hand, a fine girl of course, and all that, but—"

"Oh, I suppose we must recognise facts. Rupert, you are quite right," said Mrs. Templeton, "there must be social distinctions and there are classes. I mean," she added, as if to forestall the outburst she saw gathering behind her younger daughter's closed lips, "we must inevitably draw to our own set by our natural or acquired tastes and by our traditions and breeding."

"All very well in England, Mamma. I suppose dear Uncle Arthur and our dear cousins would hardly feel called upon to recognise Annette as a friend."

"Why should they?" challenged Rupert.

"My dear Patricia," said her father, mildly patient, "you are quite wrong. Our people at home, your uncle Arthur, I mean, and your cousins, and all well-bred folk, do not allow class distinctions to limit friendship. Friends are chosen on purely personal grounds of real worth and—well, congeniality."

"Would Uncle Arthur, or rather, Aunt Alicia have Annette to dinner, for instance?" demanded Patricia.

"Certainly not," said her mother promptly.

"She would not do anything to embarrass Annette," said her father.

"Oh, Dad, what a funk. That is quite unworthy of you."

"Would she be asked here now to dinner?" said Rupert. "I mean," he added in some confusion, "would it be, ah, suitable? You know what I mean."

"She has been here. Don't you remember, Mamma? She was often here. And every time she came she was the cleverest thing, she was the brightest, the most attractive girl in the bunch." Her mother's eyebrows went up. "In the party, I mean. And the most popular. Why, I remember quite well that Rupert was quite devoted to her."

"A mere child, she was then, you know," said Rupert.

"She is just as bright, just as attractive, as clever now, more so indeed, as fine a girl in every way. But of course she was not a factory girl then. That's what you mean," replied Patricia scornfully.

"She has found her class," persisted Rupert. "She is all you say, but surely—"

"Yes, she is working in the new box factory. Her mother, lazy, selfish thing, took her from the High School."

"My dear Patricia, you are quite violent," protested her mother.

"It's true, Mamma," continued the girl, her eyes agleam, "and now she works in the box factory while Captain Jack works in the planing mill. She is in the same class."

"And good friends apparently," said Rupert with a malicious little grin.

"Why not? We would have Captain Jack to dinner, but not Annette."

Her father smiled at her. "Well done, little girl. Annette is a fine girl and is fortunate in her champion. You can have her to dinner any evening, I am quite sure."

"Can we, Mamma?"

"My dear, we will not discuss the matter any further," said her mother. "It is a very old question and very perplexing, I confess, but—"

"We don't see Captain Jack very much since his return," said her father, turning the conversation. "You might begin with him, eh, Patsy?"

"No," said the girl, a shade falling on her face. "He is always busy. He has such long hours. He works his day's work with the men and then he always goes up to the office to his father—and—and—Oh, I don't know, I wish he would come. He's not—" Patricia fell suddenly silent.

"Jack is very much engaged," said her mother quietly.

"Naturally he is tied up, learning the business, I mean," said the elder sister quietly. "He has little time for mere social frivolities and that sort of thing."

"It's not that, Adrien," said Patricia. "He is different since he came back. I wish—" She paused abruptly.

"He is changed," said her mother with a sigh. "They—the boys are all changed."

"The war has left its mark upon them, and what else can we expect?" said Dr. Templeton. "One wonders how they can settle down at all to work."

"Oh, Jack has settled down all right," said Patricia, as if analysing a subject interesting to herself alone. "Jack's not like a lot of them. He's too much settled down. What is it, I wonder? He seems to have quit everything, dancing, tennis, golf. He doesn't care—"

"Doesn't care? What for? That sounds either as if he were an egotist or a slacker." Her sister's words rasped Patricia's most sensitive heart string. She visibly squirmed, eagerly waiting a chance to reply. "Jack is neither," continued Adrien slowly. "I understand the thing perfectly. He has been up against big things, so big that everything else seems trivial. Fancy a tennis tournament for a man that has stared into hell's mouth."

"My dear, you are right," said her father. "Patricia is really talking too much. Young people should—"

"I know, Daddy—'be seen,'" said the younger daughter, and grinning affectionately at him she blew him a kiss. "But, all the same, I wish Captain Jack were not so awfully busy or were a little more keen about things. He wants something to stir him up."

"He may get that sooner than he thinks," said Stillwell, "or wishes. I hear there's likely to be trouble in the mills."

"Trouble? Financial? I should be very sorry," said Dr. Templeton.

"No. Labour. The whole labour world is in a ferment. The Maitlands can hardly expect to escape. As a matter of fact, the row has made a little start, I happen to know."

"These labour troubles are really very distressing. There is no end to them," said Mrs. Templeton, with the resignation one shows in discussing the inscrutable ways of Providence. "It does seem as if the working classes to-day have got quite beyond all bounds. One wonders what they will demand next. What is the trouble now, Rupert? Of course—wages."

"Oh, the eternal old trouble is there, with some new ones added that make even wages seem small."

"And what are these?" enquired Dr. Templeton.

"Oh, division of profits, share in administration and control."

"Division of profits in addition to wages?" enquired Mrs. Templeton, aghast. "But, how dreadful. One would think they actually owned the factory."

"That is the modern doctrine, I believe," said Rupert.

"Surely that is an extreme statement," said Dr. Templeton, in a shocked voice, "or you are talking of the very radical element only."

"The Rads lead, of course, but you would be surprised at the demands made to-day. Why, I heard a young chap last week, a soap-box artist, denouncing all capitalists as parasites. 'Why should we work for anyone but ourselves?' he was saying. 'Why don't we take charge of the factories and run them for the general good?' I assure you, sir, those were his very words."

"Really, Rupert, you amaze me. In Blackwater here?" exclaimed Dr. Templeton.

"But, my dear papa, that sort of thing is the commonplace of Hyde Park, you know," said Adrien, "and—"

"Ah, Hyde Park, yes. I should expect that sort of thing from the Hyde Park orators. You get every sort of mad doctrine in Hyde Park, as I remember it, but—"

"And I was going to say that that sort of thing has got away beyond Hyde Park. Why, papa dear, you have been so engrossed in your Higher Mathematics that you have failed to keep up with the times." His eldest daughter smiled at him and, reaching across the corner of the table, patted his hand affectionately. "We are away beyond being shocked at profit sharing, and even sharing in control of administration and that sort of thing."

"But there remains justice, I hope," said her father, "and the right of ownership."

"Ah, that's just it—what is ownership?"

"Oh, come, Adrien," said Rupert, "you are not saying that Mr. Maitland doesn't own his factory and mill."

"It depends on what you mean by own," said the girl coolly. "You must not take too much for granted."

"Well, what my money pays for I own, I suppose," said Rupert.

"Well," said Adrien, "that depends."

"My dear Adrien," said her mother, "you have such strange notions. I suppose you got them in those Clubs in London and from those queer people you used to meet."

"Very dear people," said Adrien, with a far away look in her eyes, "and people that loved justice and right."

"All right, Ade," said her younger sister, with a saucy grin, "I agree entirely with your sentiments. I just adore that pale blue tie of yours. I suppose, now that what's yours is mine, I can preempt that when I like."

"Let me catch you at it!"

"Well done, Patricia. You see the theories are all right till we come to have them applied all round," said Rupert.

"We were talking of joint ownership, Pat," said her sister, "the joint ownership of things to the making of which we have each contributed a part."

"Exactly," said Rupert. "I guess Grant Maitland paid his own good money for his plant."

"Yes," said Adrien.

"Yes, and all he paid for he owns."

"Yes."

"Well, that's all there is to it."

"Oh, pardon me—there is a good deal more—"

"Well, well, children, we shall not discuss the subject any further. Shall we all go up for coffee?"

"These are very radical views you are advancing, Adrien," said her father, rising from his chair. "You must be careful not to say things like that in circles where you might be taken seriously."

"Seriously, Daddy? I was never more serious in my life." She put her arm through her father's. "I must give you some books, some reports to read, I see," she said, laughing up into his face.

"Evidently," said her father, "if I am to live with you."

"I wonder what Captain Jack would think of these views," said Rupert, dropping into step with Patricia as they left the dining room together.

"He will think as Adrien does," said Patricia stoutly.

"Ah, I wouldn't be too sure about that," said Rupert. "You see, it makes a difference whose ox is being gored."

"What do you mean?" cried Patricia hotly.

"Never mind, Pat," said her sister over her shoulder. "I don't think he knows Captain Jack as we do."

"Perhaps better," said Rupert in a significant tone.

Patricia drew away from him.

"I think you are just horrid," she said. "Captain Jack is—"

"Never mind, dear. Don't let him pull your leg like that," said her sister, with a little colour in her cheek. "We know Captain Jack, don't we?"

"We do!" said Patricia with enthusiasm.

"We do!" echoed Rupert, with a smile that drove Pat into a fury.

CHAPTER VI
THE GRIEVANCE COMMITTEE

There was trouble at the Maitland Mills. For the first time in his history Grant Maitland found his men look askance at him. For the first time in his life he found himself viewing with suspicion the workers whom he had always taken a pride in designating "my men." The situation was at once galling to his pride and shocking to his sense of fair play. His men were his comrades in work. He knew them—at least, until these war days he had known them—personally, as friends. They trusted him and were loyal to him, and he had taken the greatest care to deal justly and more than justly by them. No labour troubles had ever disturbed the relations which existed between him and his men. It was thus no small shock when Wickes announced one day that a Grievance Committee wished to interview him. That he should have to meet a Grievance Committee, whose boast it had been that the first man in the works to know of a grievance was himself, and that the men with whom he had toiled and shared both good fortune and ill, but more especially the good, that had befallen through the last quarter century should have a grievance against him—this was indeed an experience that cut him to the heart and roused in him a fury of perplexed indignation.

"A what? A Grievance Committee!" he exclaimed to Wickes, when the old bookkeeper came announcing such a deputation.

"That's what they call themselves, sir," said Wickes, his tone of disgust disclaiming all association with any such organization.

"A Grievance Committee?" said Mr. Maitland again. "Well, I'll be! What do they want? Who are they? Bring them in," he roared in a voice whose ascending tone indicated his growing amazement and wrath.

"Come in you," growled Wickes in the voice he generally used for his collie dog, which bore a thoroughly unenviable reputation, "come on in, can't ye?"

There was some shuffling for place in the group at the door, but finally Mr. Wigglesworth found himself pushed to the front of a committee of five. With a swift glance which touched "the boss" in its passage and then rested upon the wall, the ceiling, the landscape visible through the window, anywhere indeed rather than upon the face of the man against whom they had a grievance, they filed in and stood ill at ease.

"Well, Wigglesworth, what is it?" said Grant Maitland curtly.

Mr. Wigglesworth cleared his throat. He was new at the business and was obviously torn between conflicting emotions of pride in his present important position and a wholesome fear of his "boss." However, having cleared his throat, Mr. Wigglesworth pulled himself together and with a wave of the hand began.

"These 'ere—er—gentlemen an' myself 'ave been (h)appinted a Committee to lay before you certain grievances w'ich we feel to be very (h)oppressive, sir, so to speak, w'ich, an' meanin' no offence, sir, as men, fellow-men, as we might say—"

"What do you want, Wigglesworth? What's your trouble? You have some trouble, what is it? Spit it out, man," said the boss sharply.

"Well, sir, as I was a-sayin', this 'ere's a Committee (h)appinted to wait on you, sir, to lay before you certain facts w'ich we wish you to consider an' w'ich, as British subjecks, we feel—"

"Come, come, Wigglesworth, cut out the speech, and get at the things. What do you want? Do you know? If so, tell me plainly and get done with it."

"We want our rights as men," said Mr. Wigglesworth in a loud voice, "our rights as free men, and we demand to be treated as British—"

"Is there anyone of this Committee that can tell me what you want of me?" said Maitland. "You, Gilby, you have some sense—what is the trouble? You want more wages, I suppose?"

"I guess so," said Gilby, a long, lean man, Canadian born, of about thirty, "but it ain't the wages that's eatin' me so much."

"What then?"

"It's that blank foreman."

"Foreman?"

"That's right, sir." "Too blanked smart!" "Buttin' in like a blank billy goat!" The growls came in various undertones from the Committee.

"What foreman? Hoddle?" The boss was ready to fight for his subalterns.

"No! Old Hoddle's all right," said Gilby. "It's that young smart aleck, Tony Perrotte."

"Tony Perrotte!" Mr. Maitland's voice was troubled and uncertain. "Tony Perrotte! Why, you don't mean to tell me that Perrotte is not a good man. He knows his job from the ground up."

"Knows too much," said Gilby. "Wants to run everything and everybody. You can't tell him anything. And you'd think he was a Brigadier-General to hear him giving us orders."

"You were at the front, Gilby?"

"I was, for three years."

"You know what discipline is?"

"I do that, and I know too the difference between a Corporal and a Company Commander. I know an officer when I see him. But a brass hat don't make a General."

"I won't stand for insubordination in my mills, Gilby. You must take orders from my foreman. You know me, Gilby. You've been long enough with me for that."

"You treat a man fair, Mr. Maitland, and I never kicked at your orders. Ain't that so?"

Maitland nodded.

"But this young dude—"

"'Dude'? What do you mean, 'dude'? He's no dude!"

"Oh, he's so stuck on himself that he gives me the wearisome willies. Look here, other folks has been to the war. He needn't carry his chest like a blanked bay window."

"Look here, Gilby, just quit swearing in this room." The cold blue eyes bored into Gilby's hot face.

"I beg pardon, sir. It's a bad habit I've got, but that—that Tony Perrotte has got my goat and I'm through with him."

"All right, Gilby. If you don't like your job you know what you can do," said Maitland coldly.

"You mean I can quit?" enquired Gilby hotly.

"I mean there's only one boss in these works, and that's me. And my foreman takes my orders and passes them along. Those that don't like them needn't take them."

"We demand our rights as—" began Mr. Wigglesworth heatedly.

"Excuse me, sir. 'A should like to enquir-r-e if it is your-r or-rder-rs that your-r for-r-man should use blasphemious language to your-r men?"

The cool, firm, rasping voice cut through Mr. Wigglesworth's sputtering noise like a circular saw through a pine log.

Mr. Maitland turned sharply upon the speaker.

"What is your name, my man?" he enquired.

"Ma name is Malcolm McNish. 'A doot ye have na har-r-d it. But the name maitters little. It's the question 'A'm speerin'—asking at ye."

Here was no amateur in the business of Grievance Committees. His manner was that of a self-respecting man dealing with a fellow-man on terms of perfect equality. There was a complete absence of Wigglesworth's noisy bluster, as also of Gilby's violent profanity. He obviously knew his ground and was ready to hold it. He had a case and was prepared to discuss it. There was no occasion for heat or bluster or profanity. He was prepared to discuss the matter, man to man.

Mr. Maitland regarded him for a moment or two with keen steady gaze.

"Where do you work, McNish?" he enquired of the Scot.

"A'm workin' the noo in the sawmill. A'm a joiner to trade."

"Then Perrotte is not your foreman?"

"That is true," said McNish quietly.

"Then personally you have no grievance against him?" Mr. Maitland had the air of a man who has scored a bull at the first shot.

"Ay, A have an' the men tae—the men I represent have—"

"And you assume to speak for them?"

"They appoint me to speak for them."

"And their complaint is—?"

"Their complaint is that he is no fit to be a foreman."

"Ah, indeed! And you are here solely on their word—"

"No, not solely, but pairtly. A know by experience and A hae har-r-d the man, and he's no fit for his job, A'm tellin' you."

"I suppose you know the qualifications of a foreman, McNish?" enquired Mr. Maitland with the suspicion of sarcasm in his voice.

"Ay, A do that."

"And how, may I ask, have you come to the knowledge?"

"A dinna see—I do not see the bearing of the question."

"Only this, that you and those you represent place your judgment as superior to mine in the choice of a foreman. It would be interesting to know upon what grounds."

"I have been a foreman myself. But there are two points of view in this question—the point of view of the management and that of the worker. We have the one point of view, you have the other. And each has its value. Ours is the more important."

"Indeed! And why, pray?"

"Yours has chiefly to do with profits, ours with human life."

"Very interesting indeed," said Mr. Maitland, "but it happens that profits and human life are somewhat closely allied—"

"Aye, but wi' you profits are the primary consideration and humanity the secondary. Wi' us humanity is the primary."

"Very interesting, indeed. But I must decline your premise. You are a new man here and so I will excuse you the impudence of charging me with indifference to the well-being of my men."

"You put wur-r-ds in my mouth, Mr. Maitland. A said nae sic thing," said McNish. "But your foreman disna' know his place, and he must be changed."

"'Must,' eh?" The word had never been used to Mr. Maitland since his own father fifty years before had used it. It was an unfortunate word for the success of the interview. "'Must,' eh?" repeated Mr. Maitland with rising wrath. "I'd have you know, McNish, that the man doesn't live that says 'must' to me in regard to the men I choose to manage my business."

"Then you refuse to remove yere foreman?"

"Most emphatically, I do," said Mr. Maitland with glints of fire in his blue eyes.

"Verra weel, so as we know yere answer. There is anither matter."

"Yes? Well, be quick about it."

"A wull that. Ye dinna pay yere men enough wages."

"How do you know I don't?" said Mr. Maitland rising from his chair.

"A have examined certain feegures which I shall be glad to submit tae ye, in regard tae the cost o' leevin' since last ye fixed the wage. If yere wage was right then, it's wrang the noo." Under the strain Mr. Maitland's boring eyes and increasing impatience the Doric flavour of McNish's speech grew richer and more guttural, varying with the intensity of his emotion.

"And what may these figures be?" enquired Mr. Maitland with a voice of contempt.

"These are the figures prepared by the Labour Department of your Federal Government. I suppose they may be relied upon. They show the increased cost of living during the last five years. You know yeresel' the increase in wages. Mr. Maitland, I am told ye are a just man, an' we ask ye tae dae the r-r-right. That's all, sir."

"Thank you for your good opinion, my man. Whether I am a just man or not is for my own conscience alone. As to the wage question, Mr. Wickes will tell you, the matter had already been taken up. The result will be announced in a week or so."

"Thank you, sir. Thank you, sir," said Mr. Wigglesworth. "We felt sure it would only be necessary to point (h)out the right course to you. I may say I took the same (h)identical (h)attitude with my fellow workmen. I sez to them, sez I, 'Mr. Maitland—'

"That will do, Wigglesworth," said Mr. Maitland, cutting him short. "Have you anything more to say?" he continued, turning to McNish.

"Nothing, sir, except to express the hope that you will reconsider yere attitude as regards the foreman."

"You may take my word for it, I will not," said Mr. Maitland, snapping his words off with his teeth.

"At least, as a fair-minded man, you will look into the matter," said McNish temperately.

"I shall do as I think best," said Mr. Maitland.

"It would be wiser."

"Do you threaten me, sir?" Mr. Maitland leaned over his desk toward the calm and rugged Scot, his eyes flashing indignation.

"Threaten ye? Na, na, threats are for bairns. Yere no a bairn, but a man an' a wise man an' a just, A doot. A'm gie'in' ye advice. That's all. Guid day."

He turned away from the indignant Mr. Maitland, put his hat on his head and walked from the room, followed by the other members of the Committee, with the exception of Mr. Wigglesworth who lingered with evidently pacific intentions.

"This, sir, is a most (h)auspicious (h)era, sir. The (h)age of reason and justice 'as dawned, an' — "

"Oh, get out, Wigglesworth. Haven't you made all your speeches yet? The time for the speeches is past. Good day."

He turned to his bookkeeper.

"Wickes, bring me the reports turned in by Perrotte, at once."

Mr. Maitland's manner was frankly, almost brutally, imperious. It was not his usual manner with his subordinates, from which it may be gathered that Mr. Maitland was seriously disturbed. And with good reason. In the first place, never in his career had one of his men addressed him in the cool terms of equality which McNish had used with him in the recent interview. Then, never had he been approached by a Grievance Committee. The whole situation was new, irritating, humiliating.

As to the wages question, he would settle that without difficulty. He had never skimped the pay envelope. It annoyed him, however, that he had been forstalled in the matter by this Committee. But very especially he was annoyed by the recollection of the deliberative, rasping tones of that cool-headed Scot, who had so calmly set before him his duty. But the sting of the interview lay in the consciousness that the criticism of his foreman was probably just. And then, he was tied to Tony Perrotte by bonds that reached his heart. Had it not been so, he would have made short work of the business. As it was, Tony would have to stay at all costs. Mr. Maitland sat back in his chair, his eyes fixed upon the Big Bluff visible through the window, but his mind lingering over a picture that had often gripped hard at his heart during the last two years, a picture drawn for him in a letter from his remaining son, Jack. The letter lay in the desk at his hand. He saw in the black night that shell-torn strip of land between the lines, black as a ploughed field, lurid for a swift moment under the red glare of a bursting shell or ghastly in the sickly illumination of a Verry light, and over this black pitted earth a man painfully staggering with a wounded man on his back. The words leaped to his eyes. "He brought me out of that hell, Dad." He closed his eyes to shut out that picture, his hands clenched on the arms of his chair.

"No," he said, raising his hand in solemn affirmation, "as the Lord God liveth, while I stay he stays."

"Come in," he said, in answer to a timid tap at the office door. Mr. Wickes laid a file before him. It needed only a rapid survey of the sheets to give him the whole story. Incompetence and worse, sheer carelessness looked up at him from every sheet. The planing mill was in a state of chaotic disorganization.

"What does this mean, Mr. Wickes?" he burst forth, putting his finger upon an item that cried out mismanagement and blundering. "Here is an order that takes a month to clear which should be done within ten days at the longest."

Wickes stood silent, overwhelmed in dismayed self-condemnation.

"It seems difficult somehow to get orders through, sir, these days," he said after a pause.

"Difficult? What is the difficulty? The men are there, the machines are there, the material is in the yard. Why the delay? And look at this. Here is a lot of material gone to the scrap heap, the finest spruce ever grown in Canada too. What does this mean, Wickes?" he seemed to welcome the opportunity of finding a scapegoat for economic crimes, for which he could find no pardon.

Sheet after sheet passed in swift review under his eye. Suddenly he flung himself back in his chair.

"Wickes, this is simply damnable!"

"Yes, sir," said Wickes, his face pale and his fingers trembling. "I don't—I don't seem to be able to—to—get things through."

"Get things through? I should say not," shouted Maitland, glaring at him.

"I have tried, I mean I'm afraid I'm—that I am not quite up to it, as I used to be. I get confused—and—" The old bookkeeper's lips were white and quivering. He could not get on with his story.

"Here, take these away," roared Maitland.

Gathering up the sheets with fingers that trembled helplessly, Wickes crept hurriedly out through the door, leaving a man behind him furiously, helplessly struggling in the relentless grip of his conscience, lashed with a sense of his own injustice. His anger which had found vent upon his old bookkeeper he knew was due another man, a man with whom at any cost he could never allow himself to be angry. The next two hours were bad hours for Grant Maitland.

As the quitting whistle blew a tap came again to the office door. It was Wickes, with a paper in his hand. Without a word he laid the paper upon his chief's desk and turned away. Maitland glanced over it rapidly.

"Wickes, what does this nonsense mean?" His chief's voice arrested him. He turned again to the desk.

"I don't think—I have come to feel, sir, that I am not able for my job. I do not see as how I can go on." Maitland's brows frowned upon the sheet. Slowly he picked up the paper, tore it across and tossed it into the waste basket.

"Wickes, you are an old fool—and," he added in a voice that grew husky, "I am another and worse."

"But, sir—" began Wickes, in hurried tones.

"Oh, cut it all out, Wickes," said Maitland impatiently. "You know I won't stand for that. But what can we do? He saved my boy's life—"

"Yes, sir, and he was with my Stephen at the last, and—" The old man's voice suddenly broke.

"I remember, Wickes, I remember. And that's another reason—We must find another way out."

"I have been thinking, sir," said the bookkeeper timidly, "if you had a younger man in my place—"

"You would go out, eh? I believe on my soul you would. You—you—old fool. But," said Maitland, reaching his hand across the desk, "I don't go back on old friends that way."

The two men stood facing each other for a few minutes, with hands clasped, Maitland's face stern and set, Wickes' working in a pitiful effort to stay the tears that ran down his cheeks, to choke back the sobs that shook his old body as if in the grip of some unseen powerful hand.

"We must find a way," said Maitland, when he felt sure of his voice. "Some way, but not that way. Sit down. We must go through this together."

CHAPTER VII
THE FOREMAN

Grant Maitland's business instincts and training were such as to forbid any trifling with loose management in any department of his plant. He was, moreover, too just a man to allow any of his workmen to suffer for failures not their own. His first step was to get at the facts. His preliminary move was characteristic of him. He sent for McNish.

"McNish," he said, "your figures I have examined. They tell me nothing I did not know, but they are cleverly set down. The matter of wages I shall deal with as I have always dealt with it in my business. The other matter—" Mr. Maitland paused, then proceeded with grave deliberation, "I must deal with in my own way. It will take a little time. I shall not delay unnecessarily, but I shall accept dictation from no man as to my methods."

McNish stood silently searching his face with steady eyes.

"You are a new man here, and I find you are a good workman," continued Mr. Maitland. "I don't know you nor your aims and purposes in this Grievance Committee business of yours. If you want a steady job with a chance to get on, you will get both; if you want trouble, you can get that too, but not for long, here."

Still the Scot held him with grave steady gaze, but speaking no word.

"You understand me, McNish?" said Maitland, nettled at the man's silence.

"Aye, A've got a heid," he said in an impassive voice.

"Well, then, I hope you will govern yourself accordingly. Good-day," said Maitland, closing the interview.

McNish still stood immovable.

"That's all I have to say," said Maitland, glancing impatiently at the man.

"But it's no all A have to say, if ye will pairmit me," answered McNish in a voice quiet and respectful and apparently, except for its Doric flavour, quite untouched by emotion of any kind soever.

"Go on," said Maitland shortly, as the Scot stood waiting.

"Maister Maitland," said McNish, rolling out a deeper Doric, "ye have made a promise and a threat. Yere threat is naething tae me. As tae yere job, A want it and A want tae get on, but A'm a free man the noo an' a free man A shall ever be. Good-day tae ye." He bowed respectfully to his employer and strode from the room.

Mr. Maitland sat looking at the closed door.

"He is a man, that chap, at any rate," he said to himself, "but what's his game, I wonder. He will bear watching."

The very next day Maitland made a close inspection of his plant, beginning with the sawmill. He found McNish running one of the larger circular saws, and none too deftly. He stood observing the man for some moments in silence. Then stepping to the workman's side he said,

"You will save time, I think, if you do it this way." He seized the levers and, eliminating an unnecessary movement, ran the log. McNish stood calmly observing.

"Aye, yere r-right," he said. "Ye'll have done yon before."

"You just bet I have," said Maitland, not a little pleased with himself.

"A'm no saw man," said McNish, a little sullenly. "A dinna ken—I don't know saws of this sort. I'm a joiner. He put me off the bench."

"Who?" said Maitland quickly.

"Yon manny," replied McNish with unmistakable disgust.

"You were on the bench, eh? What sort of work were you on?"

"A was daein' a bit counter work. A wasna fast enough for him."

Mr. Maitland called the head sawyer.

"Put a man on here for a while, Powell, will you? You come with me, McNish."

Together they went into the planing mill. Asking for the foreman he found that he was nowhere to be seen, that indeed he had not been in the mill that morning.

"Show me your work, McNish," he said.

McNish led him to a corner of the mill where some fine counter work was in process.

"That's my work," he said, pointing to a piece of oak railing.

Maitland, turning the work over in his hands, ran his finger along a joint somewhat clumsily fitted.

"Not that," said McNish hastily. "Ma work stops here."

Again Maitland examined the rail. His experienced eye detected easily the difference in the workmanship.

"Is there anything else of yours about here?" he asked. McNish went to a pile of finished work and from it selected a small swing door beautifully panelled. Maitland's eye gleamed.

"Ah, that's better," he said. "Yes, that's better."

He turned to one of the workmen at the bench near by.

"What job is this, Gibbon?" he asked.

"It's the Bank job, I think," said Gibbon.

"What? The Merchants' Bank job? Surely that can't be. That job was due two weeks ago." Maitland turned impatiently toward an older man. "Ellis," he said sharply, "do you know what job this is?"

Ellis came and turned over the different parts of the work.

"That's the Merchants' Bank job, sir," he said.

"Then what is holding this up?" enquired Maitland wrathfully.

"It's the turned work, I think, sir. I am not sure, but I think I heard Mr. Perrotte asking about that two or three days ago." Mr. Maitland's lips met in a thin straight line.

"You can go back to your saw, McNish," he said shortly.

"Ay, sir," said McNish, his tone indicating quiet satisfaction. At Gibbon's bench he paused. "Ye'll no pit onything past him, a doot," he said, with a grim smile, and passed out.

In every part of the shop Mr. Maitland found similar examples of mismanagement and lack of co-ordination in the various departments of the work. It needed no more than a cursory inspection to convince him that a change of foreman was a simple necessity. Everywhere he found not only evidence of waste of time but also of waste of material. It cut him to the heart to see beautiful wood mangled and ruined. All his life he had worked with woods of different kinds. He knew them standing in all their matchless grandeur, in the primeval forest and had followed them step by step all the way to the finished product. Never without a heart pang did he witness a noble white pine, God's handiwork of centuries, come crashing to earth through the meaner growth beneath the chopper's axe. The only thing that redeemed such a deed from sacrilege, in his mind, was to see the tree fittingly transformed into articles of beauty and worth suitable for man's use. Hence, when he saw lying here and there deformed and disfigured fragments of the exquisitely grained white spruce, which during the war, he had with such care selected for his aeroplane parts, his very heart rose in indignant wrath. And filled with this wrath he made his way to the office and straightway summoned Wickes and his son Jack to conference.

"Tony will never make a worker in wood. He cares nothing for it," he said bitterly.

"Nor in anything else, Dad," said Jack, with a little laugh.

"You laugh, but it is no laughing matter," said his father reproachfully.

"I am sorry, Father, but you know I always thought it was a mistake to put Tony in charge of anything. Why, he might have had his commission if he were not such an irresponsible, downwright lazy beggar. What he needs, as my Colonel used to profanely say, is 'a good old-fashioned Sergeant-Major to knock hell out of him'. And, believe me, Tony was a rattling fine soldier if his officer would regularly, systematically and effectively expel his own special devil from his system. He needs that still."

"What can we do with him? I simply can't and won't dismiss him, as that infernally efficient and coolheaded Scot demands. You heard about the Grievance Committee?"

"Oh, the town has the story with embellishments. Rupert Stillwell took care to give me a picturesque account. But I would not hesitate, Dad. Kick Tony a good swift kick once a week or so, or, if that is beneath your dignity, fire him."

"But, Jack, lad, we can't do that," said his father, greatly distressed, "after what—"

"Why not? He carried me out of that hell all right, and while I live I shall remember that. But he is a selfish beggar. He hasn't the instinct for team play. He hasn't the idea of responsibility for the team. He gets so that he can not make himself do what he just doesn't feel like doing. He doesn't care a tinker's curse for the other fellows in the game with him."

"The man that doesn't care for other fellows will never make a foreman," said Mr. Maitland decisively. "But can't something be done with him?"

"There's only one way to handle Tony," said Jack. "I learned that long ago in school. He was a prince of half-backs, you know, but I had regularly to kick him about before every big match. Oh, Tony is a fine sort but he nearly broke my heart till I nearly broke his back."

"That does not help much, Jack." For the first time in his life Grant Maitland was at a loss as to how he should handle one of his men. Were it not for the letter in the desk at his hand he would have made short work of Tony Perrotte. But there the letter lay and in his heart the inerasible picture it set forth.

"What is the special form that Tony's devilment has taken, may I ask?" enquired Jack.

"Well, I may say to you, what Wickes knows and has known and has tried for three months to hide from me and from himself, Tony has made about as complete a mess of the organization under his care in the planing mill as can be imagined. The mill is strewn with the wreckage of unfulfilled orders. He has no sense of time value. To-morrow is as good as to-day, next week as this week. A foreman without a sense of time value is no good. And he does not value material. Waste to him is nothing. Another fatal defect. The man to whom minutes are not potential gold and material potential product can never hope to be a manufacturer. If only I had not been away from home! But the thing is, what is to be done?"

"In the words of a famous statesman much abused indeed, I suggest, 'Wait and see.' Meantime, find some way of kicking him into his job."

This proved to be in the present situation a policy of wisdom. It was Tony himself who furnished the solution. From the men supposed to be working under his orders he learned the day following Maitland's visit of inspection something of the details of that visit. He quickly made up his mind that the day of reckoning could not long be postponed. None knew better than Tony himself that he was no foreman; none so well that he loathed the job which had been thrust upon him by the father of the man whom he had carried out from the very mouth of hell. It was something to his credit that he loathed himself for accepting the position. Yet, with irresponsible procrastination, he put off the day of reckoning. But, some ten days later, and after a night with some kindred spirits of his own Battalion, a night prolonged into the early hours of the working day, Tony presented himself at the office, gay, reckless, desperate, but quite compos mentis and quite master of his means of locomotion.

He appeared in the outer office, still in his evening garb.

"Mr. Wickes," he said in solemn gravity, "please have your stenographer take this letter."

Mr. Wickes, aghast, strove to hush his vibrant tones, indicating in excited pantomime the presence of the chief in the inner office. He might as effectively have striven to stay the East wind at that time sweeping up the valley.

"Are you ready, my dear?" said Tony, smiling pleasantly at the girl. "All right, proceed. 'Dear Mr. Maitland:' Got that? 'Conscious of my unfitness for the position of foreman in—'"

"Hush, hush, Tony," implored Mr. Wickes.

Tony waved him aside.

"What have you got, eh?"

At that point the door opened and Grant Maitland stepped into the office. Tony rose to his feet and, bowing with elaborate grace and dignity, he addressed his chief.

"Good morning, sir. I am glad to see you, in fact, I wanted to see you but wishing to save your time I was in the very act of dictating a communication to you."

"Indeed, Tony?" said Mr. Maitland gravely.

"Yes, sir, I was on the point of dictating my resignation of my position of foreman."

"Step in to the office, Tony," said Mr. Maitland kindly and sadly.

"I don't wish to take your time, sir," said Tony, sobered and quieted by Mr. Maitland's manner, "but my mind is quite made up. I—"

"Come in," said Mr. Maitland, in a voice of quiet command, throwing open his office door. "I wish to speak to you."

"Oh, certainly, sir," answered Tony, pulling himself together with an all too obvious effort.

In half an hour Tony came forth, a sober and subdued man.

"Good-bye, Wickes," he said, "I'm off."

"Where are you going, Tony?" enquired Wickes, startled at the look on Tony's face.

"To hell," he snapped, "where such fools as me belong," and, jamming his hat hard down on his head, he went forth.

In another minute Mr. Maitland appeared at the office door.

"Wickes," he said sharply, "put on your hat and get Jack for me. Bring him, no matter what he's at. That young fool who has just gone out must be looked after. The boot-leggers have been taking him in tow. If I had only known sooner. Did you know, Wickes, how he has been going on? Why didn't you report to me?"

"I hesitated to do that, sir," putting his desk in order. "I always expected as how he would pull up. It's his company, sir. He is not so much to blame."

"Well, he would not take anything I had to offer. He is wild to get away. And unfortunately he has some money with him, too. But get Jack for me. He can handle him if anybody can."

Sorely perplexed Mr. Maitland returned to his office. His business sense pointed the line of action with sunlight clearness. His sense of justice to the business for which he was responsible as well as to the men in his employ no less clearly indicated the action demanded. His sane judgment concurred in the demand of his men for the dismissal of his foreman. Dismissal had been rendered unnecessary by Tony's unshakable resolve to resign his position which he declared he loathed and which he should never have accepted. His perplexity arose from the confusion within himself. What should he do with Tony? He had no position in his works or in the office for which he was fit. None knew this better than Tony himself.

"It's a joke, Mr. Maitland," he had declared, "a ghastly joke. Everybody knows it's a joke, that I should be in command of any man when I can't command myself. Besides, I can't stick it." In this resolve he had persisted in spite of Mr. Maitland's entreaties that he should give the thing another try, promising him all possible guidance and backing. But entreaties and offers of assistance had been in vain. Tony was wild to get away from the mill. He hated the grind. He wanted his freedom. Vainly Mr. Maitland had offered to find another position for him somewhere, somehow.

"We'll find a place in the office for you," he had pleaded. "I want to see you get on, Tony. I want to see you make good."

But Tony was beyond all persuasion.

"It isn't in me," he had declared. "Not if you gave me the whole works could I stick it."

"Take a few days to think it over," Mr. Maitland had pleaded.

"I know myself—only too well. Ask Jack, he knows," was Tony's bitter answer. "And that's final."

"No, Tony, it is not final," had been Mr. Maitland's last word, as Tony had left him.

But after the young man had left him there still remained the unsolved question, What was he to do with Tony? In Mr. Maitland's heart was the firm resolve that he would not allow Tony to go his own way. The letter in the desk at his hand forbade that.

At his wits' end he had sent for Jack. Jack had made a football half-back and a hockey forward out of Tony when everyone else had failed. If anyone could divert him from that desperate downward course to which he seemed headlong bent, it was Jack.

In a few minutes Wickes returned with the report that on receiving an account of what had happened Jack had gone to look up Tony.

Mr. Maitland drew a breath of relief.

"Tony is all right for to-day," he said, turning to his work and leaving the problem for the meantime to Jack.

In an hour Jack reported that he had been to the Perrotte home and had interviewed Tony's mother. From her he had learned that Tony had left the town, barely catching the train to Toronto. He might not return for a week or ten days. He could set no time for it. He was his own master as to time. He had got to the stage where he could go and come pretty much as he pleased. The mother was not at all concerned as to these goings and comings of her son. He had an assured position, all cause for anxiety in regard to him was at an end. Tony's mother was obviously not a little uplifted that her son should be of sufficient importance to be entrusted with business in Toronto in connection with the mill.

All of which tended little toward relieving the anxiety of Mr. Maitland.

"Let him take his swing, Dad, for a bit," was Jack's advice. "He will come back when he is ready, and until then wild horses won't bring him nor hold him. He is no good for his old job, and you have no other ready that he will stick at. He has no Sergeant-Major now to knock him about and make him keep step, more's the pity."

"Life will be his Sergeant-Major, I fear," said his father, "and a Sergeant-Major that will exact the utmost limit of obedience or make him pay the price. All the same, we won't let him go. I can't Jack, anyway."

"Oh, Tony will turn up, never fear, Dad," said Jack easily.

With this assurance his father had to content himself. In a fortnight's time a letter came from Tony to his sister, rosy with the brilliance of the prospects opening up before him. There was the usual irresponsible indefiniteness in detail. What he was doing and how he was living Tony did not deign to indicate. Ten days later Annette had another letter. The former prospects had not been realised, but he had a much better thing in view, something more suitable to him, and offering larger possibilities of position and standing in the community. So much Annette confided to her mother who passed on the great news with elaborations and annotations to Captain Jack. To Captain Jack himself Annette gave little actual information. Indeed, shorn of its element of prophecy, there was little in Tony's letter that could be passed on. Nor did Annette drop any hint but that all was quite well with her brother, much less that he had suggested a temporary loan of fifty dollars but only of course if she could spare the amount with perfect convenience. After this letter there was silence as far as Tony was concerned and for Annette anxiety that deepened into agony as the silence remained unbroken with the passing weeks.

With the anxiety there mingled in Annette's heart anger at the Maitlands, for she blamed them for Tony's dismissal from his position. This, it is fair to say, was a reflection from her mother's wrath, whose mind had been filled up with rumours from the mills to the effect that her son had been "fired." Annette was wise enough and knew her brother well enough to discredit much that rumour brought to her ears, but she could not rid herself of the thought that a way might have been found to hold Tony about the mills.

"He fired the boy, did the ould carmudgeon," said Madame Perrotte in one of her rages, "and druv him off from the town."

"Nonsense, Mother," Annette had replied, "you know well enough Tony left of his own accord. Why should you shame him so? He went because he wanted to go."

This was a new light upon the subject for her mother.

"Thrue for you, Annette, gurl," she said, "an' ye said it that time. But why for did he not induce the bye to remain? It would be little enough if he had made him the Manager of the hull works. That same would never pay back what he did for his son."

"Hush, Mother," said Annette, in a shocked and angry voice, "let no one hear you speak like that. Pay back! You know, Mother, nothing could ever pay back a thing like that." The anger in her daughter's voice startled the mother.

"Oui! by gar!" said Perrotte, who had overheard, with quick wrath. "Dat's foolish talk for sure! Dere's no man can spik lak dat to me, or I choke him on his fool t'roat, me."

"Right you are, mon pere!" said Annette appeasing her father. "Mother did not think what she was saying."

"Dat's no bon," replied Perrotte, refusing to be appeased. "Sacre tonnerre! Dat's one—what you call?—damfool speech. Dat boy Tony he's carry (h)on hees back his friend, le Capitaine Jack, an' le Capitaine, he's go five mile for fin' Tony on' de shell hole an' fetch heem to le docteur and stay wit' him till he's fix (h)up. Nom de Dieu! You pay for dat! Mama! You mak' shame for me on my heart!" cried the old Frenchman, beating his breast, while sobs shook his voice.

CHAPTER VIII
FREE SPEECH

Fifty years ago Blackwater town was a sawmill village on the Blackwater River which furnished the power for the first little sawmill set up by Grant Maitland's father.

Down the river came the sawlogs in the early spring when the water was high, to be caught and held by a "boom" in a pond from which they were hauled up a tramway to the saw. A quarter of a mile up stream a mill race, tapping the river, led the water to an "overshot wheel" in the early days, later to a turbine, thus creating the power necessary to drive the mill machinery. When the saw was still the water overflowed the "stop-logs" by the "spillway" into the pond below.

But that mill race furnished more than power to the mill. It furnished besides much colourful romance to the life of the village youth of those early days. For down the mill race they ran their racing craft, jostling and screaming, urging with long poles their laggard flotillas to victory. The pond by the mill was to the boys "swimming hole" and fishing pool, where, during the long summer evenings and through the sunny summer days, they spent amphibious hours in high and serene content. But in springtime when the pond was black with floating logs it became the scene of thrilling deeds of daring. For thither came the lumber-jacks, fresh from "the shanties," in their dashing, multi-colored garb, to "show off" before admiring friends and sweethearts their skill in "log-running" and "log-rolling" contests which as the spirit of venture grew would end like as not in the icy waters of the pond.

Here, too, on brilliant winter days the life of the village found its centre of vivid interest and activity. For then the pond would be a black and glittering surface whereon wheeled and curved the ringing, gleaming blades of "fancy" skaters or whereon in sterner hours opposing "shinny" teams sought glory in Homeric and often gory contest.

But those days and those scenes were now long since gone. The old mill stood a picturesque ruin, the water wheel had given place to the steam engine, the pond had shrunk to an insignificant pool where only pollywogs and minnows passed unadventurous lives, the mill race had dwindled to a trickling stream grown thick with watercress and yellow lilies, and what had once been the centre of vigorous and romantic life was now a back water eddy devoid alike of movement and of colour.

A single bit of life remained—the little log cottage, once the Manager's house a quarter of a century ago, still stood away up among the pines behind the old mill ruin and remote from the streets and homes of the present town. At the end of a little grassy lane it stood, solid and square, resisting with its well hewn pinelogs the gnawing tooth of time. Abandoned by the growing town, forgotten by the mill owner, it was re-discovered by Malcolm McNish, or rather by his keen eyed old mother on their arrival from the old land six months ago. For a song McNish bought the solid little cottage, he might have had it as a gift but that he would not, restored its roof, cleared out its stone chimney which, more than anything else, had caught the mother's eye, re-set the window panes, added a wee cunning porch, gave its facings a coat of paint, enclosed its bit of flower garden in front and its "kale yaird" in the rear with a rustic paling, and made it, when the Summer had done its work, a bonnie homelike spot which caught the eye and held the heart of the passer-by.

The interior more than fulfilled the promise of the exterior. The big living room with its great stone fireplace welcomed you on opening the porch door. From the living room on the right led two doors, each giving entrance to a tiny bedroom and flanking a larger room known as "the Room."

Within the living room were gathered the household treasures, the Lares and Penates of the little stone rose-covered cottage "at hame awa' ayont the sea." On the mantel a solid hewn log of oak, a miracle of broad-axe work, were "bits o' chiny" rarely valuable as antiques to the knowing connoisseur but beyond price to the old white-haired lady who daily dusted them with reverent care as having been borne by her mother from the Highland home in the far north country when as a bride she came by the "cadger's cairt" to her new home in the lonely city of Glasgow. Of that Glasgow home and of her own home later the walls of the log cottage were eloquent.

The character giving bit of furniture, however, in the living room was a book-case that stood in a corner. Its beautiful inlaid cabinet work would in itself have attracted attention, but not the case but the books were its distinction. The great English poets were represented there in serviceable bindings showing signs of use, Shakespeare, Wordsworth, Coleridge, Browning, Keats, and with them in various editions, Burns. Beside the poets Robert Louis had a place, and Sir Walter, as well as Kipling and Meredith and other moderns. But on the shelf that showed most wear were to be found the standard works of economists of different schools from the great Adam Smith to Marx and the lot of his imitators and disciples. This was Malcolm's book-case. There was in another corner near the fire-place a little table and above it hung a couple of shelves for books of another sort, the Bible and The Westminster Confession, Bunyan and Baxter and Fox's Book of Martyrs, Rutherford and McCheyne and Law, The Ten Years' Conflict, Spurgeon's Sermons and Smith's Isaiah, and a well worn copy of the immortal Robbie. This was the mother's corner, a cosy spot where she nourished her soul by converse with the great masters of thought and of conscience.

In this "cosy wee hoosie" Malcolm McNish and his mother passed their quiet evenings, for the days were given to toil, in talk, not to say discussion of the problems, the rights and wrongs of the working man. They agreed in much; they differed, and strongly, in point of view. The mother was all for reform of wrongs with the existing economic system, reverencing the great Adam Smith. The son was for a new deal, a new system, the Socialistic, with modifications all his own. All, or almost all, that Malcolm had read the mother had read with the exception of Marx. She "cudna thole yon godless loon" or his theories or his works. Malcolm had grown somewhat sick of Marx since the war. Indeed, the war had seriously disturbed the foundations of Malcolm's economic faith, and he was seeking a readjustment of his opinion and convictions, which were rather at loose ends. In this state of mind he found little comfort from his shrewd old mother.

"Y'e have nae anchor, laddie, and ilka woof of air and ilka turn o' the tide and awa' ye go."

As for her anchor, she made no bones of announcing that she had been brought up on the Shorter Catechism and the Confession and in consequence found a place for every theory of hers, Social and Economic as well as Ethical and Religious, within the four corners of the mighty fabric of the Calvinistic system of Philosophy and Faith.

One of the keen joys of her life since coming to the new country she found in her discussions with the Rev. Murdo Matheson, whom, after some considerable hesitation, she had finally chosen to "sit under." The Rev. Murdo's theology was a little narrow for her. She had been trained in the schools of the Higher Critics of the Free Kirk leaders at home. She talked familiarly of George Adam Smith, whom she affectionately designated as "George Adam." She would wax wrathful over the memory of the treatment meted out to Robertson Smith by a former generation of Free Kirk heresy hunters. Hence she regarded with pity the hesitation with which her Minister accepted some of the positions of the Higher Critics. Although it is to be confessed that the war had somewhat rudely shattered her devotion to German theology.

"What d'ye think o' yere friend Harnack the noo?" her son had jibed at her soon after the appearance of the great manifesto from the German professors.

"What do A think o' him?" she answered, sparring for time. "What do A think o' him?" Then, as her eye ran over her son's uniform, for he was on leave at the time, she blazed forth, "A'll tell ye what A think o' him. A think that Auld Hornie has his hook intil him and the hale kaboodle o' them. They hae forsaken God and made tae themselves ither gods and the Almichty hae gi'en them ower tae a reprobate mind."

But her Canadian Minister's economic positions satisfied her. He had specialised in Social and Economic Science in his University Course and she considered him sound "in the main."

She had little patience with half baked theorists and none at all with mere agitators. It was therefore with no small indignation that she saw on a Sunday morning Mr. Wigglesworth making his way up the lane toward her house door.

"The Lord be guid tae us!" she exclaimed. "What brings yon cratur here—and on a Sabbath mornin'? Mind you, Malcolm," she continued in a voice of sharp decision, "A'll hae nane o' his 'rights o' British citizens' clack the morn."

"Who is it, Mother?" enquired her son, coming from his room to look out through the window. "Oh, dinna fash ye're heid ower yon windbag," he added, dropping into his broadest Doric and patting his mother on the shoulder.

"He disna fash me," said his mother. "Nae fears. But A'll no pairmit him to brak the Sabbath in this hoose, A can tell ye." None the less she opened the door to Mr. Wigglesworth with dignified courtesy.

"Guid mornin', Mr. Wigglesworth," she said cordially. "Ye're airly on yere way tae the Kirk."

"Yes—that is—yes," replied Mr. Wigglesworth in some confusion, "I am a bit (h)early. Fact is, I was (h)anxious to catch Malcolm before 'e went aht. I 'ave a rather (h)important business on 'and with 'im, very (h) important business, I might say."

"'Business,' did ye say, Mr. Wigglesworth?" Mrs. McNish stood facing him at the door. "Business! On the Lord's Day?"

Mr. Wigglesworth gaped at her, hat in hand.

"Well, Mrs. McNish, not (h)exactly business. That is," he said with an apologetic smile, "(h)it depends, you see, just w'at yeh puts (h)into a word, Mrs. McNish."

Mr. Wigglesworth's head went over to one side as if in contemplation of a new and striking idea.

"A pit nae meaning into a word that's no in it on its ain accoont," she replied with uncompromising grimness. "Business is just business, an' my son diz nae business on the Lord's Day."

There was no place for casuistry in the old Scotch lady's mind. A thing was or was not, and there was an end to that.

"Certainly, Mrs. McNish, certainly! And so sez I. But there might be a slight difference of (h)opinion between you and I, so to speak, as to just w'at may constitute 'business.' Now, for (h)instance—" Mr. Wigglesworth was warming to his subject, but the old lady standing on her doorstep fixed her keen blue eyes upon him and ruthlessly swept away all argumentation on the matter.

"If it is a matter consistent with the Lord's Day, come in; if not, stay oot."

"Oh! Yes, thank you. By the way, is your son in, by (h)any chance? Per'raps 'e's shavin' 'isself, eh?" Mr. Wigglesworth indulged in a nervous giggle.

"Shavin' himsel!" exclaimed Mrs. McNish. "On the Sawbath! Man, d'ye think he's a heathen, then?" Mrs. McNish regarded the man before her with severity.

"An 'eathen? Not me! I should consider it an 'eathenish practice to go dirty of a Sunday," said Mr. Wigglesworth triumphantly.

"Hoots, man, wha's talkin' about gaein' dirty? Can ye no mak due preparation on the Saturday? What is yere Saturday for?"

This was a new view to Mr. Wigglesworth and rather abashed him.

"What is it, Mother?" Malcolm's voice indicated a desire to appease the wrath that gleamed in his mother's eye. "Oh, it is Mr. Wigglesworth. Yes, yes! I want to see Mr. Wigglesworth. Will you come in, Mr. Wigglesworth?"

"Malcolm, A was jist tellin' Mr. Wigglesworth—"

"Yes, yes, I know, Mother, but I want—"

"Malcolm, ye ken what day it is. And A wull not—"

"Yes, Mother, A ken weel, but—"

"And ye ken ye'll be settin' oot for the Kirk in half an oor—"

"Half an hour, Mother? Why, it is only half past nine—"

"A ken weel what it is. But A dinna like tae be fashed and flustered in ma mind on ma way till the Hoose o' God."

"I shall only require a very few moments, Madam," said Mr. Wigglesworth. "The matter with w'ich I am (h)entrusted need not take more than a minute or two. In fact, I simply want to (h)announce a special, a very special meetin' of the Union this (h)afternoon."

"A releegious meetin', Mr. Wigglesworth?" enquired Mrs. McNish.

"Well—not exactly—that is—I don't know but you might call it a religious meetin'. To my mind, Mrs. McNish, you know—"

But Mrs. McNish would have no sophistry.

"Mr. Wigglesworth," she began sternly.

But Malcolm cut in.

"Now, Mother, I suppose it's a regular enough meeting. Just wait till I get my hat, Mr. Wigglesworth. I'll be with you."

His mother followed him into the house, leaving Mr. Wigglesworth at the door.

"Malcolm," she began with solemn emphasis.

"Now, now, Mother, surely you know me well enough by this time to trust my judgment in a matter of this kind," said her son, hurriedly searching for his hat.

"Ay, but A'm no sae sure o' yon buddie—"

"Hoot, toot," said her son, passing out. "A'll be back in abundant time for the Kirk, Mither. Never you fear."

"Weel, weel, laddie, remember what day it is. Ye ken weel it's no day for warldly amusement."

"Ay, Mither," replied her son, smiling a little at the associating of Mr. Wigglesworth with amusement of any sort on any day.

In abundance of time Malcolm was ready to allow a quiet, unhurried walk with his mother which would bring them to the church a full quarter of an hour before the hour of service.

It happened that the Rev. Murdo was on a congenial theme and in specially good form that morning.

"How much better is a man than a sheep," was his text, from which with great ingenuity and eloquence he proceeded to develop the theme of the supreme value of the human factor in modern life, social and industrial. With great cogency he pressed the argument against the inhuman and degrading view that would make man a mere factor in the complex problem of Industrial Finance, a mere inanimate cog in the Industrial Machine.

"What did you think of the sermon, Mother?" asked Malcolm as they entered the quiet lane leading home.

"No sae bad, laddie, no sae bad. Yon's an able laddie, especially on practical themes. Ay, it was no that bad," replied his mother with cautious approval.

"What about his view of the Sabbath?"

"What about it? Wad ye no lift a sheep oot o' the muck on the Sawbath?"

"A would, of course," replied Malcolm.

"Weel, what?"

"A was jist thinkin' o' Mr. Wigglesworth this morning."

"Yon man!"

"You were rather hard on him this morning', eh, Mither?"

"Hard on him? He's no a sheep, nor in some ways as guid's a sheep, A grant ye that, but such as he is was it no ma duty to pull him oot o' the mire o' Sawbath desecration and general ungodliness?"

"Aw, Mither, Mither! Ye're incorrigible! Ye ought to come to the meeting this afternoon and give them all a lug out."

"A wull that then," said his mother heartily. "They need it, A doot."

"Hoots! Nonsense, Mither!" said her son hastily, knowing well how thoroughly capable she was of not only going to a meeting of Union workers but also of speaking her mind if in her judgment they were guilty of transgressing the Sabbath law. "The meeting will be just as religious as Mr. Matheson's anyway."

"A'm no sae sure," said his mother grimly.

Whether religious in the sense understood by Mrs. McNish, the meeting was not wanting in ethical interest or human passion. It was a gathering of the workers in the various industries in the town, Trade Unionists most of them, but with a considerable number who had never owed allegiance to any Union and a number of disgruntled ex-Unionists. These latter were very vociferous and for the most part glib talkers, with passions that under the slightest pressure spurted foaming to the surface. Returned soldiers there were who had taken on their old jobs but who had not yet settled down into the colourless routine of mill and factory work under the discipline of those who often knew little of the essentials of discipline as these men knew them. A group of French-Canadian factory hands, taken on none too willingly in the stress of war work, constituted an element of friction, for the soldiers despised and hated them. With these there mingled new immigrants from the shipyards and factories of the Old Land, all members or ex-members of Trade Unions, Socialists in training and doctrine, familiar with the terminology and jargon of those Socialistic debating schools, the Local Unions of England and Scotland, alert, keen, ready of wit and ready of tongue, rejoicing in wordy, passionate debate, ready for anything, fearing nothing.

The occasion of the meeting was the presence of a great International Official of the American Federation of Labour, and its purpose to strengthen International Unionism against the undermining of guerilla bands of non-Unionists and very especially against the new organizations emanating from the far West, the One Big Union.

At the door of the hall stood Mr. Wigglesworth, important, fussy and unctuously impressive, welcoming, directing, introducing and, incidentally but quite ineffectively, seeking to inspire with respect for his august person a nondescript crowd of small boys vainly seeking entrance. With an effusiveness amounting to reverence he welcomed McNish and directed him in a mysterious whisper toward a seat on the platform, which, however, McNish declined, choosing a seat at the side about half way up the aisle.

A local Union official was addressing the meeting but saying nothing in particular, and simply filling in till the main speaker should arrive. McNish, quite uninterested in the platform, was quietly taking note of the audience, with many of whom he had made a slight acquaintance. As his eye travelled slowly from face to face it was suddenly arrested. There beside her father was Annette Perrotte, who greeted him with a bright nod and smile. They had long ago made up their tiff. Then McNish had another surprise. At the door of the hall appeared Captain Jack Maitland who, after coolly surveying the room, sauntered down the aisle and took a seat at his side. He nodded to McNish.

"Quite a crowd, McNish," he said. "I hear the American Johnnie is quite a spouter so I came along to hear."

McNish looked at him and silently nodded. He could not understand his presence at that kind of a meeting.

"You know I am a Union man now," said Captain Jack, accurately reading his silence. "Joined a couple of months ago."

But McNish kept his face gravely non-committal, wondering how it was that this important bit of news had not reached him. Then he remembered that he had not attended the last two monthly meetings of his Union, and also he knew that little gossip of the shops came his way. None the less, he was intensely interested in Maitland's appearance. He did Captain Jack the justice to acquit him of anything but the most honourable intentions, yet he could not make clear to his mind what end the son of his boss could serve by joining a Labour Union. He finally came to the conclusion that this was but another instance of an "Intellectual" studying the social and economic side of Industry from first-hand observation. It was a common enough thing in the Old Land. He was conscious of a little contempt for this dilettante sort of Labour Unionism, and he was further conscious of a feeling of impatience and embarrassment at Captain Jack's presence. He belonged to the enemy camp, and what right had he there? From looks cast in their direction it was plain that others were asking the same question. His thought received a sudden and unexpected exposition from the platform from no less a person than Mr. Wigglesworth himself to whom as one of the oldest officials in Unionised Labour in the town had been given the honour of introducing the distinguished visitor and delegate.

In flowing periods and with a reckless but wholly unauthorised employment of aspirates he "welcomed the (h)audience, (h)especially the ladies, and other citizens among 'oom 'e was delighted to (h)observe a representative of the (h)employing class 'oo was for the present 'e believed one of themselves." To his annoyed embarrassment Captain Jack found himself the observed of many eyes, friendly and otherwise. "But 'e would assure Captain Maitland that although 'e might feel as if 'e 'ad no right to be 'ere—"

"'Ere! 'Ere!" came a piercing voice in unmistakable approval, galvanising the audience out of its apathy into instant emotional intensity.

"(H)I want most (h)emphatically to (h)assure Captain Maitland," continued Mr. Wigglesworth, frowning heavily upon the interrupter, "that 'e is as welcome—"

"No! No!" cried the same Cockney voice, followed by a slight rumbling applause.

"I say 'e is," shouted Mr. Wigglesworth, supported by hesitating applause.

"No! No! We don't want no toffs 'ere." This was followed by more definite applause from the group immediately surrounding the speaker.

Mr. Wigglesworth was much affronted and proceeded to administer a rebuke to the interrupter.

"I (h)am surprised," he began, with grieved and solemn emphasis.

"Mr. Chairman," said the owner of the Cockney voice, rising to his feet and revealing himself a small man with large head and thin wizened features, "Mr. Chairman, I rise to protest right 'ere an' naow against the presence of (h)any representative of the (h)enemy class at—"

"Aw, shut up!" yelled a soldier, rising from his place. "Throw out the little rat!"

Immediately there was uproar. On every side returned soldiers, many of whom had been in Captain Jack's battalion, sprang up and began moving toward the little Cockney who, boldly standing his ground, was wildly appealing to the chair and was supported by the furious cheering of a group of his friends, Old Country men most of whom, as it turned out, were of the extreme Socialist type. By this time it had fully been borne in upon Captain Jack's mind, somewhat dazed by the unexpected attack, that he was the occasion of the uproar. Rising from his place he tried vainly to catch the Chairman's attention.

"Come up to the platform," said a voice in his ear. He turned and saw McNish shouldering his way through the excited crowd toward the front. After a moment's hesitation he shrugged his shoulders and followed. The move caught the eye and apparently the approval of the audience, for it broke into cheers which gathered in volume till by the time that McNish and Captain Jack stood on the platform the great majority were wildly yelling their enthusiastic approval of their action. McNish stood with his hand raised for a hearing. Almost instantly there fell a silence intense and expectant. The Scotchman stood looking in the direction of the excited Cockney with cold steady eye.

"A'm for freedom! The right of public assembly! A'm feart o' nae enemy, not the deevil himself. This gentleman is a member of my Union and he stays r-r-right he-e-r-re." With a rasping roll of his r's he seemed to be ripping the skin off the little Cockney's very flesh. The response was a yell of savage cheers which seemed to rock the building and which continued while Mr. Wigglesworth in overflowing effusiveness first shook Maitland's limp hand in a violent double-handed pump handle exercise and then proceeded to introduce him to the distinguished visitor, shouting his name in Maitland's ear, "Mr 'Oward (H)E. Bigelow," adding with a sudden inspiration, "(H)Introduce 'im to the (h)audience. Yes! Yes! Most (h)assuredly," and continued pushing both men toward the front of the platform, the demonstration increasing in violence.

"I say, old chap," shouted Captain Jack in the stranger's ear, "I feel like a fool."

"I feel like a dozen of 'em," shouted Mr. Bigelow in return. "But," he added with a slow wink, "this old fool is the daddy of 'em all. Go on, introduce me, or they'll bust something loose."

Captain Jack took one step to the front of the platform and held up his hand. The cheering assumed an even greater violence, then ceased in sudden breathless silence.

"Ladies and gentlemen," he said in a slightly bored voice, "this gentleman is Mr. Howard E. Bigelow, a representative of the American Federation of Labour, whom as a member of the Woodworkers' Union, Local 197, I am anxious to hear if you don't mind."

He bowed to the visitor, bowed to the audience once more swaying under a tempest of cheers, and, followed by McNish, made his way to his seat.

From the first moment of his speech Mr. Howard E. Bigelow had to fight for a hearing. The little Cockney was the centre of a well-organised and thoroughly competent body of obstructers who by clever "heckling," by points of order, by insistent questioning, by playing now upon the anti-American string, now upon the anti-Federation string, by ribald laughter, by cheering a happy criticism, completely checked every attempt of the speaker to take flight in his oratory. The International official was evidently an old hand in this sort of game, but in the hands of these past masters in the art of obstruction he met more than his match. Maitland was amazed at his patience, his self-control, his adroitness, but they were all in vain. At last he was forced to appeal to the Chairman for British fair play. But the Chairman was helplessly futile and his futility was only emphasised by Mr. Wigglesworth's attempts now at browbeating which were met with derision and again at entreaty which brought only demands for ruling on points of order, till the meeting was on the point of breaking up in confused disorder.

"McNish, I think I'll take a hand in this," said Captain Jack in the Scotchman's ear. "Are you game?"

"Wait a wee," said McNish, getting to his feet. Slowly he once more made his way to the platform. As the crowd caught on to his purpose they broke into cheering. When he reached the side of the speaker he spoke a word in his ear, then came to the front with his hand held up. There was instant quiet. He looked coolly over the excited, disintegrating audience for a moment or two.

"A belonged tae the Feefty-fir-rst Diveesion," he said in his richest Doric. "We had a rare time wi' bullies over there. A'm for free speech! Noo, listen tae me, you Cockney wheedle doodle. Let another cheep out o' yere trap an' the Captain there will fling ye oot o' this room as we did the Kayser oot o' France."

"You said it, McNish," said Maitland, leaping to the aisle. With a roar a dozen returned men were on their feet.

"Steady, squad!" rang out Captain Jack's order. "Fall into this aisle! Shun!" As if on parade the soldiers fell into line behind their captain.

"Macnamara!" he said, pointing to a huge Irishman.

"Sir!" said Macnamara.

"You see that little rat-faced chap?"

"Yes, sir."

"Take your place beside him."

With two steps Macnamara was beside his man.

"Mr. Chairman, I protest," began the little Cockney fiercely.

"Pass him up," said the Captain sharply.

With one single motion Macnamara's hand swept the little man out of his place into the aisle.

"Chuck him out!" said Captain Jack quietly.

From hand to hand, with never a pause, amid the jeers and laughter of the crowd the little man was passed along like a bundle of old rags till he disappeared through the open door.

"Who's next?" shouted Macnamara joyfully.

"As you were!" came the sharp command.

At once Macnamara stood at attention.

Captain Jack nodded to the platform.

"All right," he said quietly.

Mr. Howard E. Bigelow finished his speech in peace. He made appeal for the closing up of the ranks of Labour in preparation for the big fight which was rapidly coming. They had just finished with Kaiserism in Europe but they were faced with only another form of the same spirit in their own land. They wanted no more fighting, God knew they had had enough of that, but there were some things dearer than peace, and Labour was resolved to get and to hold those things which they had fought for, "which you British and especially you Canadians shed so much blood to win. We are making no threats, but we are not going to stand for tyranny at the hands of any man or any class of men in this country. Only one thing will defeat us, not the traditional enemies of our class but disunion in our own ranks due to the fool tactics of a lot of disgruntled and discredited traitors like the man who has just been fired from this meeting." He asked for a committee which would take the whole situation in hand. He closed with a promise that in any struggle which they undertook under the guidance of their International Officers the American Federation of Labour to their last dollar would be behind them.

Before the formal closing of the meeting Maitland slipped quietly out. As he reached the sidewalk a light hand touched his arm. Turning he saw at his elbow Annette, her face aglow and her black eyes ablaze with passionate admiration.

"Oh, Captain Jack," she panted, her hands outstretched, "you were just wonderful! Splendid! Oh! I don't know what to say! I—" She paused in sudden confusion. A hot colour flamed in her face. Maitland took her hands in his.

"Hello, Annette! I saw you there. Why! What's up, little girl?"

A sudden rush of tears had filled her eyes.

"Oh, nothing. I am just excited, I guess. I don't know what—" She pulled her hands away. "But you were great!" She laughed shrilly.

"Oh, it was your friend McNish did the trick," said Captain Jack. "Very neat bit of work that, eh? Very neat indeed. Awfully clever chap! Are you going home now?"

"No, I am waiting." She paused shyly.

"Oh, I see!" said Captain Jack with a smile. "Lucky chap, by Jove!"

"I am waiting for my father," said Annette, tossing her head.

"Oh, then, if that's all, come along with me. Your father knows his way about." The girl paused a moment, hesitating. Then with a sudden resolve she cried gaily,

"Well, I will. I want to talk to you about it. Oh, I am so excited!" She danced along at his side in gay abandon. As they turned at the first corner Maitland glanced over his shoulder.

"Hello! Here's McNish," he cried, turning about. "Shall we wait for him?"

"Oh, never mind Malcolm," cried the girl excitedly, "come along. I don't want him just now. I want—" She checked herself abruptly. "I want to talk to you."

"Oh, all right," said Captain Jack. "He's gone back anyway. Come along Annette, old girl. I have been wanting to see you for a long time."

"Well, you see me," said the girl, laughing up into his eyes with a frank, warm admiration in hers that made Captain Jack's heart quicken a bit in its steady beat. He was a young man with a normal appreciation of his own worth. She, young, beautiful, unspoiled, in the innocence of her girlish heart was flinging at him the full tribute of a warm, generous admiration with every flash of her black eyes and every intonation of her voice. Small wonder if Captain Jack found her good to look at and to listen to. Often during the walk home he kept saying to himself, "Jove, that McNish chap is a lucky fellow!" But McNish, taking his lonely way home, was only conscious that the evening had grown chilly and grey.

CHAPTER IX
THE DAY BEFORE

Business was suspended for the day in Blackwater. That is, men went through their accustomed movements, but their thoughts were far apart from the matters that were supposed to occupy their minds during the working hours of the day. In the offices, in the stores, in the shops, on the streets, in the schools, in the homes the one, sole topic of conversation, the one mental obsession was The Great Game. Would the Maitland Mill Hockey Team pull it off? Blackwater was not a unit in desiring victory for the Maitland Mill team, for the reason that the team's present position of proud eminence in the hockey world of Eastern Ontario had been won by a series of smashing victories over local and neighbouring rival teams. They had first disposed of that snappy seven of lightning lightweights, the local High School team, the champions in their own League. They had smashed their way through the McGinnis Foundry Seven in three Homeric contests. This victory attracted the notice of the Blackwater Black Eagles, the gay and dashing representatives of Blackwater's most highly gilded stratum of society, a clever, hard-fighting, never-dying group of athletes who, summer and winter, kept themselves in perfect form, and who had moved rapidly out of obscurity into the dazzling spotlight of championship over their district. For the sake of the practice in it and in preparation for their games in the Eastern Ontario Hockey League, they took on the Maitland Mill team.

It took the Black Eagles a full week to recover sufficient control to be able to speak intelligibly as to the "how" and "why" of that match. For the Mill team with apparent ease passed in thirteen goals under and over and behind and beside the big broad goal stick of Bell Blackwood, the goal wonder of the League; and the single register for the Eagles had been netted by Fatty Findlay's own stick in a moment of aberration. During the week following the Black Eagle debacle the various Bank managers, Law Office managers and other financial magnates of the town were lenient with their clerks. Social functions were abandoned. The young gentlemen had one continuous permanent and unbreakable engagement at the rink or in preparation for it. But all was in vain. The result of the second encounter was defeat for the Eagles, defeat utter, unmistakable and inexplicable except on the theory that they had met a superior team. Throughout the hockey season the Maitland Mill maintained an unbroken record of victory till their fame flew far; and at the close of the season enthusiasts of the game had arranged a match between the winners of the Eastern Ontario Hockey League, the renowned Cornwall team and the Maitland Mill boys. To-day the Cornwalls were in town, and the town in consequence was quite unfit for the ordinary duties of life. The Eagles almost to a man were for the local team; for they were sports true to type. Not so however their friends and following, who resented defeat of their men at the hands of a working class team.

Of course it was Jack Maitland who was responsible for their humiliation. It was he who had organised his fellow workmen, put them through a blood and iron discipline, filled them with his own spirit of irresistible furious abandon in attack which carried them to victory.

It was an old game with Jack Maitland. When a High School boy he had developed that spirit of dominating and indomitable leadership that had made his team the glory of the town. Later by sound and steady grinding at the game he had developed a style and plan of team play which had produced a town team in the winter immediately preceding the war that had won championship honors. Now with his Mill team he was simply repeating his former achievements.

It had astonished his friends to learn that Captain Jack was playing hockey again. He had played no game except in a desultory way since the war. He had resisted the united efforts of the Eagles and their women friends to take the captaincy of that team. The mere thought of ever appearing on the ice in hockey uniform gave him a sick feeling at his heart. Of that noble seven whom he had in pre-war days led so often to victory four were still "over there," one was wandering round a darkened room. Of the remaining two, one Rupert Stillwell was too deeply engrossed in large financial affairs for hockey. Captain Jack himself was the seventh, and the mere sight of a hockey stick on a school boy's shoulder gave him a heart stab.

It was his loyal pal Patricia Templeton, who gave him the first impulse toward the game again. To her pleading he had yielded so far as to coach, on a Saturday afternoon, her team of High School girls to victory. But it was the Reverend Murdo Matheson who furnished the spur to conscience that resulted in the organising of the Maitland Mill team.

"You, John Maitland, more than any of us and more than all of us together can draw these lads of yours from the pool rooms and worse," the Reverend Murdo had said one day in early winter.

"Great Scott, Padre"—the Reverend Murdo had done his bit overseas—"what are you giving me now?"

"You, more than any or all of us, I am saying," repeated the minister solemnly. "For God's sake, man, get these lads on the ice or anywhere out-of-doors for the good of their immortal souls."

"Me! And why me, pray?" Captain Jack had asked. "I'm no uplifter. Why jump on me?"

"You, because God has bestowed on you the gift to lead men," said the minister with increasing solemnity. "A high gift it is, and one for which God will hold you responsible."

That very night, passing by the Lucky Strike Pool Rooms, Captain Jack had turned in to find a score and more of youths—many of them from the mills—flashing their money with reckless freedom in an atmosphere thick with foul tobacco-smoke and reeking with profane and lewd speech. On reaching his home that night Maitland went straight to the attic and dug up his hockey kit. Before he slept he had laid his plans for a league among the working lads in the various industries in the town.

It was no easy task to force these men into training habits, to hold them to the grind, to discipline them into self-control in temper and in desire. It was of vast assistance to him that three of his seven were overseas men, while some dozen or so of the twenty in the club were returned soldiers. It was part of his discipline that his team should never shirk a day's work for the game except on the rare occasions when they went on tour. Hence the management in the various mills and factories, at first hostile and suspicious, came to regard these athletic activities on the part of their employees with approval and finally came to give encouragement and support to the games.

To-day was a half holiday for the Maitland Mills and the streets were noticeably full of the men and their sweethearts and wives in their Sunday clothes. Not the team, however. Maitland knew better than that. He took his men for a run in the country before noon, bringing them home in rich warm glow. Then after a bath and a hard rubdown they dined together at the mill and then their Captain ordered them home to sleep, forbidding them the streets till they were on their way to the game.

On his way home Captain Jack was waylaid by his admirer and champion, Patricia. She, standing in front of his car, brought him to a halt.

"I have not even seen you for a whole week," she complained, getting in beside him, "and your phone is always busy in the evening. Of course no one can get you during the day. And I do want to know how the team is. Oh! do tell me they are fit for the game of their lives! Are they every one fit?"

"Fit and fine."

"And will they win?"

"Sure thing," said Captain Jack quietly.

"Oh, I hope you are right. But you are so sure," exclaimed his companion. "The Cornwalls are wonderful, Rupert says."

"He would."

"Oh! I forgot you don't think much of Rupert," sighed Patricia.

"I haven't time, you see," answered Captain Jack gravely.

"Oh, you know what I mean. It is a pity, too, for he is really very nice. I mean he is so good to me," sighed Patricia again.

"Don't sigh, Patsy, old girl. It really isn't worth it, you know. How is the supply of choc's keeping up?"

"Now you are thinking me a pig. But tell me about your men. Are they really in form?"

"Absolutely at the peak."

"And that darling Fatty Findlay. I do hope he will not lose his head and let a goal in. He is perfectly adorable with that everlasting smile of his. I do hope Fatty is at the peak, too. Is he, really?" The anxiety in Patricia's tone was more than painful.

"Dear Patsy, he is right at the pinnacle."

"Captain Jack, if you don't win to-night I shall—well, I shall just weep my eyes out."

"That settles it, Pat. We shall win. We can't—I can't spare those lovely eyes, you know," said Captain Jack, smiling at her.

One by one Captain Jack's team were passed in review—the defence, Macnamara and "Jack" Johnson, so called for his woolly white head; "Reddy" Hughes, Ross, "Snoopy" Sykes, who with Captain Jack made the forward line, all were declared to be fit to deliver the last ounce in their bodies, the last flicker in their souls.

"Do you know, Captain Jack," said Patricia gravely, "there is one change you ought to make in your forward line."

"Yes! What is that, Pat?" asked Captain Jack, with never a suggestion of a smile.

"I would change Snoopy for Geordie Ross. You know Geordie is a little too careful, and he is hardly fast enough for you. Now you and Snoopy on left wing would be oh! perfectly wonderful."

"Patsy, you are a wizard!" exclaimed Captain Jack. "That very change has been made and the improvement is unbelievable. We are both left-handers and we pull off our little specialties far more smoothly than Geordie and I could. You have exactly hit the bull. You watch for that back of the goal play to-night. Well, here we are. You have good seats, I understand."

"Oh, yes. Rupert, you see, as patron of the Eagles was able to get the very best. But won't you come in and see mother? She is really quite worked up over it, though of course she couldn't bear to go."

Captain Jack checked the refusal on his lips.

"Yes, I will go in for a few minutes," he said gravely. "No! Your mother would not—could not come, of course."

There flashed before his mind a picture from pre-war days. The rink packed with wildly excited throngs and in a certain reserved section midway down the side the Templeton-Maitland party with its distinguished looking men and beautiful women following with eager faces and shining eyes the fortunes of their sons in the fight before them. The flash of that picture was like a hand of ice upon his heart as Captain Jack entered the cosy living room.

"Here he is, Mamma!" cried Patricia as she ushered her hero into the room with a sweeping gesture. "And he brings the most cheering news. They are going to win!"

"But how delightful!" exclaimed Adrien coming from the piano where she had been playing, with Rupert Stillwell turning her music for her.

"I suppose upon the best authority," said Stillwell, grinning at Patricia.

"We are so glad you found time to run in," said Mrs. Templeton. "You must have a great deal to say to your team on the last afternoon."

"I'm glad I came too, now," said Captain Jack, holding the fragile hand in his and patting it gently. "I am afraid Patricia is responsible for my coming in. I don't really believe I could have ventured on my own."

A silence fell on the company which none of them seemed able to break. Other days were hard upon them. In this very room it was that that other seven were wont to meet for their afternoon tea before their great matches.

Mrs. Templeton, looking up at Jack, found his eyes fixed upon her and full of tears. With a swift upward reach of her arms she caught him and drew his head to her breast.

"I know, Jack dear," she said, with lips that quivered piteously. For a moment or two he knelt before her while she held him in a close embrace. Then he gently kissed her cheek and rose to his feet.

"Give him some tea, Adrien," she said, making a gallant struggle to steady her voice, "a cup of tea—and no cake. I remember, you see," she added with a tremulous smile.

Adrien came back quickly from the window.

"Yes! a fresh cup!" she cried eagerly, "and a sandwich. You, Pat, get the sandwiches. No cake. We must do nothing to imperil the coming victory."

"You have a wonderful team, Jack, I hear," said her mother. "Come and sit here beside me and tell me about them. Patricia has been keeping me informed, but she is not very coherent at times. Of course, I know about your wonderful goal keeper Findlay, is it not?" And the gentle little lady kept a stream of conversation going, for she saw how deeply moved Maitland was. It was his first visit to the Rectory since he had taken up the game again, and the rush of emotion released by the vivid memory of those old happy days when that jolly group of boys had filled this familiar room with their noisy clatter wellnigh overcame him.

For a minute or two he fussed with the tea things till he could master his voice, then he said very quietly:

"They are very decent chaps—really very good fellows and they have taken their training extraordinarily well. Of course, Macnamara and Johnson were in my old company, and that helps a lot."

"Yes, I remember Macnamara quite well. He is a fine big Irishman."

"Fancy you remembering him, Mrs. Templeton," said Captain Jack.

"Of course, I remember him. He is one of our boys."

"Let's see, he is one of your defence, isn't he?" said Stillwell, who had felt himself rather out of the conversation. Maitland nodded. The presence of Stillwell in that room introduced a painful element. Once he had been one of the seven and though never so intimately associated with the Rectory life as the others, yet at all team gatherings he had had his place. But since the war Maitland had never been able to endure his presence in that room. To-day, with the memory of those old thrilling days pressing hard upon his heart, he could not bear to look upon a man, once one of them, now forever an outsider. The tea coming in brought to Maitland relief.

"Ah, here you are," he cried anticipating Stillwell in relieving Adrien of part of her load. "You are a life saver. Tea is the thing for this hour."

"Three lumps, is it not?" said the girl, smiling at him. "You see, I remember, though you really don't deserve it. And here is Pat with the sandwiches."

"Yes! a whole plate for yourself, Captain Jack," said Patricia. "Come and sit by me here."

"No indeed!" said her sister with a bright glow on her cheeks. "Jack is going to sit right here by the tea-pot, and me," she added, throwing him a swift glance.

"No! you are both wrong, children," said their mother. "Jack is coming to sit beside me. He's my boy this afternoon."

"Mother, we will all share him," said Patricia, placing chairs near her mother. "I must talk about the match, I simply must."

A shadow for a moment wiped the brightness from the face and eyes of the elder sister, but yielding to her mother's appeal, she joined the circle, saying to Maitland,

"I don't believe you want to talk about the match, do you? That is not supposed to be good psychology before a match. What you really want is a good sleep. Isn't that right?"

"He has just sent his men off to bed, I know," said Patricia, "and we will send him off when he has had his tea."

"I am so glad you are playing again," said Mrs. Templeton to Maitland as he sat down by her side. "You need more recreation than you have been taking, I believe."

A shadow crossed Maitland's face.

"I don't believe I need recreation very much, but these chaps of mine do," he said simply.

"The workmen, you mean!"

"Yes. They lead rather a dull life, you know. Not much colour. A pool room on the whole has rather a rotten effect upon a chap who has been nine or ten hours indoors already and who sticks at the same thing day in and day out for months at a time."

"Ah, I see. You mean you took up hockey for—ah—to help—"

"Well, I don't want to pose as a workingman's advocate and that sort of thing. But really he has a slow time."

"Then, why doesn't he get busy and do something for himself," broke in Stillwell, impatiently. "The Lord knows he is getting most of the money these days and has more spare time than anyone else in the community."

But Maitland ignored him, till Patricia intervened.

"Tell me about that," she demanded.

"Look here!" said her sister. "You are not going to get Jack into a labour controversy this afternoon. But I would just like to ask you, Pat, how keen you'd be on organising and conducting a Literary and Debating Society after you had put in not five and a half hours' lessons, but eight or nine hours'! It would take some doing, eh? But let's cut out the labour trouble. It is nearly time for his sleep, isn't it?"

"Is it, Captain Jack? If so, we won't keep you a minute," said Patricia anxiously. "No, mother! you must not keep him. He must be on tip-toe to-night."

Captain Jack rose. "Patricia would make an ideal trainer," he said. "I fear I must really go. I am awfully glad to have come in and seen you all. Somehow I feel a whole lot better."

"And so do we, Jack," said the old lady in a wistful voice. "Won't you come again soon?"

Maitland hesitated a moment, glancing at Adrien.

"Oh, do!" said the girl, with a little colour coming into her face. "It has been a little like old times to see you this way."

"Yes, hasn't it?" said Stillwell. "Awfully jolly."

Maitland stiffened and turned again to the old lady whose eyes were turned on him with sad entreaty.

"Yes, I shall come to see you," said Maitland, bowing over her hand in farewell.

"We shall expect you to come and see us to-night at the match, remember, Captain Jack," said Patricia, as he passed out of the room. "Now be sure to go and have your sleep."

But there was no sleep that afternoon for Captain Jack. On his way through the town he was halted by McNish.

"The boys want to see you," he said briefly.

"What boys? What do you mean, McNish?"

"At the rooms. Will you come down now?"

"Now? I can't come now, McNish. I have to be on the ice in three hours and I must get a little rest. What's up, anyway? Tell them I'll see them to-morrow."

"No! they want you now!" said McNish firmly. "I would advise that you come."

"What do you mean, McNish? Well, get in here and I'll go to see them." McNish got into the car. "Now, what's all the mystery?"

"Better wait," said McNish, grimly.

"Well, it is a dog's trick," said Maitland wrathfully, "to get on to a chap before a big match like this."

In the Union Committee rooms a group of men were awaiting them, among them Mr. Wigglesworth and the little cockney who had made himself so obnoxious at the public meeting.

"What's all this tomfoolery, Wigglesworth?" demanded Captain Jack, striding in among them.

"(H)excuse me," said the little cockney. "You are a member of the Woodworkers' Union I (h)understand."

"Who the devil are you, may I ask?" said Maitland in a rage.

"(H)allow me," said Mr. Wigglesworth. "Mister Simmons, Mr. Maitland—Mr. Simmons is our new secretary, (h)elected last meetin'."

"Well, what do you want of me?" demanded Maitland. "Don't you know I am tied up this afternoon?"

"Tied (h)up?" asked Simmons coolly, "'ow?"

"With the match, confound you."

"Oh, the match! And w'at match may that be? (H)Anythin' to do with your Union?"

Maitland glared at him, too dumfounded to speak.

"You see, Mr. Maitland," began Mr. Wigglesworth in a hurried and apologetic manner.

"'Ere! you keep aht o' this," said Simmons sharply, "this 'ere's my job. I shall tell Brother Maitland all that is necessary."

"I was only going to (h)explain—" began Mr. Wigglesworth.

"Naw then! IS this your job or mine? Was you (h)appointed or was I? When I find myself (h)unable to discharge my dooty to the Union I might per'aps call on you, Brother Wigglesworth; but until I find myself in that situation I 'ope you will refrain from shovin' in your 'orn." Brother Simmons' sarcasm appeared to wither Brother Wigglesworth into silence.

"Naw then, Brother Maitland, we shall get (h)on."

Maitland glanced round on the group of half a dozen men. Some of them he knew; others were strangers to him.

"I don't know what the business is, gentlemen," he said, curbing his wrath, "but I want to know if it can't wait till to-morrow? You know our boys are going on the ice in a couple of hours or so—"

"Goin' on the (h)ice! Goin' on the (h)ice! W'at's that to do with Union business?" snarled Simmons. "This 'ere's no silly kids' gaime! It's a man's work we ave in 'and, if you don't want to do the business to w'ich you are (h)appointed w'y just say so and we shall know 'ow to (h)act. There 'as been too much o' this gaime business to suit me. If we are men let us (h)act like men."

"Better get on wi' it," said McNish curtly.

"I shall get on w'en I am good and ready, Brother McNish," answered Simmons.

"All r-r-right, brother, but A doot ye're oot o' order. Who is the chairman o' this Committee?" asked McNish calmly.

"Brother Phillips," answered two or three voices.

"All right. I suggest you proceed regularly and call the meeting to order," said McNish quietly. Simmons, recognising that it was Greek meeting Greek, agreed to this.

Clumsily and hesitatingly Brother Phillips began stating the business of the Committee. He had not gone far before Simmons interrupted.

"Mr. Chairman, with your permission I would just like to say that the resolution passed at the representative joint meetin' of the Maitland Mills and Box Factory (h)employees last night will sufficiently (h)explain the (h) object of this meetin' 'ere." Brother Simmons' tone suggested infinite pity for the lumbering efforts of the chairman.

"Yes, I guess it will," said the chairman, blushing in his confusion. Brother Phillips was new to his position and its duties.

"I would suggest that that resolution be read," said Brother Simmons, the pity in his tone hardly veiling his contempt.

"Yes! Yes! Of course!" said Brother Phillips hurriedly. "Eh—would you please read it, Mr.—that is—Brother Simmons?"

With great show of deliberation and of entire mastery of the situation Mr. Simmons produced a Minute Book and began:

"Mr. Chairman and brothers, I may say that this 'ere resolution was passed at a joint representative meetin' of all the (h)employees of the Maitland Company—"

"There is no sich company, Mr. Chairman," said McNish. "A say let us hear the resolution. We'll hear the speech afterwards if we must." It was again Greek meeting Greek, and the little man turned with a sarcastic smile to McNish.

"I suppose Brother McNish is (h)anxious to get ready for this gaime we've bin 'earing abaht. I should just like to remind 'im that we 'ave a bigger gaime on 'and, if 'e wants to get into it. Personally I don't 'ave no use for these 'ere gaimes. I 'ave seen the same kind of capitalistic dodge to distract the workin' man's (h)attention from 'is real gaime in life. These circumventions—"

"Maister Chair-r-man! A rise—"

"Mr. Chairman, I 'ave the floor and if Brother McNish knows (h) anythink abaht constitootional proceedin's—"

"Maister Chair-r-man—Maister-r Chair-r-r-man!" Brother McNish's Doric was ominously rasping. "A rise tae a pint of or-r-de-r-r. And Brother Simmons, who claims to be an expert in constitutional law and procedure knows I have the floor. Ma pint of order is this, that there is no business before the meeting and as apparently only aboot half the members are absent—"

"And 'oo's fault is that? 'E was to get them 'isself," shouted Mr. Simmons.

"A searched the toon for them but cudna find them, but as A was sayin'—as the secretary has no business tae bring before the meeting but a wheen havers, A move we adjourn tae tomorrow at 12:30 p. m. in this place, and I believe that as Brither Maitland is also a member o' this committee he will second the motion."

Maitland, not knowing in the least what the whole thing was about, but seeing a way out of the present mix-up, promptly seconded the motion.

"Mr. Chairman!" shouted Simmons. "I am prepared to—"

"Maister Chair-r-man, A need not remind you that there is no discussion on a motion to adjourn."

"That is quite right," said the chairman, in whose memory by some obscure mental process this fact seemed to have found a lodging.

"It is moved that this committee do now adjourn."

"Mr. Chairman! I protest," shrieked Brother Simmons frantically.

"Ay, he's a grand protester!" said Brother McNish.

The motion was carried by a majority of one, Brothers Wigglesworth, McNish and Maitland voting in the affirmative.

"Traitors!" shrieked Brother Simmons. "Capitalistic traitors!"

"Hoot mon! Ye're no in Hyde Park. Save yere breath for yere porritch the morn—" said McNish, relaxing into a grim smile as he left the rooms.

"We'll get 'im," said Simmons to his ally and friend. "'E's in with that there young pup. 'E knows 'ow to work 'im and 'e'd sell us all up, 'e would." Brother Simmons' brand of profanity strongly savoured of the London pavements in its picturesque fluency.

"Get in here, McNish," said Maitland, who was waiting at the door. With some hesitation McNish accepted the invitation.

"Now, what does this mean?" said Maitland savagely, then checking his rage, "but I ought to thank you for getting me out of the grip of that frantic idiot. What is this fool thing?"

"It's nae that," said McNish shortly. "It is anything but that. But I grant ye this was no time to bring it on. That was beyond me. A doot yon puir cratur had a purpose in it, however. He disna—does not think much of these games of yours. But that's anither—another"—McNish was careful of his speech—"matter."

"But what in—"

"I am just telling you. There is a strong, a very strong movement under way among the unions at present."

"A movement? Strike, do you mean?"

"It may be, or worse." McNish's tone was very grave. "And as a good union man they expect your assistance."

"Wages again?"

"Ay, and condeetions and the like."

"But it is not six months since the last agreement was signed and that agreement is running still."

"Ay, it is, but condeetions, conditions have changed since that date," said McNish, "and there must be readjustment—at least, there is a feeling that way."

"Readjustment? But I have had no hint of this in our meetings. This has not come up for discussion."

A gentle pity smiled from the rugged face of the man beside him.

"Hardly," he said. "It's no done that way."

They came to McNish's door.

"Will you come in?" he said courteously. A refusal was at Maitland's lips when the door was opened by an old lady in a white frilled cap and without being able to explain how it came about he found himself in the quaintly furnished but delightfully cosy living-room, soaking in the comfort of a great blazing fire.

"This is really solid comfort," he said, spreading his hands to the glowing pine slabs.

"Ay, ye need it the day. The fire cheers the heart," said the old lady.

"But you don't need it for that, Mrs. McNish," said her visitor, smiling at the strong, serene face under the white frilled cap.

"Do I not then? An' what aboot yersel'?" The keen grey eye searched his face. Maitland was immediately conscious of a vast dreariness in his life. He sat silent looking into the blazing fire.

"Ay," continued the old lady, "but there are the bright spots tae, an' it's ill tae glower at a cauld hearth stone." Maitland glanced quickly at the shrewd and kindly face. What did she know about him and his life and his "cauld hearth stone"? So he said nothing but waited. Suddenly she swerved to another theme.

"Malcolm," she said, "have ye secured the tickets for the match?"

"Aw, mither, now it is the terrible auld sport ye are. She drags me out to all these things." His eyes twinkled at Maitland. "I can't find time for any study."

"Hoots ye and ye're study. A doot a rale heartening scramble on the ice wad dae ye mair guid than an oor wi' yon godless Jew buddie."

"She means Marx, of course," said McNish, in answer to Maitland's look of perplexity. "She has no use for him."

"But the tickets, Malcolm," insisted his mother.

"Well, mither, A'll confess I clean forgot them. Ye see," he hurried to say, "A was that fashed over yon Committee maitter—"

"Committee maitter!" exclaimed the old lady indignantly. "Did I not tell ye no to heed yon screamin' English cratur wi' his revolutionary nonsense?"

"She means Simmons," interjected Malcolm with a little smile. "He means well, mither, but A'm vexed aboot the tickets."

"Mrs. McNish," said Maitland, "I happen to have two tickets that I can let you have." For an instant she hesitated.

"We can find a way in, I think, Mr. Maitland," said Malcolm, forestalling his mother's answer. But with simple dignity his mother put him aside.

"A shall be verra pleased indeed to have the tickets, provided you can spare them, Mr. Maitland. Never mind, noo, Malcolm. A ken well what ye're thinkin'. He's gey independent and his mind is on thae revolutionary buddies o' his. A'm aye tellin' him this is nae land for yon nonsense. Gin we were in Rooshie, or Germany whaur the people have lived in black slavery or even in the auld land whaur the fowk are haudden doon wi' generations o' class bondage, there might be a chance for a revolutionary. But what can ye dae in a land whaur the fowk are aye climbin' through ither, noo up, noo down, noo maister, noo man? Ye canna make Canadians revolutionaries. They are a' on the road to be maisters. Malcolm is a clever loon but he has a wee bee in his bonnet." The old lady smiled quizzically at her big, serious-faced son.

"Noo, mither, ye're just talkin' havers," he said. "My mother is as great a Socialist as I am."

"Ay, but A keep ma heid."

"That ye do, mither. Ye're gey cannie," replied her son, shaking his head, and so they passed the word to and fro, and Maitland sat listening to the chat. The delightful spirit of camaraderie between mother and son reminded him of a similar relationship between mother and sons in his own home in pre-war days. He could not tear himself away. It was well on to his dinner hour before he rose to go.

"You have given me a delightful hour, Mrs. McNish," he said as he shook hands. "You made me think of my own home in the old days,—I mean before the war came and smashed everything." The old lady's eyes were kindly scanning his face.

"Ay, the war smashed yere hame?" Maitland nodded in silence.

"His brither," said Malcolm, quietly.

"Puir laddie," she said, patting his hand.

"And my mother," added Maitland, speaking with difficulty, "and that, of course, meant our home—and everything. So I thank you for a very happy hour," he added with a smile.

"Wad ye care to come again?" said the old lady with a quiet dignity. "We're plain fowk but ye'll be always welcome."

"I just will, Mrs. McNish. And I will send you the tickets."

"Man! I wish ye grand luck the night. A grand victory."

"Thank you. We are going to make a try for it," said Maitland. "You must shout for us."

"Ay, wull I," she answered grimly. And she kept her word for of all the company that made up the Maitland party, none was more conspicuously enthusiastic in applause than was a white-haired old lady in a respectable black bonnet whose wild and weird Doric expletives and exclamations were the joy of the whole party about her.

CHAPTER X
THE NIGHT OF VICTORY

It was an hour after the match. They were gathered in the old rendezvous of the hockey teams in pre-war days. And they were all wildly excited over the Great Victory.

"Just think of it, Mamma, dear," Patricia shouted, pirouetting now on one foot and then on the other, "Eight to six! Oh, it is too glorious to believe! And against that wonderful team, the Cornwalls! Now listen to me, while I give you a calm and connected account of the game. I shall always regret that you were not present, Mamma. Victory! And at half time we were down, five to two! I confess disaster and despair stared me in the face. And we started off so gloriously! Captain Jack and Snoopy in the first five minutes actually put in two goals, with that back goal play of theirs. You know, I explained it to you, Mamma."

"Yes, dear, I know," said her mother, "but if you will speak a little more quietly and slowly—"

"I will, Mamma," said her daughter, sitting down with great deliberation, in front of her. "I will explain to you again that 'round the goal' play."

"I am afraid, my dear, that I could hardly grasp just what you mean."

"Well, never mind, Mamma. It is a particular and special play that Captain Jack worked out. They rush down to the goal and instead of trying to shoot, the one with the puck circles round the back and delivers the puck immediately in front of the goal, where another takes and slips it in. Two goals in about five minutes, wasn't it, Hugh?"

"About eight minutes, I should say," replied Hugh Maynard, the big Captain of the Eagles.

"Well, eight minutes," continued Patricia, taking up the tale, "and then they began the roughhouse business. Jumbo Larson—a terribly big Swede, Mamma—put it all over little Snoopy. Chucked him about, wiped the ice with him!"

"My dear!" exclaimed her mother.

"Well, you know what I mean. A great big, two-hundred-pound monster, who simply threw Snoopy and Georgie Ross all about the rink. It took Captain Jack all his time to stand up against him. And then they ran in goals at a perfectly terrific rate. Two—three—four—five! And only Fatty Findlay's marvelous play kept down the score. I adore Fatty! You know, Mamma, that dear old Scotchwoman—"

"Scotchwoman?" exclaimed Mrs. Templeton.

"Yes. Oh! you don't know about her. Captain Jack brought her along. Mrs. Mc-something."

"McNish," supplied Adrien.

"Yes, McNish," continued Patricia, "a perfect dear! She did everything but swear. Indeed, she may have been swearing for I could not understand half of what she said."

Adrien interrupted: "She is perfectly priceless, Mother. I wish you could meet her—so dignified and sweet."

"Sweet!" exclaimed Patricia, with a laugh. "Well, I didn't see the sweetness, exactly. But at half time, Mamma, fancy! they stood five to two against us. It was a truly awful moment for all of us. And then, after half time, didn't those Cornwalls within five minutes run in another goal, and, worse than all, Jumbo Larson laid out Snoopy flat on the ice! Now the game stood six to two! Think of it, Mamma!"

Then Adrien put in: "It was at this point that the old lady made a remark which, I believe, saved the day. What was it exactly, Hugh?"

"I didn't quite get it."

"I know," said little Vic Forsythe, himself a star of the Eagle forward line. "You poor Sassenach! You couldn't be expected to catch the full, fine flavour of it. Maitland was trying to cheer the old lady up when she said to him: 'Yon half backs, A'm thinkin''—she was a soccer fan in the old land, I believe—'yon half backs, A'm thinkin', are gey confident. It is a peety they cudna be shaken a bit in their nerves.' By Jove! Maitland jumped at it. 'Mrs. McNish, you're right! you're right. I wonder I did not think of it before.'"

Then Adrien broke in: "Yes, from that moment there was a change in our men's tactics."

Then Patricia broke in: "Well, then, let me go on. Captain Jack knew quite well there was no use of allowing those little chaps, Snoopy and Geordie Ross, to keep feeding themselves to those horrid monsters, Jumbo Larson and Macnab, so what did they do but move up 'Jack' Johnson and Macnamara. That is, you see, Mamma, the forwards would take down the puck and then up behind them would come the backs, Macnamara and 'Jack' Johnson, like a perfect storm, and taking the puck from the forwards, who would then fall back to defence, would smash right on the Cornwall defence. The very first time when 'Jack' Johnson came against Jumbo, Jumbo found himself sitting on the ice. Oh! it was lovely! Perfectly lovely! And the next time they did it, Jumbo came at him like a bull. But that adorable 'Jack' Johnson just lifted him clear off his feet and flung him against the side. It seemed to me that the whole rink shook!"

Here Vic broke in: "You didn't hear what the old lady said at this point, I suppose. I was sitting next to her. She was really a whole play by herself. When Jumbo went smashing against the side, the old lady gave a grunt. 'Hum, that wull sort ye a doot.' Oh! she is a peach!"

"And the next time they came down," cried Patricia, taking up the tale again, "Jumbo avoided him. For Macnamara, 'Jack' Johnson and Captain Jack came roaring down the ice at a terrific pace, and with never a stop, smashed head on into Jumbo and Macnab and fairly hurled them in on Hepburn—that is their goal keeper, you know—and scored. Oh! Oh! Oh! Such a yell! Six to three, and ten minutes to play."

"But Patricia," said Mrs. Templeton, "do moderate your tone. We are not in the rink. And this terrible excitement can't be good for you."

"Good for me?" cried Patricia. "What difference does that make? Ten minutes to play, Mamma! But that was the end of the roughhouse game by the Cornwall defence."

Then Hugh stepped in: "It really did break up that defence. It was a wonderful piece of generalship, I must say. They never seemed to get together after that."

"Let me talk, Hugh," exclaimed Patricia, "I want to tell Mamma what happened next, for this was really the most terribly exciting part of the game. And I think it was awfully clever of Captain Jack. You know, next time, Mamma, when they came down—I mean our men—they pretended to be playing the same game, but they weren't. For Captain Jack and Snoopy went back to their old specialty, and before the Cornwalls knew where they were at, they ran in three goals—one-two-three, just like that! Oh! you ought to have seen that rink, Mamma, and you ought to have heard the yelling! I wish you had been there! And then, just at that last goal didn't that horrid Jumbo make a terrible and cruel swing at Snoopy's ankle, just as he passed. Knocked him clean off his feet so that poor Snoopy lay on the ice quite still! He was really nearly killed. They had to carry him off!"

"Well, I wouldn't say that exactly," said Hugh. "The fact of the matter is, Snoopy is a clever little beggar and I happened to catch his wink as Maitland was bending over him. I was helping him off the ice, you know, and I heard him whisper, 'Don't worry, Captain, I'm all right. Get me another pair of skates. It will take a little time.'"

"Do you mean he wasn't hurt?" exclaimed Patricia indignantly. "Indeed he was; he was almost killed, I am sure he was."

"Oh, he was hurt right enough," said Hugh, "but he wasn't killed by any means!"

"And then," continued Patricia, "there was the most terrible riot and uproar. Everybody seemed to be on the ice and fighting. Hugh ran in, and Vic—I should loved to have gone myself—Hugh was perfectly splendid—and all the Eagles were there and—"

Then Mrs. Templeton said: "What do you mean—a fight, a riot?"

"A real riot, Mother," said Adrien, "the whole crowd demanding Jumbo's removal from the ice."

"Yes," continued Patricia impatiently, pushing her sister aside, "Hugh went straight to the umpire and it looked almost as though he was going to fight, the way he tore in. But he didn't. He just spoke quietly to the umpire. What did you say, Hugh?"

"Oh," cried Vic, "Hugh was perfectly calm and superior. He knows the umpire well. Indeed, I think the umpire owes his life to Hugh and his protecting band of Eagles."

"What did he say," cried Patricia. "I wish I could have heard that."

"Oh," said Vic, "there was an interesting conversation. 'Keep out of this, Maynard. You ought to know better,' the umpire said, 'keep out.' 'Baker, that man Larson must go off.' 'Rubbish,' said the umpire, 'they were both roughing it.' 'Look here, Baker, that's rot and you know it. It was a deliberate and beastly trick. Put him off!' 'He stays on!' said the umpire, and he stuck to it, I'll give him credit for that. It was old Maitland that saved the day. He came up smiling. 'I hope you are taking off the time, umpire,' he said, with that little laugh of his. 'I am not going to put Larson off,' shouted the umpire to him. 'Who asked you to?' said Maitland. 'Go on with the game.' That saved the day. They all started cheering. The ice was cleared and the game went on."

"Oh, that was it. I couldn't understand. They were so savage first, and then suddenly they all seemed to quiet down. It was Captain Jack. Well,

Mamma, on they came again! But when poor Snoopy came out, all bandaged round the head and the blood showing through—"

"Quite a clever little beggar," murmured Vic.

"Clever? What do you mean?" cried Patricia.

"Oh, well, good psychology, I mean—that's all. Bloody bandages—demanding vengeance, Jack's team, you know—Macnamara, for instance, entreating his captain for the love of heaven to put him opposite Jumbo—shaking the morale of the enemy and so forth—mighty good psychology."

"I don't know exactly what you mean," said Patricia, "but the Cornwall defence was certainly rattled. They pulled their men back and played defence like perfect demons, with the Mill men on to them like tigers."

"But Patricia, my dear," said her mother, "those are terrible words."

"But, Mamma, not half so terrible as the real thing. Oh, it was perfectly splendid! And then how did it finish, Hugh? I didn't quite see how that play came about."

"I didn't see, either," said Hugh.

"Didn't you?" cried Adrien, "I did. Jack and Geordie Ross were going down the centre at a perfectly terrific speed, big Macnamara backing them up. Out came Macnab and Jumbo Larson following him. Macnab checked Geordie, who passed to Jack, who slipped it back to Macnamara. Down came Jumbo like a perfect thunderbolt and fairly hurled himself upon Macnamara. I don't know what happened then, but—"

"Oh, I do!" cried Vic. "When old Jumbo came hurtling down upon Macnamara, this was evidently what Macnamara was waiting for. Indeed, what he had been praying for all through the game. I saw him gather himself, crouch low, lurch forward with shoulder well down, a wrestler's trick—you know Macnamara was the champion wrestler of his division in France—he caught Jumbo low. Result, a terrific catapult, and the big Swede lay on his back some twenty feet away. Everybody thought he was dead."

"Oh, it was perfectly lovely!" exclaimed Patricia, rapturously.

"But, my dear," said her mother, "lovely, and they thought the man was dead!"

"Oh, but he wasn't dead. He came to. I will say he was very plucky. Then just as they faced off, time was called. Six to six! Think of it, Mamma, six to six! And we had been five to two at half time!"

"Six to six?" said Mrs. Templeton. "But I thought you said we won?"

"Oh, listen, Mamma, this is the most wonderful thing of the whole match," said Adrien, trying to break in on the tornado of words from her younger sister.

"No, let me, Adrien! I know exactly how it was done. Captain Jack explained it to me before. It was Captain Jack's specialty. It was what they call the double-circle. Here is the way it was worked." Patricia sprang to her feet, arranged two chairs for goal and proceeded to demonstrate. "You see, Mamma, in the single circle play, Captain Jack and Snoopy come down—say Snoopy has the puck. Just as they get near the goal Snoopy fools the back, rushes round the goal and passes to Jack, who is standing in front ready to slip it in. But of course the Cornwalls were prepared for the play. But that is where the double-circle comes in. This time Geordie had the puck, with Captain Jack immediately at his left and Snoopy further out. Well, Geordie had the puck, you see. He rushes down and pretends to make the circle of the goal. But this time he doesn't. He tears like mad around the goal with the puck, Snoopy tears like mad around the goal from the other side, the defence all rush over to the left to check them, leaving the right wide open. Snoopy takes the ball from Geordie, rushes around the goal the other way, Mamma, do you see?—passes back to Reddy, his partner, who slips it in! And poor Jumbo was unable to do anything. I believe he was still dazed from his terrible fall!"

Then Hugh breaks in: "It really was beautifully done."

"It certainly was," said Vic.

"Seven to six, Mamma, think of it! Seven to six, and two minutes of the first overtime to play. Two minutes! It just seemed that our men could do as they liked. The last time the whole forward lines came down, with Macnamara and 'Jack' Johnson roaring and yelling like—like—I don't know what. And they did the double-circle again! Think of it! And then time was called. Oh, I am perfectly exhausted with this excitement!" said Patricia, sinking back into her chair. "I don't believe I could go down to that rink, not even for another game. It is terribly trying!"

At this moment Rupert Stillwell came in, full of enthusiasm for the Cornwalls' scientific hockey, and with grudging praise for the local team, deploring their roughhouse tactics. But he met a sharp and unexpected check, for Adrien took him in hand, in her quiet, cool, efficient manner.

"Roughhouse!" she said. "What do you mean exactly by that?"

"Well," said Rupert, somewhat taken aback, "for instance that charge of Macnamara on Jumbo Larson at the last."

"I saw that quite clearly," said Adrien, "and it appeared to me quite all right. It was Larson who made the most furious charge upon Macnamara."

"Of course it was," cried Patricia, indignantly. "Jumbo deserved all he got. Why, the way he mauled little Snoopy and Geordie Ross in the first part of the game was perfectly horrid. Don't you think so, Hugh?"

"Oh, well, hockey is not tiddly-winks, you know, Patricia, and—"

"As if I didn't know that!" broke in the girl indignantly.

"And Jumbo and Macnab," continued Hugh, "really had to break up the dangerous combination there. Of course that was a rotten assault on Snoopy. It wasn't Jumbo's fault that he didn't break an ankle. As it was, he gave him a very bad fall."

At this Rupert laughed scornfully. "Rot," he said, "the whole town is laughing at all that bloody bandage business. It was a bit of stage play. Very clever, I confess, but no hockey. I happen to know that Maitland was quite hot about it."

But Hugh and Vic only laughed at him.

"He is a clever little beggar, is Snoopy," said Vic.

"But, meantime," said Mrs. Templeton, "where is Jack! He was going to be here, was he not?"

"Feasting and dancing, I expect," said Rupert. "There is a big supper on, given by the Mill management, and a dance afterwards—'hot time in the old town,' eh?"

"A dance?" gasped Patricia. "A dance! Where?"

"Odd Fellows' Hall," said Rupert. "Want to go? I have tickets. Don't care for that sort of thing myself. Rather a mixed affair, I guess. Mill hands and their girls."

"Oh," breathed Patricia, "I should love to go. Couldn't we?"

"But my dear Patricia," said her mother, "a dance, with all those people? What nonsense. But I wish Jack would drop in. I should so like to congratulate him on his great victory."

"Oh, do let us go, just for a few minutes, Mamma" entreated Patricia. "Hugh, have you tickets?"

The men looked at each other.

"Well," confessed Vic, "I was thinking of dropping in myself. After all, it is our home team and they are good sports. And Maitland handled them with wonderful skill."

"Yes, I am going," said Hugh. "I am bound to go as Captain of the Eagles, and that sort of thing, but I would, anyway. Would you care to come, Adrien, if Mrs. Templeton will allow you? Of course there are chaperons. Maitland would see to that."

"I should like awfully to go," said Adrien eagerly. "We might, for a few minutes, Mother? Of course, Patricia should be in bed, really."

Poor Patricia's face fell.

"It is no place for any of you," said the mother, decidedly. "Just think of that mixed multitude! And you, Patricia, you should be in bed."

"But oh, Mamma, dear," wailed Patricia, "I can rest all day to-morrow."

At this point a new voice broke in to the discussion and Doctor Templeton appeared. "Well, what's the excitement," he enquired. "Oh, the match, of course! Well, what was the result?"

"Oh, Daddy, we won, we won!" cried Patricia, springing at him. "The most glorious match! Big Jumbo Larson, a perfect monster on the Cornwall defence, was knocked out! Oh, it was a glorious match! And can't I go down to see the dance? Adrien and Hugh and Vic are going. Only for a few minutes," she begged, with her arms around her father's neck. "Say yes, Daddy!"

"Give me time; let me get my breath, Patricia. Now, do begin somewhere—say, with the score."

They all gave him the score.

"Hurrah!" cried the old doctor. "No one hurt—seriously, I mean?"

"No," said Patricia, "except perhaps Jumbo Larson," she added hopefully.

"The Lord was merciful to this family when he made you a girl, Patricia," said her father.

"But, Daddy, it was a wonderful game." Quite breathlessly, she went once more over the outstanding features of the play.

"Sounds rather bloody, I must say," said her father, doubtfully.

But Hugh said: "It was not really—not quite so bad as Patricia makes it, sir. Rough at times, of course, but, on the whole, clean."

"Clean," cried Patricia, "what about Jumbo's swing at Snoopy?"

"Oh, well, Snoopy had the puck, you know. It was a little off-colour, I must confess."

"And now, Daddy," said Patricia, going at her father again, "we all want to go down to the dance. There will be speeches, you know, and I do want to hear Captain Jack," she added, not without guile. "Won't you let me go with them? Hugh will take care of me."

"I think I should rather like to go myself," said her father. A shout of approval rose from the whole company. "But," continued the doctor, "I don't think I can. My dear, I think they might go for a few minutes—and you can bring me in a full account of the speeches, Patricia," he added, with a twinkle in his eye.

"But, my dear," exclaimed his wife, "this is one of those awful public affairs. You can't imagine what they are like. The Mill hands will all be there, and that sort of people."

"Well, my dear, Jack Maitland will be there, I fancy, and you were thinking of going, Hugh?"

"Yes, sir, I am going. Of course there will be a number of the friends of both teams, townspeople. Of course the Mill hands will be there, too, in large numbers. It will be great fun."

"Well, my dear," said the doctor, "I think they might go down for a few minutes. But be sure to be back before midnight. Remember, Patricia, you are to do exactly as your sister says."

Then Vic said: "I shall keep a firm hand on her, sir."

"Oh, you darling," Patricia cried, hugging her father rapturously. "I will be so good; and won't it be fun!"

Odd Fellows' Hall was elaborately decorated with bunting and evergreens. The party from the Rectory, arriving in time to hear the closing speeches of the two team captains, took their places in the gallery. The speeches were brief and to the point.

The Captain of the visiting team declared that he had greatly enjoyed the game. He was not quite convinced that the best team had won, but he would say that the game had gone to the team that had put up the best play. He complimented Captain Maitland upon his generalship. He had known Captain Maitland in the old days and he ought to have been on the lookout for the kind of thing he had put over. The Maitland Mill team had made a perfectly wonderful recovery in the last quarter, though he rather thought his friend Macnamara had helped it a little at a critical point.

"He did that," exclaimed Jumbo Larson, with marked emphasis.

After the roar of laughter had quieted down, the Cornwall Captain closed by expressing the hope that the Maitland Mill team would try for a place next season in the senior hockey. In which case he expressed the hope that he might have the pleasure of meeting them again.

Captain Maitland's speech was characteristic. He had nothing but praise for the Cornwalls. They played a wonderful game and a clean game. He shared in the doubt of their Captain as to which was the better team. He frankly confessed that in the last quarter the luck came to his team.

"Not a bit of it," roared the Cornwalls with one voice.

As to his own team, he was particularly proud of the way they had taken the training—their fine self-denial, and especially the never-dying spirit which they showed. It was a great honour for his team to meet the Cornwalls. A hard team to meet—sometimes—as Snoopy and himself had found out that evening—but they were good sports and he hoped some day to meet them again.

After the usual cheers for the teams, individually and collectively, for their supporters, for the Mill management and for the ladies, the dinner came to an end, the whole party joining with wide open throats and all standing at attention, in the Canadian and the Empire national anthems.

While the supper table was being cleared away preparatory to the dance, Captain Jack rushed upstairs to the party in the gallery. Patricia flung herself at him in an ecstasy of rapture.

"Oh! Captain Jack, you did win! You did win! You did win! It was glorious! And that double-circle play that you and Snoopy put up—didn't it work beautifully!"

"We were mighty lucky," said Captain Jack.

The others, Hugh, Vic and Rupert, crowded round, offering congratulations. Adrien waited behind, a wonderful light shining in her eyes, a faint colour touching her pale cheek. Captain Jack came slowly forward.

"Are you not going to congratulate us, too, Adrien?" he said.

She moved a pace forward.

"Oh, Jack," she whispered, leaning toward him and breathing quickly, "it was so like the old, the dear old days."

Into Maitland's eyes there flashed a look of surprise, of wonder, then of piercing scrutiny, while his face grew white.

"Adrien," he said, in a voice low, tense, almost stern, which she alone heard. "What do you mean? Then do you—"

"Oh, Captain Jack," cried Patricia, catching his arm, "are you going to dance? You are, aren't you? And will you give me—Oh, I daren't ask! You are such a great hero to-night!"

"Why, Patsy, will you give me a dance?"

The girl stood gazing at him with eyes that grew misty, the quick beating of her loyal heart almost suffocating her.

"Oh, Captain Jack," she gasped, "how many?"

Maitland laughed at her, and turned to her sister.

"And you, Adrien, may I have a dance?"

Again Adrien leaned toward him.

"One?" she asked.

"And as many more as you can spare."

"My program is quite empty, you see," she said, flinging out her hands and laughing joyously into his face.

"What about me? And me? And me?" said the other three men.

"I suppose we are all nowhere to-night," added Rupert, with a touch of bitterness in his voice.

"Well, there is only one conquering hero, you know," replied Adrien, smiling at them all.

"Now I must run off," said Maitland. "You see, I am on duty, as it were. Come down in a few minutes."

"Yes, go, Jack," said Adrien, throwing him a warm smile. "We will follow you in a few minutes."

"Oh, I am so excited!" said Patricia, as Maitland disappeared down the stairs. "I mean to dance with every one of the team. I know I am going to have a perfectly lovely time! But I would give them all up if I could have Captain Jack all the time."

"Pig," said her sister, smiling at her.

"Wretch," cried Vic, making a face.

But Patricia was quite unabashed. "I am going to have him just as often as I can," she said, brazenly.

For a few minutes they stood watching the dancers on the floor below. It was indeed, as Mrs. Templeton had said, a "mixed multitude." Mill hands and their girls, townsfolk whose social standing was sufficiently assured to endure the venture. A mixed multitude, but thoroughly jolly, making up in vigour what was lacking in grace in their exposition of the Terpsichorean art.

"Rather ghastly," said Rupert, who appeared to be quite disgusted with the whole evening's proceedings.

"Lovely!" exclaimed Patricia.

"They are enjoying themselves, at any rate," said Adrien, "and, after all, that is what people dance for."

"Stacks of fun. I am all for it, eh, Pat?" said Vic, making adoring eyes at the young girl.

But Patricia severely ignored him.

"Oh, Adrien, look!" she cried suddenly. "There is Annette, and who is the big man with her? Oh, what an awful dancer he is! But Annette, isn't she wonderful! What a lovely dress! I think she is the most beautiful thing." And Patricia was right, for Annette was radiant in colour and unapproachable in the grace of her movement.

"By Jove! She is a wonder!" said Vic. "Some dancer, if she only had a chance."

"Well, why don't you go down, Vic," said Patricia sharply. "You know you are just aching to show off your fox trot. Run away, little boy, I won't mind."

"I don't believe you would," replied Vic ruefully.

For some minutes longer they all stood watching the scene below.

"They are a jolly crowd," said Adrien. "I don't think we have half the fun at our dances."

"They certainly get a lot for their money," said Vic. "But wait till they come to 'turkey-in-the-straw!' That is where they really cut loose."

"Oh, pshaw!" cried Patricia. "I can 'turkey' myself. Just wait and you'll see."

"So can I," murmured Vic. "Will you let me in on it? Hello," he continued, "there is the Captain and Annette. Now look out for high art. I know the Captain's style. And a two-step! My eye! She is a little airy fairy!"

"How beautifully she dances," said Adrien. "And how charmingly she is dressed."

"They do hit it off, don't they," said Rupert. "They evidently know each other's paces."

Suddenly Adrien turned to Hugh: "Don't you think we should go down?" she asked. "You know we must not stay late."

"Yes, do come along!" cried Patricia, seizing Victor by the arm and hurrying to the stairs, the others making their way more leisurely to the dancing room.

The hall was a scene of confused hilarity. Maitland was nowhere to be seen.

"Oh! let us dance, Vic!" cried Patricia. "There is really no use waiting for Captain Jack. At any rate, Adrien will claim the first dance."

No second invitation was needed and together they swung off into the medley of dancers.

"We may as well follow," said Hugh. "We shall doubtless run into Maitland somewhere before long."

But not in that dance, nor in the three successive dances did Maitland appear. The precious moments were slipping by. Patricia was becoming more and more anxious and fretful at the non-appearance of her hero. Also, Hugh began to notice and detect a lagging in his partner's step.

"Shall we go out into the corridor?" he said. "This air is beginning to be rather trying."

From the crowded hall they passed into the corridor, from which opened side rooms which were used as dressing and retiring rooms, and whose entrances were cleverly screened by a row of thick spruce trees set up for the occasion.

"This is better," said Hugh, drawing a deep breath. "Shall we sit a bit and rest?"

"Oh, do let us," said Adrien. "This has been a strenuous and exciting evening. I really feel quite done out. Here is a most inviting seat."

Wearily she sat down on a bench which faced the entrance to one of the rooms.

"Shall I bring you a glass of water or an ice, Adrien?" inquired Hugh, noting the pallor in her face.

"Thank you. A glass of water, if you will be so kind. How deliciously fragrant that spruce is."

As her partner set off upon his errand, Adrien stepped to the spruce tree which screened the open door of the room opposite, and taking the bosky branches in her hands, she thrust her face into the aromatic foliage.

"How deliciously fragrant," she murmured.

Suddenly, as if stabbed by a spine in the trees, she started back and stood gazing through the thick branches into the room beyond There stood Maitland and Annette, the girl, with her face tearfully pale and pleading, uplifted to his and with her hands gripped tight and held fast in his, clasped against his breast. More plainly than words her face, her eyes, her attitude told her tale. She was pouring out her very soul to him in entreaty, and he was giving eager, sympathetic heed to her appeal.

Swiftly Adrien stepped back from the screening tree, her face white as if from a stunning blow, her heartbeats checking her breath. Quickly, blindly, she ran down the corridor. At the very end she met Hugh with a glass of water in his hand.

"What is the matter, Adrien? Have you seen a ghost?" he cried in an anxious voice.

She caught the glass from his hand and began to drink, at first greedily, then more slowly.

"Ah!" she said, drawing a deep breath. "That is good. Do you know, I was almost overcome. The air of that room is quite deadly. Now I am all right. Let us get a breath from the outside, Hugh."

Taking him by the arm, she hastened him to the farther end of the corridor and opened the door. "Oh, delicious!" She drew in deep breaths of the cold, fresh air.

"How wonderful the night is, Hugh." She leaned far out, "and the snow was like a cloth of silver and diamonds in this glorious moon." She stooped, and from a gleaming bank beside the door she caught up a double handful of the snow and, packing it into a little ball, flung it at her partner, catching him fairly on the ear.

"Aha!" she cried. "Don't ever say a woman is a poor shot. Now then," she added, stamping her feet free from the clinging flakes and waving her hands in the air to dry them, "I feel fit for anything. Let us have one more dance before we go home, for I feel we really must go."

"You are sure you are quite fit?" inquired Hugh, still anxious for her.

"Fit? Look at me!" Her cheeks were bright with colour, her eyes with light.

"You surely do look fit," said Hugh, beaming at her with frank admiration. "But you were all in a few moments ago."

"Come along. There is a way into the hall by this door," she cried, catching his hand and hurrying him into the dancing room again.

At the conclusion of their dance they came upon Patricia near the main entrance, in great distress. "I have not seen Captain Jack anywhere," she lamented. "Have you, Adrien? I have just sent Vic for a final search. I simply cannot go home till I have had my dance." The girl was almost in tears.

"Never mind, dear," said Adrien. "He has many duties to-night with all these players to look after. I think we had better go whenever Vic returns. I am awfully sorry for you, Patricia," she added. "No! Don't! You simply must not cry here." She put her arm around her sister's shoulder, her own lips trembling, and drew her close. "Where has Vic gone, I wonder?"

That young man, however, was having his own trials. In his search for Maitland he ran across McNish, whom he recognised as Annette's partner in the first dance.

"Hello!" he cried. "Do you know where Captain Maitland is, by any chance?"

"No, how should I know," replied McNish, in a voice fiercely guttural.

"Oh!" said Vic, somewhat abashed. "I saw you dance with Annette—with Miss Perrotte—and I thought perhaps you might know where the Captain was."

McNish stood glowering at him for a moment or two, then burst forth:

"They are awa'—he's ta'en her awa'."

"Away," said Vic. "Where?"

"To hell for all I ken or care."

Then with a single stride McNish was close at his side, gripping his arm with fingers that seemed to reach the bone.

"Ye're a friend o' his. Let me say tae ye if ony ill comes tae her, by the leevin' God above us he wull answer tae me." Hoarse, panting, his face that of a maniac, he stood glaring wild-eyed at the young man before him. To say that Vic was shaken by this sudden and violent onslaught would be much within the truth. Nevertheless he boldly faced the passion-distracted man.

"Look here! I don't know who you are or what you mean," he said, in as steady tones as he could summon, "but if you suggest that any girl will come to harm from Captain Maitland, then I say you are a liar and a fool." So speaking, little Vic set himself for the rush which he was firmly convinced would come. McNish, however, stood still, fighting for control. Then, between his deep-drawn breaths, he slowly spoke:

"Ye may be richt. A hope tae God A am baith liar and fule." The agony in his face moved Vic to pity.

"I say, old chap," he said, "you are terribly mistaken somehow, I can swear to that. Where is Maitland, anyway, do you know?"

"They went away together." McNish had suddenly gotten himself in hand. "They went away in his car, secretly."

"Secretly," said Vic, scornfully. "Now, that is perfect rot. Look here, do you know Captain Maitland? I am his friend, and let me tell you that all I ever hope to own, here and hereafter, and all my relatives and friends, I would gladly trust with him."

"Maybe, maybe," muttered McNish. "Ye may be richt. A apologise, sir, but if—" His eyes blazed again.

"Aw, cut out the tragedy stuff," said Vic, "and don't be an ass. Goodnight."

Vic turned on his heel and left McNish standing in a dull and dazed condition, and made his way toward the ballroom.

"Who is the Johnny, anyway?" he said to himself. "He is mad—looney—utterly bughouse. Needs a keeper in the worst way. But what about the Captain—must think up something. Let's see. Taken suddenly ill? Hardly—there is the girl to account for. Her mother—grandmother—or something—stricken—let's see. Annette has a brother—By Jove! the very thing—I've got it—brother met with an accident—run over—fell down a well—anything. Hurry call—ambulance stuff. Good line. Needs working up a bit, though. What has happened to my grey matter? Let me think. Ah, yes—when that Johnny brought word of an accident, a serious accident to her brother, Maitland, naturally enough, the gallant soul, hurries her off in his car, sending word by aforesaid mad Johnny."

Vic went to the outer door, feeling the necessity for a somewhat careful conning of his tale to give it, as he said himself, a little artistic verisimilitude. Then, with his lesson—as he thought—well learned, and praying for aid of unknown gods, he went back to find his partner.

"If only Patricia will keep out of it," he said to himself as he neared the hall door, "or if I could only catch old Hugh first. But he is not much of a help in this sort of thing. Dash it all! I am quite nervous. This will never do. Must find a way—good effect—cool and collected stuff." So, ruminating and praying and moving ever more slowly, he reached the door. Coming in sight of his party, he hurried to meet them. "Awfully sorry!" he exclaimed excitedly. "The most rotten luck! Old Maitland's just been called off."

"Called off!" cried Patricia, in dismay. "Where to!"

"Now, don't jump at me like that. Remember my heart. Met that Johnny—the big chap dancing with Annette, you know—just met him—quite worked up—a hurry call for the girl—for the girl, Annette, you know."

"The girl!" exclaimed Patricia. "You said Captain Jack."

"I know! I know!" replied Vic, somewhat impatiently. "I am a bit excited, I confess. Rather nasty thing—Annette's brother, you know—something wrong—accident, I think. Couldn't get the particulars."

"But Annette's brother is in Toronto," said Adrien, gravely.

"Exactly!" cried Vic. "That is what I have been telling you. A hurry call—phone message for Annette—horrible accident. Maitland rushed her right away in his car to catch the midnight to Toronto."

"By Jove! That is too bad," said Hugh, a genuine sympathy in his honest voice. "That is hard luck on poor Annette. Tony is not exactly a safe proposition, you know."

"Was he—is he killed?" cried Patricia, in a horror-stricken voice.

"Killed! Not a bit of it," said Vic cheerfully. "Slight injury—but serious, I mean. You know, just enough to cause anxiety." Vic lit another cigarette with ostentatious deliberation. "Nasty shock, you know," he said.

"Who told you all this?" inquired Rupert.

"Who told me?" said Vic. "Why, that mad Johnny."

"Mad Johnny? What mad Johnny?"

Vic said: "Eh! What? You know, that—ahr—big chap who was falling over her in the fox trot. Looked kind of crazy, you know—big chap—Scotch."

"Where is he now?" enquired Rupert.

"Oh, I fancy about there, somewhere," replied Vic, remembering that he had seen McNish moving toward the door. "Better go and look him up and get more particulars. Might help some, you know."

"Oh, Adrien, let us go to her," said Patricia. "I am sure Annette would love to have you. Poor Annette!"

"Oh! I say!" interposed Vic hurriedly. "There is really no necessity. I shouldn't like to intrude in family affairs and that sort of thing, you know what I mean."

Adrien's grave, quiet eyes were upon Vic's face. "You think we had better not go, then," she said slowly.

"Sure thing!" replied Vic, with cheerful optimism. "There is no necessity—slight accident—no need to make a fuss about it."

"But you said it was a serious accident—a terrible thing," said Patricia.

"Oh, now, Patricia, come out of it. You check a fellow up so hard. Can't you understand the Johnny was so deucedly worked up over it he couldn't give me the right of it. Dash it all! Let's have another turn, Patricia!"

But Adrien said: "I think we will go home, Hugh."

"Very well, if you think so, Adrien. I don't fancy you need worry over Annette. The accident probably is serious but not dangerous. Tony is a tough fellow."

"Exactly!" exclaimed Vic. "Just as I have been telling you. Serious, but not dangerous. At least, that was the impression I got."

"Oh, Vic, you are so terribly confusing!" exclaimed Patricia. "Why can't you get things straight? I say, Adrien, we can ride round to Annette's on our way home, and then we will get things quite clearly."

"Certainly," said Hugh. "It will only take us a minute. Eh, what!" he added to Vic, who was making frantic grimaces at him. "Well, if you ladies will get your things, we will go."

"But I am so disappointed," said Patricia to Adrien, as they went to their dressing room together.

After they had gone, Hugh turned upon Vic: "Now then, what the deuce and all are you driving at?"

"Driving at!" cried Vic, in an exasperated tone. "You are a sweet support for a fellow in distress. I am a nervous wreck—a perfect mess. Another word from that kid and I should have run screaming into the night. And as for you, why the deuce didn't you buck up and help a fellow out?"

"Help you out? How in the name of all that is reasonable could I help you out? What is all the yarn about? Of course I know it isn't true. Where's Maitland?"

"Search me," said Vic. "All I know is that I hit upon that Scotch Johnny out in the hall—he nearly wrenched an arm off me and did everything but bite—spitting out incoherent gaspings indicating that Maitland had 'gone awa' wi' his gur-r-l, confound him!' and suggesting the usual young Lochinvar stuff. You know—nothing in it, of course. But what was I to do? Some tale was necessary! Fortunately or unfortunately, brother Tony sprang to the thing I call my mind and—well, you know the mess I made of it. But Hugh, remember, for heaven's sake, make talk about something—about the match—and get that girl quietly home. I bag the back seat and Adrien. It is hard on me, I know, but fifteen minutes more of Patsy and I shall be counting my tootsies and prattling nursery rhymes. Here they come," he breathed. "Now, 'a little forlorn hope, deadly breach act, if you love me, Hardy.' Play up, old boy!"

And with commendable enthusiasm and success, Hugh played up, supported—as far as his physical and mental condition allowed—by the enfeebled Vic, till they had safely deposited their charges at the Rectory door, whence, refusing an invitation to stop for cocoa, they took their homeward way.

"'And from famine, pestilence and sudden death,' and from the once-over by that penetrating young female, 'good Lord, deliver us,'" murmured Vic, falling into the seat beside his friend. "Take me home to mother," he added, and refused further speech till at his own door. He waved a weak adieu and staggered feebly into the house.

CHAPTER XI
THE NEW MANAGER

Grant Maitland sat in his office, plainly disturbed in his mind. His resolute face, usually reflecting the mental repose which arises from the consciousness of a strength adequate to any emergency, carried lines which revealed a mind which had lost its poise. Reports from his foremen indicated brooding trouble, and this his own observation within the last few weeks confirmed. Production was noticeably falling low. The attitude of the workers suggested suspicion and discontent. That fine glow of comradeship which had been characteristic of all workers in the Maitland Mills had given place to a sullen aloofness and a shiftiness of eye that all too plainly suggested evil forces at work.

During the days immediately preceding and following the Great Match, there had been a return of that frank and open bearing that had characterised the employees of the Maitland Mills in the old days, but that fleeting gleam of sunshine had faded out and the old grey shadow of suspicion, of discontent, had fallen again. To Maitland this attitude brought a disappointment and a resentment which sensibly added to his burden, already heavy enough in these days of weakening markets and falling prices. In his time he had come through periods of financial depression. He was prepared for one such period now, but he had never passed through the unhappy experience of a conflict with his own employees. Not that he had ever feared a fight, but he shrank from a fight with his own men. It humiliated him. He felt it to be a reflection upon his system of management, upon his ability to lead and control, indeed, upon his personality. But, more than all, it grieved him to feel that he had lost that sense of comradeship which for forty years he had been able to preserve with those who toiled with him in a common enterprise.

A sense of loneliness fell upon him. Like many a man, self-made and self-sufficing, he craved companionship which his characteristic qualities of independence and strength seemed to render unnecessary and undesired. The experience of all leaders of men was his, for the leader is ever a lonely man.

This morning the reports he had just received convinced him that a strike with his workers would not long be delayed. "If I only knew what they really wanted," he bitterly mused. "It cannot be wages. Their wages are two or three times what they were before the war—shop conditions are all that could be desired—the Lord knows I have spent enough in this welfare stuff and all that sort of thing during these hard times. I have heard of no real grievances. I am sick of it all. I guess I am growing too old for this sort of thing."

There was a tap at the door and his son appeared, with a cheery greeting.

"Come in, Jack," said his father, "I believe you are the very man I want."

"Hello, Dad. You look as if you were in trouble."

"Well," replied his father with a keen look at him, "I think I may return the compliment."

"Well, yes, but perhaps I should not bother you. You have all you can carry."

"All I can carry," echoed Maitland, picking up the reports from his desk and handing them to his son, who glanced over them. "Things are not going well at the mills. No, you needn't tell me. You know I never ask you for any confidences about your brother unionists."

"Right you are, Dad. You have always played the game."

"Well, I must confess this is beyond me. Everywhere on the men's faces I catch that beastly look of distrust and suspicion. I hate to work with men like that. And very obviously, trouble is brewing, but what it is, frankly, it is beyond me to know."

"Well, it is hardly a secret any longer," said Jack. "Trouble is coming, Dad, though what form it shall take I am not in a position to say. Union discipline is a fierce thing. The rank and file are not taken into the confidence of the leaders. Policies are decided upon in the secret councils of the Great Ones and handed down to us to adopt. Of course, it is open to any man to criticise, and I am bound to say that the rankers exercise that privilege with considerable zest. All the same, however, it is difficult to overturn an administration, hard to upset established order. The thing that is, is the thing that ought to be. Rejection of an administration policy demands revolution."

"Well," said his father, taking the sheets from Jack's hand, "we needn't go to meet the trouble. Now, let us have yours. What is your particular grief?"

"Tony," said Jack shortly.

"Tony?" echoed his father in dismay. "Heaven help us! And what now has come to Tony? Though I must confess I have been expecting this for some time. It had to come."

"It is a long story, Dad, and I shan't worry you with the details. As you know, after leaving us, Tony went from one job to another with the curve steadily downwards. For the last few months, I gather, he has been living on his wits, helped out by generous contributions from his sister's wages. Finally he was given a subordinate position under 'The Great War Veterans' who have really been very decent to him. This position involved the handling of funds—no great amount. Then it was the old story—gambling and drinking—the loss of all control—desperate straits—hoping to recoup his losses—and you know the rest."

"Embezzlement?" asked Maitland.

"Yes, embezzlement," said Jack. "Tony is not a thief. He didn't deliberately steal, you understand."

"Jack," said his father, sharply, "get that out of your head. There is no such distinction in law or in fact. Stealing is stealing, whatever the motive behind it, whatever the plan governing it, by whatever name called."

"I didn't really mean anything else, Dad. Tony did the thing, at any rate, and the cops were on his trail. He got into hiding, sent an S. O. S. to his sister. Annette, driven to desperation, came to me with her story the night of the Match. She was awfully cut up, poor girl. I had to leave the dance and go right off to Toronto. Too late for the train, I drove straight through,—ghastly roads,—found Tony, fetched him back, and up till yesterday he has been hiding in his own home. Meantime, I managed to get things fixed up—paid his debts, the prosecution is withdrawn and now he wants,—or, rather, he doesn't want but needs, a job."

Maitland listened with a grave face. "Then the little girl was right, after all," he said.

"Meaning?"

"Patricia," said his father. "She told me a long story of a terrible accident to Tony that had called you away to Toronto. I must say it was rather incoherent."

"But who told her? I swear not a soul knew but his people and myself," said Jack.

"Strange how things get out," said his father. "Well, where is Tony now?"

"Here, in the outer office."

"But," said Maitland, desperately, "where can we place him? He is impossible in any position—dangerous in the office, useless as a foreman, doubtful and uncertain as a workman."

"One thing is quite certain," said Jack decidedly, "he must be under discipline. He is useless on his own. I thought that perhaps he might work beside me. I could keep an eye on him. Tony has nothing in him to work with. I should like to hear old Matheson on him—the Reverend Murdo, I mean. That is a great theme of his—'To the man who has nothing you can give nothing.'"

"Matheson?" said Maitland. "A chum of yours, I understand. Radical, eh?"

"A very decent sort, father," replied Jack. "I have been doing a little economics with him during the winter. His radicalism is of a sound type, I think. He is a regular bear at economics and he is even better at the humanity business, the brother-man stuff. He is really sound there."

"I can guess what you mean," said his father, "though I don't quite catch on to all your jargon. But I confess that I suspect there is a whole lot of nonsense associated with these theories."

"You will pardon me, Dad," said Jack, "if I suggest that your education is really not yet complete."

"Whose is?" inquired his father, curtly.

"But about Tony," continued Jack, "I wish I had him in a gang under me. I would work him, or break his neck."

His father sat silently pondering for some minutes. Then, as if making a sudden resolve, he said: "Jack, I have been wanting to speak with you about something for some weeks. I have come to a place where it is imperative that I get some relief from my load. You see, I am carrying the whole burden of management practically alone. I look after the financing, the markets, I keep an eye on production and even upon the factory management. In normal conditions I could manage to get along, but in these critical days, when every department calls for close, constant and sane supervision, I feel that I must have relief. If I could be relieved of the job of shop management, I could give myself to the other departments where the situation at present is extremely critical. I want a manager, Jack. Why not take the job? Now," he continued, holding up his hand, as his son was about to speak, "listen for a moment or two. I have said the situation is serious. Let me explain that. The financing of this business in the present crisis requires a man's full time and energy. Markets, credits, collections, all demand the very closest attention."

Jack glanced at his father's face. For the first time he noticed how deep-cut were the lines that indicated care, anxiety and worry. A sudden remorse seized him.

"I am awfully sorry, sir," he said, "I have not been of much help to you."

Maitland waved his hand as if dismissing the suggestion. "Now you know nothing of the financial side, but you do know men and you can handle them. You proved that in the war, and, in another way, you proved that during this recent athletic contest. I followed that very closely and I say without hesitation that it was a remarkably fine bit of work and the reactions were of the best. Jack, I believe that you would make a great manager if you gave yourself to it, and thought it worth while. Now, listen to me." Thereupon the father proceeded to lay before his son the immediately pressing problems in the business—the financial obligations already assumed, the heavy accumulation of stock for which there were no markets, the increasing costs in production with no hope of relief, but rather every expectation of added burdens in this direction.

As he listened to his father, Jack was appalled with what he considered the overwhelmingly disastrous situation in which the business was placed. At the same time he saw his father in a new light. This silent, stern, reserved man assumed a role of hero in his eyes, facing desperate odds and silently fighting a lonely and doubtful battle. The son was smitten with a sense of his own futility. In him was born a desire and a resolve to stand beside his father in this conflict and if the battle went against them, to share in the defeat.

"Dad," cried his son impulsively, "I am a rotter. I have been of no help to you, but only a burden. I had no idea the situation was so serious." Remorse and alarm showed in his tone.

"Don't misunderstand me," said his father. "This is new to you and appears more serious than it is. There is really no ground, or little ground, for anxiety or alarm. Let me give you the other side." Then he proceeded to set forth the resources of the business, the extent of his credit, his plans to meet the present situation and to prepare for possible emergencies. "We are not at the wall yet, by any means, Jack," he said, his voice ringing out with a resolute courage. "But I am bound to say that if any sudden or untoward combination of circumstances, a strike, for instance, should arise, disaster might follow."

Jack's heart sank still lower. He was practically certain that a strike was imminent. Although without any official confirmation of his suspicions, he had kept his eyes and ears opened and he was convinced that trouble was unavoidable. As his father continued to set forth his plans, his admiration for him grew. He brought to bear upon the problems with which he was grappling a clear head, wide knowledge and steady courage. He was a general, planning a campaign in the face of serious odds. He recalled a saying of his old Commander-in-Chief in France: "War is a business and will be won by the application of business principles and business methods. Given a body of fighting men such as I command, the thing becomes a problem of transportation, organization, reserve, insurance. War is a business and will be won by fighting men directed or governed by business principles." He was filled with regret that he had not given himself more during these last months to the study of these principles. The prospect of a fight against impending disaster touched his imagination and stimulated him like a bugle call.

"I see what you want, father," he said. "You want to have some good N. C. O.'s. The N. C. O. is the backbone of the army," he quoted with a grin.

"N. C. O?" echoed his father. He was not sufficiently versed in military affairs to catch the full meaning of the army rag.

"What I mean is," said Jack, "that no matter how able a military commander is, he must have efficient subordinates to carry on. No Colonel can do his own company and platoon work."

His father nodded: "You've got it, Jack. I want a manager to whom I can entrust a policy without ever having to think of it again. I don't want a man who gets on top of the load, but one who gets under it."

"You want a good adjutant, father, and a sergeant-major."

"I suppose so," said the father, "although your military terms are a little beyond me. After all, the thing is simple enough. On the management side, we want increase in production, which means decrease in production costs, and this means better organization of the work and the workers."

Jack nodded and after a moment, said: "May I add, sir, one thing more?"

"Yes," said his father.

"Team play," said Jack. "That is my specialty, you know. Individualism in a game may be spectacularly attractive, but it doesn't get the goal."

"Team play," said his father. "Co-operation, I suppose you mean. My dear boy, this is no time for experimentation in profit-sharing schemes, if that is what you are after. Anyway, the history of profiteering schemes as I have read it is not such as to warrant entire confidence in their soundness. You cannot change the economic system overnight."

"That is true enough, Dad," said his son, "and perhaps I am a fool. But I remember, and you remember, what everybody said, and especially what the experts said, about the military methods and tactics before the war. You say you cannot change the economic system overnight, and yet the whole military system was changed practically overnight. In almost every particular, there was a complete revolution. Cavalry, fortress defences, high explosives, the proper place for machine guns, field tactics, in fact, the whole business was radically changed. And if we hadn't changed, they would be speaking German in the schools of England, like enough, by this time."

"Jack, you may be right," said his father, with a touch of impatience, "but I don't want to be worried just now. It is easy enough for your friend, Matheson, and other academic industrial directors, to suggest experiments with other people's money. If we could only get production, I would not mind very much what wages we had to pay. But I confess when industrial strife is added to my other burdens, it is almost more than I can bear."

"I am awfully sorry, Dad," replied his son. "I have no wish to worry you, but how are you going to get production? Everybody says it has fallen off terribly during and since the war. How are you going to bring it up? Not by the pay envelope, I venture to say, and that is why I suggested team play. And I am not thinking about co-operative schemes of management, either. Some way must be found to interest the fellows in their job, in the work itself, as distinct from the financial returns. Unless the chaps are interested in the game, they won't get the goals."

"My boy," said his father wearily, "that old interest in work is gone. That old pride in work which we used to feel when I was at the job myself, is gone. We have a different kind of workman nowadays."

"Dad, don't believe that," said Jack. "Remember the same thing was said before the war. We used to hear all about that decadent race stuff. The war proved it to be all rot. The race is as fine as ever it was. Our history never produced finer fighting men."

"You may be right," said his father. "If we could only get rid of these cursed agitators."

"There again, Dad, if you will excuse me, I believe you are mistaken. I have been working with these men for the last nine months, I have attended very regularly the meetings of their unions and I have studied the whole situation with great care. The union is a great institution. I am for it heart and soul. It is soundly and solidly democratic, and the agitators cut very little figure. I size up the whole lot about this way: Fifty per cent of the men are steady-going fellows with ambition to climb; twenty-five per cent are content to grub along for the day's pay and with no great ambition worrying them. Of the remainder, ten per cent are sincere and convinced reformers, more or less half-baked intellectuals; ten per cent love the sound of their own voices, hate work and want to live by their jaw, five per cent only are unscrupulous and selfish agitators. But, Dad, believe me, fire-brands may light fires, but solid fagots only can keep fires going. You cannot make conflagrations out of torches alone."

"That is Matheson, I suppose," said his father, smiling at him.

"Well, I own up. I have got a lot of stuff from Matheson. All the same I believe I have fairly sized up the labour situation."

"Boy, boy," said his father, "I am tired of it all. I believe with some team play you and I could make it go. Alone, I am not so sure. Will you take the job?"

There was silence between them for a few minutes. Then Jack answered slowly: "I am not sure of myself at all, Dad, but I can see you must have someone and I am willing to try the planing mill."

"Thank you, boy," said his father, stretching his hand quickly across the table, "I will back you up and won't worry you. Within reasonable limits I will give you a free hand."

"I know you will, Dad," said Jack, "and of course I have been in the army long enough to know the difference between the O. C. and the sergeant-major."

"Now, what about Tony?" inquired Maitland, reverting suddenly to what both felt to be a painful and perplexing problem. "What are we to do with him?"

"I will take him on," said Jack. "I suppose I must."

"He will be a heavy handicap to you, boy. Is there no other way?"

"I see no other way," Jack replied. "I will give him a trial. Shall I bring him in?"

"Bring him in."

In a minute or two Jack returned with Tony. As Maitland's eyes fell upon him, he could not prevent a start of shocked surprise.

"Why, Tony!" he exclaimed. "What in all the world is wrong with you? You are ill." Trembling, pale, obviously unstrung, Tony stood before him, his shifty eyes darting now at one face, then at the other, his hands restless, his whole appearance suggesting an imminent nervous collapse. "Why, Tony, boy, what is wrong with you?" repeated Maitland. The kindly tone proved too much for Tony's self-control. He gulped, choked, and stood speechless, his eyes cast down to the floor.

"Sit down, Tony," said Maitland. "Give him a chair, Jack."

But Jack said, "He doesn't need a chair. He is not here for a visit. You wanted to say something to him, did you not?" Jack's dry, matter-of-fact and slightly contemptuous tone had an instant and extraordinary effect upon the wretched man beside him.

Instantly, Tony stiffened up. His head went back, he cast a swift glance at Jack's face, whose smile, slightly quizzical, slightly contemptuous, appeared to bite into his vitals. A hot flame of colour swept his pale and pasty face.

"I want a job, sir," he said, in a tone low and fierce, looking straight at Mr. Maitland.

Maitland, taking his cue from his son, replied in a quiet voice: "Can you hold a job?"

"God knows," said Tony.

"He does," replied Maitland, "but what about you?"

Tony stood for a few moments saying nothing, darting uncertain glances now and then at Jack, on whose face still lingered the smile which Tony found so disturbing.

"If you want work," continued Mr. Maitland, "and want to make it go, Tony, you can go with Jack. He will give it to you."

"Jack!" exclaimed Tony. His face was a study. Uncertainty, fear, hope, disappointment were all there.

"Yes, Jack," said Mr. Maitland. "He is manager in these works now."

Tony threw back his head and laughed. "I guess I will have to work, then," he said.

"You just bet you will, Tony," replied Jack. "Come along, we will go."

"Where?"

"I am taking you home. See you to-night, sir," Jack added, nodding to his father.

The two young men passed out together to the car.

"Yes, Tony," said Jack, "I have taken over your job."

"My job? What do you mean by that?" asked Tony, bitter and sullen in face and tone.

"I am the new manager of the planing mill. Dad had you slated for that position, but you hadn't manager-timber in you."

Tony's answer was an oath, deep and heartfelt.

"Yes," continued Jack, "manager-timber is rare and slow-growing stuff, Tony."

Again Tony swore but kept silence, and so remained till they had reached his home. Together they walked into the living room. There they found Annette, and with her McNish. Both rose upon their entrance, McNish showing some slight confusion, and assuming the attitude of a bulldog on guard, Annette vividly eager, expectant, anxious.

"Well," she cried, her hands going fluttering to her bosom.

"I have got a job, Annette," said Tony, with a short laugh. "Here is my boss."

For a moment the others stood looking at Jack, surprised into motionless silence.

"I tell you, he is the new manager," repeated Tony, "and he is my boss."

"What does he mean, Jack?" cried the girl, coming forward to Maitland with a quick, impulsive movement.

"Just what he says, Annette. I am the new manager of the planing mill and I have given Tony a job."

Again there fell a silence. Into the eyes of the bulldog McNish there shot a strange gleam of something that seemed almost like pleasure. In those brief moments of silence life was readjusting itself with them all. Maitland had passed from the rank and file of the workers into the class of those who direct and control their work. Bred as they were and trained as they were in the democratic atmosphere of Canada, they were immediately conscious of the shifting of values.

Annette was the first to break silence. "I wish I could thank you," she said, "but I cannot. I cannot." The girl's face had changed. The eager light had faded from her dark eyes, her hands dropped quietly to her side. "But I am sure you know," she added after a pause, "how very, very grateful I am, how grateful we all are, Mr. Maitland."

"Annette," said Jack severely, "drop that 'Mr.' stuff. I was your friend yesterday. Am I any less your friend to-day? True enough, I am Tony's boss, but Tony is my friend—that is, if he wants to have it so. You must believe this, Annette."

He offered her his hand. With a sudden impulse she took it in both of hers and held it hard against her breast, her eyes meanwhile burning into his with a look of adoration, open and unashamed. She apparently forgot the others in the room.

"Jack," she cried, her voice thrilling with passion, "I don't care what you are. I don't care what you think. I will never, never forget what you have done for me."

Maitland flung a swift glance at McNish and was startled at the look of rage, of agonised rage, that convulsed his face.

"My dear Annette," he said, with a light laugh, "don't make too much of it. I was glad to help Tony and you. Why shouldn't I help old friends?"

As he was speaking they heard the sound of a door closing and looking about, Jack found that McNish had gone, to be followed by Tony a moment or two later.

"Oh, never mind him," cried Annette, answering Jack's look of surprise. "He has to go to work. And it doesn't matter in the least."

Jack was vaguely disturbed by McNish's sudden disappearance.

"But, Annette," he said, "I don't want McNish to think that I—that you—"

"What?" She leaned toward him, her face all glowing with warm and eager light, her eyes aflame, her bosom heaving. "What, Jack?" she whispered. "What does it matter what he thinks?"

He put out his hands. With a quick, light step she was close to him, her face lifted up in passionate surrender. Swiftly Jack's arms went around her and he drew her toward him.

"Annette, dear," he said, and his voice was quiet and kind, too kind. "You are a dear girl and a good girl, and I am glad to have helped you and shall always be glad to help you."

The door opened and Tony slipped into the room. With passionate violence, Annette threw away the encircling arms.

"Ah!" she cried, a sob catching her voice. "You—you shame me. No—I shame myself." Rigid, with head flung back, she stood before him, her eyes ablaze with passionate anger, her hands clenched tight. She had flung herself at him and had been rejected.

"What the devil is this?" cried Tony, striding toward them. "What is he doing to you, Annette?"

"He?" cried Annette, her breath coming in sobs. "To me? Nothing! Keep out of it, Tony." She pushed him fiercely aside. "He has done nothing! No! No! Nothing but what is good and kind. Ah! kind. Yes, kind." Her voice rose shrill in scorn of herself and of him. "Oh, yes, he is kind." She laughed wildly, then broke into passionate tears. She turned from them and fled to her room, leaving the two men looking at each other.

"Poor child," said Jack, the first to recover speech. "She is quite all in. She has had two hard weeks of it."

"Two hard weeks," repeated Tony, his eyes glaring. "What is the matter with my sister? What have you done to her?" His voice was like the growl of a savage dog.

"Don't be a confounded fool, Tony," replied Jack. "You ought to know what is the matter with your sister. You have had something to do with it. And now your job is to see if you can make it up to her. To-morrow morning, at seven o'clock, remember," he said curtly, and, turning on his heel, he passed out.

It seemed to Jack as he drove home that life had suddenly become a tangle of perplexities and complications. First there was Annette. He was genuinely distressed as he thought of the scene through which they had just passed. That he himself had anything to do with her state of mind did not occur to him.

"Poor little girl," he said to himself, "she really needs a change of some sort, a complete rest. We must find some way of helping her. She will be all right in a day or two." With which he dismissed the subject.

Then there was McNish. McNish was a sore puzzle to him. He had come to regard the Scotchman with a feeling of sincere friendliness. He remembered gratefully his ready and efficient help against the attacks of the radical element among his fellow workmen. On several occasions he, with the Reverend Murdo Matheson, had foregathered in the McNish home to discuss economic problems over a quiet pipe. He was always conscious of a reserve deepening at times to a sullenness in McNish's manner, the cause of which he could not certainly discover. That McNish was possessed of a mentality of more than ordinary power there was no manner of doubt. Jack had often listened with amazement to his argumentation with the Reverend Murdo, against whom he proved over and over again his ability to hold his own, the minister's superiority as a trained logician being more than counterbalanced by his antagonist's practical experience.

As he thought of these evenings, he was ready to believe that his suspicion of the Scotchman's ill-will toward himself was due largely to imagination, and yet he could not rid himself of the unpleasant memory of McNish's convulsed face that afternoon.

"What the deuce is the matter with the beggar, anyway?" he said to himself.

Suddenly a new suggestion came to him.

"It can't be," he added, "surely the idiot is not jealous." Then he remembered Annette's attitude at the moment, her hands pressing his hard to her breast, her face lifted up in something more than appeal. "By Jove! I believe that may be it," he mused. "And Annette? Had she observed it? What was in her heart? Was there a reason for the Scotchman's jealousy on that side?"

This thought disturbed him greatly. He was not possessed of a larger measure of self-conceit than falls to the lot of the average young man, but the thought that possibly Annette had come to regard him other than as a friend released a new tide of emotion within him. Rapidly he passed in review many incidents in their association during the months since he returned from the war, and gradually the conviction forced itself upon him that possibly McNish was not without some cause for jealousy. It was rotten luck and was bound to interfere with their present happy relations. Yet none the less was he conscious that it was not altogether an unpleasant thought to him that in some subtle way a new bond had been established between this charming young girl and himself.

But he must straighten things out with McNish at the very first opportunity. He was a decent chap and would make Annette a first-rate husband. Indeed, it pleased Jack not a little to feel that he would be able to further the fortunes of both. McNish had good foreman timber in him and would make a capable assistant. As to this silly prejudice of his, Jack resolved that he would take steps immediately to have that removed. That he could accomplish this he had little doubt.

But the most acutely pressing of the problems that engaged his mind were those that arose out of his new position as manager. The mere organizing and directing of men in their work gave him little anxiety. He was sure of himself as far as that was concerned. He was sure of his ability to introduce among the men a system of team play that would result in increased production and would induce altogether better results. He thought he knew where the weak spots were. He counted greatly upon the support of the men who had been associated with him in the Maitland Mills Athletic Association. With their backing, he was certain that he could eliminate most of that very considerable wastage in time that even a cursory observation had revealed to him in the shops, due to such causes as dilatory workers, idle machines, lack of co-ordination, improper routing of work, and the like. He had the suspicion that a little investigation would reveal other causes of wastage as well.

There was one feature in the situation that gave him concern and that was the radical element in the unions. Simmons and his gang had from the very first assumed an attitude of hostility to himself, had sought to undermine his influence and had fought his plans for the promotion of clean sport among the Mill men. None knew better than Simmons that an active interest in clean and vigorous outdoor sports tended to produce contentment of mind, and a contented body of men offered unfertile soil for radical and socialistic doctrines. Hence, Simmons had from the first openly and vociferously opposed with contemptuous and bitter indignation all Jack's schemes and plans for the promotion of athletic sports. But Jack had been able to carry the men with him and the recent splendid victory over a famous team had done much to discredit brother Simmons and his propaganda.

Already Jack was planning a new schedule of games for the summer. Baseball, football, cricket, would give occupation and interest to all classes of Mill workers. And in his new position he felt he might be able, to an even greater degree, to carry out the plans which he had in mind. On the other hand, he knew full well that men were apt to be suspicious of welfare schemes "promoted from above." His own hockey men he felt sure he could carry with him. If he could only win McNish to be his sergeant-major, success would be assured. This must be his first care.

He well knew that McNish had no love for Simmons, whom the Scotchman despised first, because he was no craftsman, and chiefly because he had no soundly-based system of economics but was governed by the sheerest opportunism in all his activities. A combination between McNish and Simmons might create a situation not easy to deal with. Jack resolved that that combination should be prevented. He would see McNish at once, after the meeting of his local, which he remembered was set for that very night.

This matter being settled, he determined to proceed immediately to the office for an interview with Wickes. He must get to know as speedily as possible something of the shop organization and of its effect upon production. He found Mr. Wickes awaiting him with tremulous and exultant delight, eager to put himself, his experience, his knowledge and all that he possessed at the disposal of the new manager. The whole afternoon was given to this work, and before the day was done, Jack had in his mind a complete picture of the planing mill, with every machine in place and an estimate, more or less exact, of the capacity of every machine. In the course of this investigation, he was surprised to discover that there was no detailed record of the actual production of each machine, nor, indeed, anything in the way of an accurate cost system in any department of the whole business.

"How do you keep track of your men and their work, Wickes?" he inquired.

"Oh!" said the old man, "the foremen know all about that, Mr. Jack."

"But how can they know? What check have they?"

"Well, they are always about, Mr. Jack, and keep their eyes on things generally."

"I see," said Jack. "And do you find that works quite satisfactorily?"

"Well, sir, we have never gone into details, you know, Mr. Jack, but if you wish—"

"Oh, no, Wickes, I am just trying to get the hang of things, you know." Jack was unwilling to even suggest a criticism of method at so early a stage in his managerial career. "I want to know how you run things, Wickes, and at any time I shall be glad of assistance from you."

The old bookkeeper hastened to give him almost tearful assurance of his desire to assist to the utmost of his power.

The meeting of Local 197 of the Woodworkers' Union was largely attended, a special whip having been sent out asking for a full meeting on the ground that a matter of vital importance to unionised labour was to be considered.

The matter of importance turned out to be nothing less than a proposition that the Woodworkers' Union should join with all other unions in the town to make a united demand upon their respective employers for an increase in wages and better conditions all around, in connection with their various industries. The question was brought up in the form of a resolution from their executive, which strongly urged that this demand should be approved and that a joint committee should be appointed to take steps for the enforcement of the demand. The executive had matters thoroughly in hand. Brother Simmons and the more radical element were kept in the background, the speakers chosen to present the case being all moderates. There was no suggestion of extreme measures. Their demands were reasonable, and it was believed that the employers were prepared to give fair consideration—indeed, members had had assurance from an authoritative quarter on the other side that such was the case.

Notwithstanding the moderate tone adopted in presenting it, the resolution met with strenuous opposition. The great majority of those present were quiet, steady-going men who wanted chiefly to be let alone at their work and who were hostile to the suggested action, which might finally land them in "trouble." The old-time workers in the Maitland Mills had no grievances against their employer. They, of course, would gladly accept an increase in wages, for the cost of living was steadily climbing, but they disliked intensely the proposed method of making a general demand for an increase in wages and for better conditions.

The sporting element in the meeting were frankly and fiercely antagonistic to anything that would disturb the present friendly relation with their employers in the Maitland Mills. "The old man" had always done the square thing. He had shown himself a "regular fellow" in backing them up in all their games during the past year. He had always given them a fair hearing and a square deal. They would not stand for any hold-up game of this sort. It was a low-down game, anyway.

The promoters of the resolution began to be anxious for their cause. They had not anticipated any such a strong opposition and were rather nonplussed as to the next move. Brother Simmons was in a fury and was on the point of breaking forth into a passionate denunciation of scabs and traitors generally when, to the amazement of all and the intense delight of the supporters of the administration, McNish arose and gave unqualified support to the resolution.

His speech was a masterpiece of diplomacy, and revealed his long practice in the art of oratory in that best of all training schools, the labour union of the Old Land. He began by expressing entire sympathy with the spirit of the opposition. The opposition, however, had completely misunderstood the intent and purport of the resolution. None of them desired trouble. There need not be, indeed, he hoped there would not be trouble, but there were certain very ugly facts that must be faced. He then, in terse, forceful language, presented the facts in connection with the cost of living, quoting statistics from the Department of Labour to show the steady rise in the price of articles of food, fuel and clothing since the beginning of the war, a truly appalling array. He had secured price lists from dealers in these commodities, both wholesale and retail, to show the enormous profits made during the war. There were returned soldiers present. They had not hesitated at the call of duty to give all they had for their country. They had been promised great things when they had left their homes, their families, their business and their jobs. How had they found things upon their return? He illustrated his argument from the cases of men present. It was a sore spot with many of them and he pressed hard upon it. They were suffering to-day; worse, their wives and children were suffering. Had anyone heard of their employers suffering? Here again he offered illustrations of men who had made a good thing out of the war. True, there were many examples of the other kind of employer, but they must deal with classes and not individuals in a case like this. This was part of a much bigger thing than any mere local issue. He drew upon his experience in the homeland with overwhelming effect. His voice rose and rolled in his richest Doric as he passionately denounced the tyranny of the masters in the coal and iron industries in the homeland. He was not an extremist; he had never been one. Indeed, all who knew him would bear him out when he said that he had been an opponent of Brother Simmons and those who thought with him on economic questions. This sudden change in attitude would doubtless surprise his brothers. He had been forced to change by the stern logic of facts. There was nothing in this resolution which any reasonable worker might object to. There was nothing in the resolution that every worker with any sympathy with his fellow workers should not support. Moreover, he warned them that if they presented a united front, there would be little fear of trouble. If they were divided in their ranks, or if they were halfhearted in their demands, they would invite opposition and, therefore, trouble. He asked them all to stand together in supporting a reasonable demand, which he felt sure reasonable men would consider favorably.

The effect of his speech was overwhelming. The administration supporters were exuberant in their enthusiastic applause and in their vociferous demands for a vote. The opposition were paralysed by the desertion of one whom they had regarded and trusted as a leader against the radical element and were left without answer to the masterly array of facts and arguments which he had presented.

At this point, the door opened and Maitland walked in. A few moments of tense silence, and then something seemed to snap. The opposition, led by the hockey men and their supporters, burst into a demonstration of welcome. The violence of the demonstration was not solely upon Maitland's account. The leaders of the opposition were quick to realise that his entrance had created a diversion for them which might save them from disastrous defeat. They made the most of this opportunity, prolonging the demonstration and joining in a "chair procession" which carried Maitland shoulder-high about the room, in the teeth of the violent protest of Brother Simmons and his following.

Order being restored, business was again resumed, when Brother Macnamara rose to his feet and, in a speech incoherent at times, but always forceful, proposed that the usual order be suspended and that here and now a motion be carried expressing their gratification at the recent great hockey victory and referring in highly laudatory terms to the splendid work of Brother Captain Maitland, to whose splendid efforts victory was largely due.

It was in vain that Brother Simmons and those of his way of thinking sought to stem the tide of disorder. The motion was carried with acclaim.

No sooner had this matter been disposed of than Maitland rose to his feet and said:

"Mr. President, I wish to thank you all for this very kind reference to my team and myself. I take very little credit for the victory which we won. We had a good team, indeed, quite a remarkable team. I have played in a good many athletic teams of various kinds, but in two particulars the Maitland Mills Hockey Team is the most remarkable of any I have known—first, in their splendid loyalty in taking their training and sticking together; that was beyond all praise; and, secondly, in the splendid grit which they showed in playing a losing game. Now, Mr. President, I am going to do something which gives me more regret than any of you can understand. I have to offer my resignation as a member of this union. I have accepted the position of manager of the planing mill and I understand that this makes it necessary that I resign as a member of this union. I don't really see why this should be necessary. I don't believe myself that it should, and, brothers, I expect to live long enough to belong to a union that will allow a fellow like me to be a member with chaps like you. But meantime, for the present I must resign. You have treated me like a brother and a chum. I have learned a lot from you all, but one thing especially, which I shall never forget: that there is no real difference in men that is due to their position in life; that a man's job doesn't change his heart."

He paused for a few moments as if to gather command of his voice, which had become suddenly husky.

"I am sorry to leave you, boys, and I want to say to you from my heart that though I cannot remain a member of this union, I can be and I will be a brother to you all the same. And I promise you that, as far as I can, I will work for the good of the union in the future as I have done in the past."

McNish alone was prepared for this dramatic announcement, although they all knew that Maitland sooner or later would assume a position which would link him up with the management of the business. But the suddenness of the change and the dramatic setting of the announcement created an impression so profound as to neutralise completely the effect of McNish's masterly speech.

Disappointed and enraged at the sudden turn of events, he was too good a general to allow himself to be routed in disorder. He set about to gather his disordered forces for a fresh attack, when once more the hockey men took command of the field. This time it was Snoopy Sykes, the most voiceless member of the union.

After a few moments of dazed silence that followed Maitland's announcement of his resignation, Snoopy rose and, encouraged by the cheers of his astonished comrades, began the maiden speech of his life.

"Mr. President," he shouted.

"Go to it, Snoopy, old boy."

"I never made a speech in my life, never—"

"Good, old scout, never begin younger! Cheerio, old son!"

"And I want to say that he don't need to. I once heard of a feller who didn't. He kept on and he didn't do no harm to nobody. And the Captain here wouldn't neither. So what I say is he don't need to," and Snoopy sat down with the whole brotherhood gazing at him in silence and amazed perplexity, not one of them being able to attach the faintest meaning to Snoopy's amazing oration.

At length Fatty Findlay, another of the voiceless ones, but the very special pal of Snoopy Sykes, broke forth in a puzzled voice:

"Say it again, Snoopy."

There was a roar of laughter, which only grew in volume as Snoopy turned toward his brothers a wrathful and bewildered countenance.

"No," said another voice. "Say something else, Snoopy. Shoot a goal this time."

Again Snoopy rose. "What I said was this," he began indignantly. Again there was a roar of laughter.

"Say, you fellers, shut up and give a feller a chance. The Captain wants to resign. I say 'No.' He is a darned good scout. We want him and we won't let him go. Let him keep his card."

"By the powers," roared Macnamara, "it is a goal, Snoopy. It's a humdinger. I second the motion."

It was utterly in vain that Brother Simmons and his whole following pointed out unitedly and successively the utter impossibility and absurdity of the proposal which was unconstitutional and without precedent. The hockey team had the company with them and with the bit in their teeth swept all before them.

At this point, McNish displayed the master-hand that comes from long experience. He saw his opportunity and seized it.

"Mr. President," he said, and at once he received the most complete attention. "A confess this is a most extraordinary proposal, but A'm goin' tae support it." The roar that answered told him that he had regained control of the meeting. "Brother Simmons says it is unconstitutional and without precedent. He is no correct in this. A have known baith maisters and managers who retained their union cards. A grant ye it is unusual, but may I point oot that the circumstances are unusual?"—Wild yells of approval—"And Captain Maitland is an unusual man"—louder yells of approval—"It may that there is something in the constitution o' this union that stands in the way—Cries of "No! No!" and consignment of the constitution to a nameless locality.—"A venture to suggest that a committee be appointed, consisting of Brothers Sykes, Macnamara and the chairman, wi' poors tae add, tae go into this maitter with Captain Maitland and report."

It was a master-stroke. A true union man regards with veneration the constitution and hesitates to tamper with it except in a perfectly constitutional manner. The opposition to the administration's original resolution had gained what they sought, a temporary stay. The committee was appointed and the danger to both the resolution and the constitution for the present averted.

Again Mr. McNish took command. "And noo, Mr. President," he said, "the oor is late. We are all tired and we all wish to give mair thocht to the main maitter before us. A move, therefore, that we adjourn to the call o' the Executive."

Once more Brother Simmons found himself in a protesting minority, and the meeting broke up, the opposition jubilant over their victory, the supporters of the administration determined to await a more convenient time.

CHAPTER XII
LIGHT THAT IS DARKNESS

At the next monthly meeting of Local 197 of the Woodworkers' Union, the executive had little difficulty in finally shelving the report of its committee appointed to deal with the resignation of Captain Maitland, and as little difficulty in passing by unanimous vote their resolution held up at the last meeting. The allied unions had meantime been extended to include the building trades. Their organization had been perfected and their discipline immensely strengthened. Many causes contributed to this result. A month's time had elapsed and the high emotional tides due to athletic enthusiasm, especially the hockey victory, had had space to subside. The dead season for all outdoor games was upon them and the men, losing touch with each other and with their captain, who was engrossed in studying his new duties, began to spend their leisure hours in loafing about the streets or lounging in the pool rooms.

All over the country the groundswell of unrest was steadily and rapidly rising. The returned soldiers who had failed to readjust themselves to the changed conditions of life and to the changes wrought in themselves by the war, embittered, disillusioned and disappointed, fell an easy prey to unscrupulous leaders and were being exploited in the interests of all sorts of fads and foolish movements. Their government bonuses were long since spent and many of them, through no fault of their own, found themselves facing a situation full of difficulty, hardship, and often of humiliation.

Under the influence of financial inflation and deceived by the abundant flow of currency in every department of business, industries by the score started up all over the land. Few could foresee the approach of dark and stern days. It was in vain that financial leaders began to sound a note of warning, calling for retrenchment and thrift. And now the inevitable results were beginning to appear. The great steel and coal industries began to curtail their operations, while desperately striving to maintain war prices for their products. Other industries followed their example. All the time the cost of living continued to mount. Foodstuffs reached unheard-of prices, which, under the manipulations of unscrupulous dealers, continued to climb.

Small wonder that working men with high wages and plenty of money in their hands cherished exaggerated ideas of their wealth and developed extravagant tastes in dress, amusements and in standard of living. With the rest of the world, they failed to recognise the fact that money was a mere counter in wealth and not wealth itself. To a large extent, thrift was abandoned and while deposits in the savings banks grew in volume, the depositors failed to recognise the fact that the value of the dollar had decreased fifty per cent. Already the reaction from all this had begun to set in. Nervousness paralysed the great financial institutions. The fiat went forth "No more money for industrial enterprises. No more advances on wholesale stocks." The order was issued "Retrench. Take your losses, unload your stocks." This men were slow to do, and while all agreed upon the soundness of the policy, each waited for the other to begin.

Through the month of April anxiety, fear and discontent began to haunt the minds of business men. In the labour world the High Command was quick to sense the approach of a crisis and began to make preparations for the coming storm. The whole industrial and commercial world gradually crystallised into its two opposing classes. A subsidised press began earnestly to demand lower cost in productions retrenchment in expenditure, a cut in labour costs, a general and united effort to meet the inevitable burden of deflation.

On the other hand, an inspired press began to raise an outcry against the increasing cost of living, to point out the effect of the house famine upon the income of the working man, and to sound a warning as to the danger and folly of any sudden reduction in the wage scale.

Increased activity in the ranks of organised labour began to be apparent. Everywhere the wild and radical element was gaining in influence and in numbers, and the spirit of faction and internecine strife became rampant.

It was due to the dominating forcefulness of McNish, the leader of the moderates, that the two factions in the allied unions had been consolidated, and a single policy agreed upon. His whole past had been a preparation for just a crisis as the present. His wide reading, his shrewd practical judgment, his large experience in labour movements in the Old Land, gave him a position of commanding influence which enabled him to dominate the executives and direct their activities. His sudden and unexplained acceptance of the more radical program won for him an enthusiastic following of the element which had hitherto recognised the leadership of Brother Simmons. Day and night, with a zeal that never tired, he laboured at the work of organising and disciplining the various factions and parties in the ranks of labour into a single compact body of fighting men under a single command. McNish was in the grip of one of the mightiest of human passions. Since that day in the Perrotte home, when he had seen the girl that he loved practically offer herself, as he thought, to another man, he had resolutely kept himself away from her. He had done with her forever and he had torn out of his heart the genuine friendship which he had begun to hold toward the man who had deprived him of her love. But deep in his heart he nourished a passion for vengeance that became an obsession, a madness with him. He merely waited the opportunity to gratify his passion.

He learned that the Maitland Mills were in deep water, financially. His keen economic instinct and his deep study of economic movements told him that a serious financial crisis, continent-wide, was inevitable and imminent. It only needed a successful labour war to give the final touch that would bring the whole industrial fabric tumbling into ruin. The desire for immediate revenge upon the man toward whom he had come to cherish an implacable hatred would not suffer him to await the onset of a nation-wide industrial crisis. He fancied that he saw the opportunity for striking an immediate blow here in Blackwater.

He steadily thwarted Maitland's attempts to get into touch with him, whether at the works or in his own home, where Maitland had become a frequent visitor. He was able only partially to allay his mother's anxiety and her suspicion that all was not well with him. That shrewd old lady knew her son well enough to suspect that some untoward circumstance had befallen him, but she knew also that she could do no more than bide her time.

With the workers of the Maitland Mills circumstances favoured the plans of McNish and the Executive of the allied unions. The new manager was beginning to make his hand felt upon the wheel. Checks upon wastage in labour time and in machine time were being instituted; everywhere there was a tightening up of loose screws and a knitting up of loose ends, with the inevitable consequent irritation. This was especially true in the case of Tony Perrotte, to whom discipline was ever an external force and never an inward compulsion. Inexact in everything he did, irregular in his habits, irresponsible in his undertakings, he met at every turn the pressure of the firm, resolute hand of the new manager. Deep down in his heart there was an abiding admiration and affection for Jack Maitland, but he loathed discipline and kicked against it.

The first of May is ever a day of uncertainty and unrest in the world of labour. It is a time for readjustment, for the fixing of wage scales, for the assertion of labour rights and the ventilating of labour wrongs. It is a time favourable to upheaval, and is therefore awaited by all employers of labour with considerable anxiety.

On the surface there was not a ripple to indicate that as far as the Maitland Mills were concerned there was beneath a surging tide of unrest. So undisturbed indeed was the surface that the inexperienced young manager was inclined to make light of the anxieties of his father, and was confident in his assurance that the danger of a labour crisis had, for the present at least, been averted.

Out of the blue heaven fell the bolt. The mails on May Day morning brought to the desk of every manager of every industry in Blackwater, and to every building contractor, a formal document setting forth in terms courteous but firm the demands of the executives of the allied unions of Blackwater.

"Well, it has come, boy," was Maitland's greeting to his son, who came into the office for the usual morning consultation.

"What?" said Jack.

"War," replied his father, tossing him the letter and watching his face as he read it.

Jack handed him the letter without a word.

"Well, what do you think of it?" said his father.

"It might be worse."

"Worse?" roared his father. "Worse? How can it be worse?"

"Well, it is really a demand for an increase in wages. The others, I believe, are mere frills. And between ourselves, sir, though I haven't gone into it very carefully, I am not sure but that an increase in wages is about due."

Maitland glowered at his son in a hurt and hopeless rage.

"An increase in wages due?" he said. "After the increase of six months ago? The thing is preposterous. The ungrateful scoundrels!"

At this point the telephone upon his desk rang. Jack took up the receiver.

"Good morning, Mr. McGinnis. . . . Yes, he is here. Yes. . . . At least, I suppose so. . . . Oh, I don't know. . . . It is rather peremptory. . . . All right, sir, I shall tell him."

"Let me talk to him," said his father, impatiently.

"Never mind just now, Dad," said Jack, with his hand over the receiver. Then through the telephone he said: "All right, sir; he will await you here. Good morning."

"... The old boy is wild," said Jack with a slight laugh. "The wires are quite hot."

"This is no joke, Jack, I can tell you. McGinnis is coming over, is he?"

"Yes," replied Jack, "but we won't get much help from him."

"Why not?" inquired his father. "He is a very shrewd and able business man."

"He may be all that, sir, but in a case like this, if you really want my opinion, and I have no wish to be disrespectful, he is a hot-headed ass. Just the kind of employer to rejoice the heart of a clever labour leader who is out for trouble. Dad," and Jack's voice became very earnest, "let's work this out by ourselves. We can handle our own men better without the help of McGinnis or any other."

"That is just the trouble. Look at this precious document, 'The Allied Unions.' What have I got to do with them? And signed by Simmons and McDonough. Who is McDonough, pray?"

"McDonough? Oh, I know McDonough. He is a little like McGinnis— big-hearted, hot-headed, good in a scrap, useless in a conference. But I suggest, sir, that we ignore the slight unpleasant technicalities in the manner and method of negotiation and try to deal with our own people in a reasonable way."

"I am ready always to meet my own people, but I refuse utterly to deal with this committee!" It was not often that Mr. Maitland became profane, but in his description of this particular group of individuals his ordinary English suffered a complete collapse.

"Dad, McGinnis will be here in a few minutes. I should like to suggest one or two things, if you will allow me."

"Go on," said his father quickly.

"Dad, this is war, and I have learned a little about that game 'over there.' And I have learned something about it in my athletic activities. The first essential is to decline to play the enemy's game. Let's discover his plan of campaign. As I read this document, the thing that hits my eye is this: do they really want the things they ask for, or is the whole thing a blind? What I mean is, do they really want war or peace? I say let's feel them out. If they are after peace, the thing is easy. If they want war, this may come to be a very serious thing. Meantime, Dad, let's not commit ourselves to McGinnis. Let's play it alone."

Mr. Maitland's lips had set in a thin, hard line. His face was like a mask of grey steel. He sat thinking silently.

"Here he comes," said Jack, looking out of the window. "Dad, you asked me to come into this with you. Let's play the game together. I found it wise to place the weight on the defence line. Will you play defence in this?"

The lines in his father's face began to relax.

"All right, boy, we'll play it together, and meantime I shall play defence."

"By Jove, Dad," cried Jack, in a tone of exultant confidence, "we'll beat 'em. And now here comes that old Irish fire-eater. I'll go. No alliance, Dad, remember." His father nodded as Jack left the room, to return almost immediately with Mr. McGinnis, evidently quite incoherent with rage.

In the outer office Jack paused beside the desk of the old bookkeeper. From behind the closed door came the sound of high explosives.

"Rough stuff in there, eh, Wickes," said Jack, with a humorous smile. For some moments he stood listening. "War is a terrible thing," he added with a grin.

"What seems to be the matter, Mr. Jack?"

Jack laid before him the document sent out by the Allied Unions.

"Oh, this is terrible, Mr. Jack! And just at this time. I am very much afraid it will ruin us."

"Ruin us? Rot. Don't ever say that word again. We will possibly have a jolly good row. Someone will be hurt and perhaps all of us, more or less, but I don't mean to be beaten, if I know myself," he added, with the smile on his face that his hockey team loved to see before a match. "Now, Wickes," continued Jack, "get that idea of failure out of your mind. We are going to win. And meantime, let us prepare for our campaign. Here's a bit of work I want you to do for me. Get four things for me: the wages for the last three years—you have the sheets?"

"Yes, sir."

"—The cost of living from the Labour Gazette for the last three years—you have them here—and the rates of increase in wages. Plot a diagram showing all these things. You know what I mean?"

"Yes, sir, I understand."

"And find out the wages paid at our competing points."

"All right, Mr. Jack. I know what you want. I can give you the necessary information in regard to the first three points almost at once. It will take some days, however, to get the wages of our competing points."

"All right, old boy. Carry on!" said Jack, and with the same smile on his face he passed out of the office into the shops.

It amused him slightly to observe the change in the attitude and bearing of his men. They would not look at him fairly in the face. Even Snoopy Sykes and Macnamara avoided his glance. But he had for everyone his usual cheery word. Why should he not? These chaps had no hatred for him, nor he for them. He had come to understand union methods of discipline and recognised fully the demands for loyalty and obedience imposed upon its members by the organisation. These men of his were bound to the union by solemn obligations. He bore them no ill-will on that score. Rather he respected them the more for it. If a fight was inevitable, he would do his best to beat them but he would allow no spirit of hatred to change his mind toward them nor cloud his judgment.

The day was full of excursions and alarms. A hurry call was sent out by McGinnis to all employers who had received copies of the document from the Allied Unions. In the afternoon a meeting was held in the Board of Trade Building, but it was given over chiefly to vituperation and threatening directed toward their variously described employees. With one heart and voice all affirmed with solemn, and in many cases with profane oaths that they would not yield a jot to the insolent demands of this newly organised body.

"I have already sent my answer," shouted Mr. McGinnis.

"What did you say, Mac?"

"Told 'em to go to hell, and told 'em that if any of these highly coloured committee men came on my premises, I would kick 'em into the middle of next week."

Jack, who was present at the meeting, sat listening with silent and amused pity. They seemed to him so like a group of angry children whose game had suddenly been interfered with and whose rage rendered them incapable of coherent thought.

Grant Maitland, who, throughout the meeting had sat silent, finally rose and said: "Gentlemen, the mere expression of feeling may afford a sort of satisfaction but the question is, What is to be done? That the situation is grave for all of us we know too well. Not many of us are in a position to be indifferent to a strike. Let us get down to business. What shall we do?"

"Fight them to a finish! Smash the unions!" were the suggestions in various forms and with various descriptive adjectives.

"It may come to a fight, gentlemen, but however gratifying a fight may be to our feelings, a fight may be disastrous to our business. A strike may last for weeks, perhaps months. Are we in a position to stand that? And as for smashing the unions, let us once and for all put such a thought out of our minds. These unions have all international affiliations. It is absurd to imagine that we here in Blackwater could smash a single union."

Fiercely McGinnis made reply. "I want to tell you right here and now that I am prepared to close down and go out of business but I will have no outside committee tell me how to run my job."

But no one took this threat seriously, and no one but knew that a shut-down for any of them might mean disaster. They all recalled those unfilled orders which they were straining every nerve to complete before the market should break, or cancellation should come. It added not a little to their rage that they knew themselves to be held in the grip of circumstances over which they had little control.

After much angry deliberation it was finally agreed that they should appoint a committee to consider the whole situation and to prepare a plan of action. Meantime the committee were instructed to temporise with the enemy.

The evening papers announced the imminence of a strike the extent and magnitude of which had never been experienced in the history of Blackwater. Everywhere the citizens of the industrial town were discussing the disturbing news anxiously, angrily, indifferently, according as they were variously affected. But there was a general agreement among all classes of citizens that a strike in the present industrial and financial situation which was already serious enough, would be nothing short of a calamity, because no matter what the issue would be, no matter which of the parties won in the conflict, a fight meant serious loss not only to the two parties immediately concerned, but to the whole community as well. With the rank and file of the working people there was little heart for a fight. More especially, men upon whom lay the responsibility for the support of homes shrank from the pain and the suffering, as well as from the loss which experience taught them a strike must entail. It is safe to say that in every working man's home in Blackwater that night there was to be found a woman who, as she put her children to bed, prayed that trouble might be averted, for she knew that in every war it is upon the women and children that in the last analysis the sorest burden must fall. To them even victory would mean for many months a loss of luxuries for the family, it might be of comforts; and defeat, which would come not until after long conflict, would mean not only straitened means but actual poverty, with all the attendant humiliation and bitterness which would kill for them the joy of life and sensibly add to its already heavy burden.

That night Jack Maitland felt that a chat with the Reverend Murdo Matheson might help to clear his own mind as to the demands of the Allied Unions. He found the minister in his study and in great distress of soul.

"I am glad to see you, Maitland," he said, giving him a hearty greeting. "My hope is largely placed in you and you must not fail me in this crisis. What exactly are the demands of the unions?"

Maitland spread before him the letter which his father had received that morning. The Reverend Murdo read it carefully over, then, with a sigh of relief, he said: "Well, it might be worse. There should not be much difficulty in coming to an agreement between people anxious for peace."

After an hour spent in canvassing the subject from various points of view, the Reverend Murdo exclaimed: "Let us go and see McNish."

"The very thing," said Maitland. "I have been trying to get in touch with him for the last month or so, but he avoids me."

"Ay," replied the Reverend Murdo, "he has a reason, no doubt."

To Maitland's joy they found McNish at home. They were received with none-too-cordial a welcome by the son, with kindly, even eager greeting by the mother.

"Come awa in, Minister; come awa, Mr. Maitland. You have come to talk about the 'trouble,' a doot. Malcolm does-na want to talk about it to me, a bad sign. He declines to converse even, wi' me, Mr. Matheson. Perhaps ye may succeed better wi' him."

"Mr. Matheson can see for himself," said her son, using his most correct English, "the impropriety of my talking with an employer in this way."

"Nonsense, McNish," said the minister briskly. "You know me quite well and we both know Maitland. It is just sheer nonsense to say that you cannot talk with us. Everyone in town is talking. Every man in your union is talking, trying to justify their present position, which, I am bound to say, takes some justifying."

"Why?" asked McNish hotly.

"Because the demands are some of them quite unsound. Some other than you had a hand in drawing up your Petition of Right, McNish, and some of the demands are impossible."

"How do you—" began McNish indignantly, but the minister held up his hand and continued:

"And some of them are both sound and reasonable."

"What's wrang with the demands?" said McNish.

"That's what I am about to show you," said the minister with grave confidence.

"Aye, minister," said the mother with a chuckle of delight. "That's you! That's you! Haud at him! Haud at him! That's you!"

They took seats about the blazing fire for the evening was still shrewd enough to make the fire welcome.

"Noo, Mr. Matheson," said the old lady, leaning toward him with keen relish in her face, "read me the union demands. Malcolm wadna read nor talk nor anything but glower."

The Reverend Murdo read the six clauses.

"Um! They're no bad negotiating pints."

"Negotiatin' pints!" exclaimed her son indignantly. "Noo, mither, ye maun play the game. A'm no gaun tae argue with ye to-night. Nor wi' any of ye," he added.

"Nonsense, Malcolm. You can't object to talk over these points with us. You must talk them over before you're done with them. And you'll talk them over before the whole town, too."

"What do you mean, 'before the whole town'?" said Malcolm.

"This is a community question. This community is interested and greatly interested. It will demand a full exposition of the attitude of the unions."

"The community!" snorted McNish in contempt.

"Aye, the community," replied the minister, "and you are not to snort at it. That's the trouble with you labour folk. You think you are the whole thing. You forget the third and most important party in any industrial strife, the community. The community is interested first, in justice being done to its citizens—to all its citizens, mind you; second, in the preservation of the services necessary to its comfort and well-being; third, in the continuance of the means of livelihood to wage earners."

"Ye missed one," said McNish grimly. "The conserving of the profits of labour for the benefit of the capitalist."

"I might have put that in, too," said the minister, "but it is included in my first. But I should have added another which, to my mind, is of the very first importance, the preservation of the spirit of brotherly feeling and Christian decency as between man and man in this community."

"Aye, ye might," replied Malcolm in bitter irony, "and ye might begin with the ministers and the churches."

"Whisht, laddie," said his mother sharply, "Mind yer manners."

"He doesn't mean me specially, Mrs. McNish, but I will not say but what he is right."

"No," replied McNish, "I don't mean you exactly, Mr. Matheson."

"Don't take it back, McNish," said the minister. "I need it. We all need it in the churches, and we will take it, too. But come now, let us look at these clauses. You are surely not standing for them all, or for them all alike?"

"Why not, then?" said McNish, angrily.

"I'll tell you," replied the minister, "and won't take long, either." He proceeded to read over carefully the various clauses in the demands of the allied unions, emphasizing and explaining the meaning of each clause. "First, as to wages. This is purely a matter for adjustment to the cost of living and general industrial conditions. It is a matter of arithmetic and common sense. There is no principle involved."

"I don't agree with you," said McNish. "There is more than the cost of living to be considered. There is the question of the standard of living. Why should it be considered right that the standard of living for the working man should be lower than that for the professional man or the capitalist?"

"There you are again, McNish," said the minister. "You are not up to your usual to-night. You know quite well that every working man in my parish lives better than I do, and spends more money on his living. The standard of living has no special significance with the working man to-day as distinguished from the professional man. We are not speaking of the wasteful and idle rich. So I repeat that here it is a matter of adjustment and that there is no principle involved. Now, as regard to hours. You ask an eight-hour day and a Saturday half-holiday. That, too, is a matter of adjustment."

"What about production, Mr. Matheson?" said Maitland. "And overhead? Production costs are abnormally high to-day and so are carrying charges. I am not saying that a ten-hour day is not too long. Personally, I believe that a man cannot keep at his best for ten hours in certain industries—not in all."

"Long hours do not mean big production, Maitland. Not long hours but intensive and co-ordinated work bring up production and lower production costs."

"What about idle machines and overhead?" inquired Maitland.

"A very important consideration," said the minister. "The only sound rule governing factory industry especially is this: the longest possible machine time, the shortest possible man time. But here again it is a question of organisation, adjustment and co-ordination of work and workers. We all want education here."

"If I remember right," said McNish, and he could not keep the bitterness out of his voice, "I have heard you say something in the pulpit at times in regard to the value of men's immortal souls. What care can men take of their bodies and minds, let alone their souls, if you work them ten hours a day?"

"There is a previous question, McNish," said the minister. "Why give more leisure time to men who spend their leisure hours now in pool rooms and that sort of nonsense?"

"And whose fault is that," replied McNish sharply. "Who is responsible that they have not learned to use their leisure more wisely? And further, what about your young bloods and their leisure hours?"

"Ay, A doot he has ye there, minister," said Mrs. McNish with a quiet chuckle.

"He has," said the minister. "The point is well taken and I acknowledge it freely. My position is that the men need more leisure, but, more than that, they need instruction as to how to use their leisure time wisely. But let us get on to the third point. 'A Joint Committee of References demanded to which all complaints shall be referred.' Now, that's fine. That's the Whitley plan. It is quite sound and has proved thoroughly useful in practice."

"I quite agree," said Maitland frankly. "But certain conditions must be observed."

"Of course, of course," replied the minister. "Conditions must be observed everywhere. Now, the fourth point: 'The foreman must be a member of the union.' Thoroughly unsound. They can't ride two horses at once.

"I am not so sure of that," said Maitland. "For my part, I should like to have retained my membership in the union. The more that both parties meet for conference, the better. And the more connecting links between them, the better. I should like to see a union where employers and employees should have equal rights of membership."

McNish grunted contemptuously.

"It would be an interesting experiment," said the minister. "An interesting experiment, McNish, and you are not to grunt like that. The human element, of course, is the crux here. If we had the right sort of foreman he might be trusted to be a member of the union, but a man cannot direct and be directed at the same time. But that union of yours, Maitland, with both parties represented in it, is a big idea. It is worth considering. What do you think about it, McNish?"

"What do I think of it? It is sheer idealistic nonsense."

"It is a noble idea, laddie, and no to be sneered at, but A doot it needs a better world for it than we hae at the present."

"I am afraid that is true," said the minister. "But meantime a foreman is a man who gives orders and directs work, and, generally speaking, he must remain with a directorate in any business. There may be exceptions. You must acknowledge that, McNish."

"I'll acknowledge nothing of the sort," replied McNish, and entered into a long argument which convinced no one.

"Now we come to the next, number five: 'a voice in the management,' it means. Come now, McNish, this is rather much. Do you want Mr. Maitland's job here, or is there anyone in your shop who would be anything but an embarrassment trying running the Maitland Mills, and you know quite well that the men want nothing of the sort. It may be as Mrs. McNish said, 'a good negotiating point,' but it has no place in practical politics here in Blackwater. How would you like, for instance, to take orders from Simmons?"

The old lady chuckled delightedly. "He has you there, laddie, he has you there!"

But this McNish would not acknowledge, and proceeded to argue at great length on purely theoretical grounds for joint control of industries, till his mother quite lost patience with him.

"Hoots, laddie, haud yer hoofs on mither earth. Would ye want yon radical bodies to take chairge o' ony business in which ye had a baubee? Ye're talkin' havers."

"Now, let us look at the last," said Mr. Matheson. "It is practically a demand for the closed shop. Now, McNish, I ask you, man to man, what is the use of putting that in there? It is not even a negotiating point."

At that McNish fired up. "It is no negotiating point," he declared. "I stand for that. It is vital to the very existence of unionised labour. Everyone knows that. Unionism cannot maintain itself in existence without the closed shop. It is the ideal toward which all unionised labour works."

"Now, McNish, tell me honestly," said the minister, "do you expect or hope for an absolutely closed shop in the factories here in Blackwater, or in the Building Industries? Have you the faintest shadow of a hope?"

"We may not get it," said McNish, "but that is no reason why we should not fight for it. Men have died fighting for the impossible because they knew it was right, and, by dying for it, they have brought it to pass."

"Far be it from me, McNish, to deny that. But I am asking you now, again as man to man, do you know of any industry, even in the Old Land, where the closed shop absolutely prevails, and do you think that conditions in Blackwater give you the faintest hope of a closed shop here?"

"Yes," shouted McNish, springing to his feet, "there is hope. There is hope even in Blackwater."

"Tut, tut, laddie," said his mother. "Dinna deeve us. What has come ower ye that ye canna talk like a reasonable man? Noo, Mr. Matheson, ye've had enough of the labour matters. A'll mak ye a cup of tea."

"Thank you, Mrs. McNish," said the minister gravely, "but I cannot linger. I have still work to do to-night." He rose from his chair and found his coat. His manner was gravely sad and gave evidence of his disappointment with the evening's conversation.

"Dinna fash yersel, minister," said the old lady, helping him on with his coat. "The 'trouble' will blow ower, a doot. It'll a' come oot richt."

"Mrs. McNish, what I have seen and heard in this house to-night," said the minister solemnly, "gives me little hope that it will all come right, but rather gives me grave concern." Then, looking straight into the eyes of her son, he added: "I came here expecting to find help and guidance in discovering a reasonable way out of a very grave and serious difficulty. I confess I have been disappointed."

"Mr. Matheson," said McNish, "I am always glad to discuss any matter with you in a reasonable and kindly way."

"I am afraid my presence has not helped very much, Mrs. McNish," said Maitland. "I am sorry I came tonight. I did come earnestly desiring and hoping that we might find a way out. It seems I have made a mistake."

"You came at my request, Maitland," said the minister. "If a mistake has been made, it is mine. Good-night, Mrs. McNish. Good-night, Malcolm. I don't pretend to know or understand what is in your heart, but I am going to say to you as your minister that where there is evil passion there can be no clear thinking. And further, let me say that upon you will devolve a heavy responsibility for the guidance you give these men. Good-night again. Remember that One whom we both acknowledge as the source of all true light said: 'If the light that is in thee be darkness, how great is that darkness.'" He shook hands first with the mother, then with the son, who turned away from him with a curt "Good-night" and nodded to Maitland.

For a moment or two neither of the men spoke. They were both grievously disappointed in the interview.

"I never saw him like that," said the Reverend Murdo at length. "What can be the matter with him? With him passion is darkening counsel."

"Well," said Maitland, "I have found out one thing that I wanted."

"And what is that?"

"These men clearly do not want what they are asking for. They want chiefly war—at least, McNish does."

"I am deeply disappointed in McNish," replied the minister, "and I confess I am anxious. McNish, above all others, is the brains of this movement, and in that mood there is little hope of reason from him. I fear it will be a sore fight, with a doubtful issue."

"Oh, I don't despair," said Maitland cheerily. "I have an idea he has a quarrel with me. He wants to get me. But we can beat him."

The Reverend Murdo waited for a further explanation, but was too much of a gentleman to press the point and kept silent till they reached his door.

"You will not desert us, Mr. Matheson," said Maitland earnestly.

"Desert you? It is my job. These people are my people. We cannot desert them."

"Right you are," said Maitland. "Cheerio. We'll carry on. He shook hands warmly with the minister and went off, whistling cheerily.

"That is a man to follow," said the minister to himself. "He goes whistling into a fight."

CHAPTER XIII
THE STRIKE

The negotiations between the men and their employers, in which the chief exponents of the principles of justice and fair play were Mr. McGinnis on the one hand and Brother Simmons on the other, broke down at the second meeting, which ended in a vigorous personal encounter between these gentlemen, without, however, serious injury to either.

The following day a general strike was declared. All work ceased in the factories affected and building operations which had begun in a moderate way were arrested. Grant Maitland was heartily disgusted with the course of events and more especially with the humiliating and disgraceful manner in which the negotiations had been conducted.

"You were quite right, Jack," he said to his son the morning after which the strike had been declared. "That man McGinnis is quite impossible."

"It really made little difference, Dad. The negotiations were hopeless from the beginning. There was no chance of peace."

"Why not?"

"Because McNish wants war." He proceeded to give an account of the evening spent at the McNish home. "When McNish wants peace, we can easily end the strike," concluded Jack.

"There is something in what you say, doubtless," replied his father, "but meantime there is a lot to be done."

"What do you mean exactly, Father?"

"We have a lot of stock made up on hand. The market is dead at present prices. There is no hope of sales. The market will fall lower still. I propose that we take our loss and unload at the best rate we can get."

"That is your job, Dad. I know little about that, but I believe you are right. I have been doing a lot of reading in trade journals and that sort of thing, and I believe that a big slump is surely coming. But there is a lot to do in my department at the Mills, also. I am not satisfied with the inside arrangement of our planing mill. There is a lot of time wasted and there is an almost complete lack of co-ordination. Here is a plan I want to show you. The idea is to improve the routing of our work."

Maitland glanced at the plan perfunctorily, more to please his son than anything else. But, after a second glance, he became deeply interested and began to ask questions. After half an hour's study he said:

"Jack, this is really a vast improvement. Strange, I never thought of a great many of these things."

"I have been reading up a bit, and when I was on my trip two weeks ago I looked in upon two or three of the plants of our competitors. I believe this will be more up-to-date and will save time and labour."

"I am sure it will, boy. And we will put this in hand at once. But what about men?"

"Oh, we can pick up labourers, and that is all we want at the present time."

"All right, go at it. I will give you a hand myself."

"Then there is something else, Dad. We ought to have a good athletic field for our men."

His father gasped at him.

"An athletic field for those ungrateful rascals?"

"Father, they are not rascals," said his son. "They are just the same to-day as they ever were. A decent lot of chaps who don't think the same as we do on a number of points. But they are coming back again some time and we may as well be ready for them. Look at this."

And before Grant Maitland could recover his speech he found himself looking at a beautifully-drawn plan of athletic grounds set out with walks, shade trees and shrubbery, and with a plain but commodious club-house appearing in the background.

"And where do you get this land, and what does it cost you?"

"The land," replied Jack, "is your land about the old mill. It will cost us nothing, I hope. The old mill site contains two and one-half acres. It can be put in shape with little work. The mill itself is an eyesore; ought to have been removed long ago. Dad, you ought to have seen the plant at Violetta, that is in Ohio, you know. It is a joy to behold. But never mind about that. The lumber in the old mill can be used up in the club-house. The timbers are wonderful; nothing like them to-day anywhere. The outside finishing will be done with slabs from our own yard. They will make a very pretty job."

"And where do you get the men for this work?" inquired his father.

"Why, our men. It is for themselves and they are our men."

"Voluntary work, I suppose?" inquired Maitland.

"Voluntary work?" said Jack. "We couldn't have men work for us for nothing."

"And you mean to pay them for the construction of their own athletic grounds and club-house?"

"But why not?" inquired Jack in amazement.

His father threw back his head and began to laugh.

"This is really the most extraordinary thing I have ever heard of in all my life," he said, after he had done with his laugh. "Your men strike; you prepare for them a beautiful club-house and athletic grounds as a reward for their loyalty. You pay them wages so that they may be able to sustain the strike indefinitely." Again he threw back his head and continued laughing as Jack had never in his life heard him laugh.

"Why not, Dad?" said Jack, gazing at his father in half-shamed perplexity. "The idea of athletic grounds and club-house is according to the best modern thought. These are our own men. You are not like McGinnis. You are not enraged at them. You don't hate them. They are going to work for us again in some days or weeks. They are idle and therefore available for work. You can get better work from them than from other men. And you wouldn't take their work from them for nothing."

Again his father began to laugh. "Your argument, Jack," he said when he was able to control his speech, "is absolutely unanswerable. There is no answer possible on any count; but did ever man hear of such a scheme? Did you?"

"I confess not. But, Dad, you are a good sport. We are out to win this fight, but we don't want to injure anybody. We are going to beat them, but we don't want to abuse them unnecessarily. Besides, I think it is good business. And then, you see, I really like these chaps."

"Simmons, for instance?" said his father with an ironical smile.

"Well, Simmons, just as much as you can like an ass."

"And McNish?" inquired Maitland.

"McNish," echoed Jack, a cloud falling upon his face. "I confess I don't understand McNish. At least," he added, "I am sorry for McNish. But what do you say to my scheme, Dad?"

"Well, boy," said his father, beginning to laugh again, "give me a night to think it over."

Then Jack departed, not quite sure of himself or of the plan which appeared to give his father such intense amusement. "At any rate," he said to himself as he walked out of the office, "if it is a joke it is a good one. And it has given the governor a better laugh than he has had for five years."

The Mayor of Blackwater was peculiarly sensitive to public opinion and acutely susceptible of public approval. In addition, he was possessed of a somewhat exalted idea of his powers as the administrator in public affairs, and more particularly as a mediator in times of strife. He had been singularly happy in his mediation between the conflicting elements in his Council, and more than once he had been successful in the composing of disputes in arbitration cases submitted to his judgment. Moreover, he had an eye to a second term in the mayor's chair, which gubernatorial and majestical office gave full scope to the ruling ambition of his life, which was, in his own words, "to guard the interests and promote the well-being of my people."

The industrial strike appeared to furnish him with an opportunity to gratify this ambition. He resolved to put an end to this unnecessary and wasteful struggle, and to that end he summoned to a public meeting his fellow citizens of all classes, at which he invited each party in the industrial strife to make a statement of their case, in the hope that a fair and reasonable settlement might be effected.

The employers were more than dubious of the issue, having but a small idea of the mayor's power of control and less of his common-sense. Brother Simmons, however, foreseeing a magnificent field for the display of his forensic ability, a thing greatly desired by labour leaders of his kidney, joyfully welcomed the proposal. McNish gave hesitating assent, but, relying upon his experience in the management of public assemblies and confident of his ability to shape events to his own advantage, he finally agreed to accept the invitation.

The public meeting packed the City Hall, with representatives of both parties in the controversy in about equal numbers and with a great body of citizens more or less keenly interested in the issue of the meeting and expectant of a certain amount of "fun." The Mayor's opening speech was thoroughly characteristic. He was impressed with the responsibility that was his for the well-being of his people. Like all right-thinking citizens of this fair town of Blackwater, he deeply regretted this industrial strife. It interfered with business. It meant loss of money to the strikers. It was an occasion of much inconvenience to the citizens and it engendered bitterness of feeling that might take months, even years, to remove. He stood there as the friend of the working man. He was a working man himself and was proud of it.

He believed that on the whole they were good fellows. He was a friend also of the employers of labour. What could we do without them? How could our great industries prosper without their money and their brains? The one thing necessary for success was co-operation. That was the great word in modern democracy. In glowing periods he illustrated this point from their experiences in the war. All they wanted to do was to sit down together, and, man to man, talk their difficulties over. He would be glad to assist them, and he had no doubt as to the result. He warned the working man that hard times were coming. The spectre of unemployment was already parading their streets. Unemployment meant disorder, rioting. This, he assured them, would not be permitted. At all costs order would be maintained. He had no wish to threaten, but he promised them that the peace would be preserved at all costs. He suggested that the strikers should get back at once to work and the negotiations should proceed in the meantime.

At this point Brother Simmons rose.

"The mayor (h)urges the workers to get back to work," he said. "Does 'e mean at (h)increased pay, or not? 'E says as 'ow this strike interferes with business. 'E doesn't tell us what business. But I can tell 'im it (h)interferes with the business of robbery of the workin' man. 'E deplores the loss of money to the strikers. Let me tell 'im that the workin' men are prepared to suffer that loss. True, they 'ave no big bank accounts to carry 'em on, but there are things that they love more than money—liberty and justice and the rights of the people. What are we strikin' for? Nothin' but what is our own. The workin' man makes (h)everything that is made. What percentage of the returns does 'e get in wages? They won't tell us that. Last year these factories were busy in the makin' o' munitions. Mr. McGinnis 'ere was makin' shells. I'd like to (h)ask, Mr. Mayor, what profit Mr. McGinnis made out of these shells."

Mr. McGinnis sprang to his feet, "I want to tell you," he said in a voice choking with rage, "that it is none of your high-explosive business."

"'E says as it is none o' my business," cried Brother Simmons, joyously taking Mr. McGinnis on. "Let me (h)ask 'im who paid for these shells? I did, you did, all of us did. Not my business? Then 'ose business is it? (H)If 'e was paid a fair price for 'is shells, (h)all right, I say nothin' against it. If 'e was paid more than a fair price, then 'e is a robber, worse, 'e is a blood robber, because the price was paid in blood."

At once a dozen men were on their feet. Cries of "Order! Order!" and "Put him out!" arose on every hand. The mayor rose from his chair and, in an impressive voice, said: "We must have order. Sit down, Mr. Simmons." Simmons sat down promptly. Union men are thoroughly disciplined in points of order. "We must have order," continued the mayor. "I will not permit any citizen to be insulted. We all did our bit in this town of Blackwater. Some of us went to fight, and some that could not go to fight 'kept the home fires burning'." A shout of derisive laughter from the working men greeted this phrase. The mayor was deeply hurt. "I want to say that those who could not go to the war did their bit at home. Let the meeting proceed, but let us observe the courtesies that are proper in debate."

Again Simmons took the floor. "As I was sayin', Mr. Mayor—"

Cries of "Order! Order! Sit down!"

"—Mr. Mayor, I believe I 'ave the floor?"

"Yes, you have. Go on. But you must not insult."

"(H)Insult? Did I (h)insult anybody? I don't know what Mr. McGinnis made from 'is shells. I only said that if—you (h)understand—if 'e made more than e ought to, 'e is a robber. And since the price of our freedom was paid in blood, if 'e made more than was fair, 'e's a blood robber."

Again the cries arose. "Throw him out!" Once more the mayor rose. "You must not make insinuations, sir," he cried angrily. "You must not make insinuations against respectable citizens."

"(H)Insinooations," cried Simmons. "No, sir, I never make no (h)insinooations. If I knew that (h)any man 'ere 'ad made (h)unfair profits I wouldn't make no (h)insinooations. I would charge 'im right 'ere with blood robbery. And let me say," shouted Simmons, taking a step into the aisle, "that the time may come when the working men of this country will make these charges, and will (h)ask the people who kept the ''ome fires burning'—"

Yells of derisive laughter.

"—what profits came to them from these same 'ome fires. The people will (h)ask for an (h)explanation of these bank accounts, of these new factories, of these big stores, of these (h)autermobiles. The people that went to the war and were (h)unfortoonate enough to return came back to poverty, while many of these 'ere 'ome fire burners came (h)out with fortunes." At this point brother Simmons cast a fierce and baleful eye upon a group of the employers who sat silent and wrathful before him. "And now, what I say," continued Brother Simmons—

At this point a quiet voice was heard.

"Mr. Mayor, I rise to a point of order."

Immediately Simmons took his seat.

"Mr. Farrington," said the mayor, recognising one of the largest building contractors in the town.

"Mr. Mayor, I should like to ask what are we discussing this afternoon? Are we discussing the war records of the citizens of Blackwater? If so, that is not what I came for. It may be interesting to find out what each man did in the war. I find that those who did most say least. I don't know what Mr. Simmons did in the war. I suppose he was there."

With one spring Simmons was on his feet and in the aisle. He ripped off coat and vest, pulled his shirt over his head and revealed a back covered with the network of ghastly scars. "The gentleman (h)asks," he panted, "what I done in the war. I don't know. I cannot say what I done in the war, but that is what the war done to me." The effect was positively overwhelming.

A deadly silence gripped the audience for a single moment. Then upon every hand rose fierce yells, oaths and strange cries. Above the uproar came Farrington's booming voice. Leaving his seat, which was near the back of the hall, he came forward, crying out:

"Mr. Mayor! Mr. Mayor! I demand attention!" As he reached Simmons's side, he paused and, facing about, he looked upon the array of faces pale and tense with passion. "I want to apologise to this gentleman," he said in a voice breaking with emotion. "I should not have said what I did. The man who bears these scars is a man I am proud to know." He turned swiftly toward Simmons with outstretched hand. "I am proud to know you, sir. I could not go to the war. I was past age. I sent my two boys. They are over there still." As the two men shook hands, for once in his life Simmons was speechless. His face was suffused with uncontrollable feeling. On every side were seen men, strong men, with tears streaming down their faces. A nobler spirit seemed to fall upon them all. In the silence that followed, Mr. Maitland rose.

"Mr. Mayor," he said quietly, "we have all suffered together in this war. I, for one, want to do the fair thing by our men. Let us meet them and talk things over before any fair-minded committee. Surely we who have suffered together in war can work together in peace." It was a noble appeal, and met with a noble response. On all sides and from all parties a storm of cheers broke forth.

Then the Reverend Murdo Matheson rose to his feet. "Mr. Mayor," he said, "I confess I was not hopeful of the result of this meeting. But I am sure we all recognise the presence and influence of a mightier Spirit than ours. From the outset I have been convinced that the problems in the industrial situation here are not beyond solution, and should yield to fair and reasonable consideration. I venture to move that a committee of five be appointed, two to be chosen by each of the parties in this dispute, who would in turn choose a chairman; that this committee meet with representatives of both parties; and that their decision in all cases be final."

Mr. Farrington rose and heartily seconded the motion.

At this point Jack, who was sitting near the platform and whose eyes were wandering over the audience, was startled by the look on the face of McNish. It was a look in which mingled fear, anxiety, wrath. He seemed to be on the point of starting to his feet when McGinnis broke in:

"Do I understand that the decision of this committee is to be final on every point?"

"Certainly," said the Reverend Murdo. "There is no other way by which we can arrive at a decision."

"Do you mean," cried McGinnis, "that if this committee says I must hire only union men in my foundry that I must do so?"

"I would reply," said the Reverend Murdo, "that we must trust this committee to act in a fair and reasonable way."

But Mr. McGinnis was not satisfied with this answer.

"I want to know," he cried in growing anger, "I want to know exactly where we are and I want a definite answer. Will this committee have the right to force me to employ only union men?"

"Mr. Mayor," replied the Reverend Murdo, "Mr. McGinnis is right in asking for definiteness. My answer is that we must trust this committee to do what is wise and reasonable, and we must accept their decision as final in every case."

Thereupon McGinnis rose and expressed an earnest desire for a tragic and unhappy and age-long fate if he would consent to any such proposition. With terrible swiftness the spirit of the meeting was changed. The moment of lofty emotion and noble impulse passed. The opportunity for reason and fair play to determine the issue was lost, and the old evil spirit of suspicion and hate fell upon the audience like a pall.

At this point McNish, from whose face all anxiety had disappeared, rose and said:

"For my part, and speaking for the working men of this town, I am ready to accept the proposal that has been made. We have no fear for the justice of our demands like some men here present. We know we have the right on our side and we are willing to accept the judgment of such a committee as has been proposed." The words were fair enough, but the tone of sneering contempt was so irritating that immediately the position assumed by McGinnis received support from his fellow employers on every hand. Once more uproar ensued. The mayor, in a state of angry excitement, sought in vain to restore order.

After some minutes of heated altercation with Mr. McGinnis, whom he threatened with expulsion from the meeting, the mayor finally left the chair and the meeting broke up in disorder which threatened to degenerate into a series of personal encounters.

Again McNish took command. Leaping upon a chair, with a loud voice which caught at once the ears of his following, he announced that a meeting was to be held immediately in the union rooms, and he added: "When these men here want us again, they know where to find us." He was answered with a roar of approval, and with an ugly smile on his face he led his people in triumph from the hall, leaving behind the mayor, still engaged in a heated argument with McGinnis and certain employers who sympathised with the Irishman's opinions. Thus the strike passed into another and more dangerous phase.

CHAPTER XIV
GATHERING CLOUDS

On the Rectory lawn a hard-fought game had just finished, bringing to a conclusion a lengthened series of contests which had extended over a whole week, in which series Patricia, with her devoted cavalier, Victor Forsythe, had been forced to accept defeat at the hands of her sister and her partner, Hugh Maynard.

"Partner, you were wonderful in that last set!" said Patricia, as they moved off together to offer their congratulations to their conquerors.

"Patsy," said her partner, in a low voice, "as ever, you are superb in defeat as in victory. Superb, unapproachable, wonderful."

"Anything else, Vic?" inquired Patsy, grinning at the youth.

"Oh, a whole lot more, Pat, if you only give me a chance to tell you."

"No time just now," cried Patricia as she reached the others. "Well, you two deserved to win. You played ripping tennis," she continued, offering Hugh her hand.

"So did you, Pat. You were at the very top of your form."

"Well, some other day," said Vic. "I think we are improving a bit, partner. A little more close harmony will do the trick."

"Come away, children," said Mrs. Templeton, calling to them from the shade at the side of the courts. "You must be very tired and done out. Why, how hot you look, Patricia."

"Stunning, I should say!" murmured Vic, looking at her with adoring eyes.

And a truly wonderful picture the girl made, in her dainty muslin frock, her bold red hair tossed in a splendid aureole about her face. Care-free, heart-free, as she flashed from her hearty blue eyes her saucy and bewitching glances at her partner's face, her mother sighed, thinking that her baby girl was swiftly slipping away from her and forever into that wider world of womanhood where others would claim her.

In lovely contrast stood her sister, dressed in flannel skirt and sweater of old gold silk, fair, tall, beautiful, a delicate grace in every line of her body and a proud, yet gentle strength in every feature of her face. There dwelt in her deep blue eyes a look of hidden, mysterious power which had wrought in her mother a certain fear of her eldest daughter. The mother never quite knew what to expect from Adrien. Yet, for all, she carried an assured confidence that whatever she might do, her daughter never would shame the high traditions of her race.

The long shadows from the tall elms lay across the velvet sward of the Rectory lawn. The heat of the early June day had given place to the cool air of the evening. The exquisitely delicate colouring from the setting sun flooded the sky overhead and deepened into blues and purples behind the elms and the church spire. A deep peace had fallen upon the world except that from the topmost bough of the tallest elm tree a robin sang, pouring his very heart out in a song of joyous optimism.

The little group, disposed upon the lawn according to their various desires, stood and sat looking up at the brave little songster.

"How happy he is," said Mrs. Templeton, a wistful cadence of sadness in her voice.

"I wonder if he is, Mamma. Perhaps he is only pretending," said Adrien.

"Cheerio, old chap!" cried Vic, waving his hand at the gallant little songster. "You are a regular grouch killer."

"He has no troubles," said Mrs. Templeton, with a sigh.

"I wonder, Mamma. Or is he just bluffing us all?"

"He has no strike, at any rate, to worry him," said Patricia, "and, by the way, what is the news to-day? Does anybody know? Is there any change?"

"Oh," cried Vic, "there has been a most exciting morning at the E. D. C.—the Employers' Defence Committee," he explained, in answer to Mrs. Templeton's mystified look.

"Do go on!" cried Patricia impatiently. "Was there a fight? They are always having one."

"Of course there was the usual morning scrap, but with a variation to-day of a deputation from the brethren of the Ministerial Association. But, of course, Mrs. Templeton, the Doctor must have told you already."

"I hardly ever see him these days. He is dreadfully occupied. There is so much trouble, sickness and that sort of thing. Oh, it is all terribly sad. The Doctor is almost worn out."

"He made a wonderful speech to the magnates, my governor says."

"Oh, go on, Vic!" cried Patricia. "Why do you stop? You are so deliberate."

"I was thinking of that speech," replied Victor more quietly than was his wont. "It came at a most dramatic moment. The governor was quite worked up over it and gave me a full account. They had just got all their reports in—'all safe along the Potomac'—no break in the front line—Building Industries slightly shaky due to working men's groups taking on small contracts, which excited great wrath and which McGinnis declared must be stopped."

"How can they stop them? This is a free country," said Adrien.

"Aha!" cried Victor. "Little you know of the resources of the E. D. C. It is proposed that the supply dealers should refuse supplies to all builders until the strike is settled. No more lumber, lime, cement, etc., etc."

"Boycott, eh? I call that pretty rotten," said Adrien.

"The majority were pretty much for it, however, except Maitland and my governor, they protesting that this boycott was hardly playing the game. Your friend Captain Jack came in for his licks," continued Vic, turning to Patricia. "It appears he has been employing strikers in some work or other, which some of the brethren considered to be not according to Hoyle."

"Nonsense!" cried Patricia indignantly. "Jack took me yesterday to see the work. He showed me all the plans and we went over the grounds. It is a most splendid thing, Mamma! He is laying out athletic grounds for his men, with a club house and all that sort of thing. They are going to be perfectly splendid! Do you mean to say they were blaming him for this? Who was?" And Patricia stood ready for battle.

"Kamerad!" cried Vic, holding up his hands. "Not me! However, Jack was exonerated, for it appears he sent them a letter two weeks ago, telling them what he proposed to do, to which letter they had raised no objection."

"Well, what then?" inquired Patricia.

"Oh, the usual thing. They all resolved to stand pat—no surrender—or, rather, let the whole line advance—you know the stuff—when into this warlike atmosphere walked the deputation from the Ministerial Association. It gave the E. D. C. a slight shock, so my Dad says. The Doctor fired the first gun. My governor says that it was like a breath from another world. His face was enough. Everybody felt mean for just being what they were. I know exactly what that is, for I know the way he makes me feel when I look at him in church. You know what I mean, Pat."

"I know," said Patricia softly, letting her hand fall upon her mother's shoulder.

"Well," continued Vic, "the Doctor just talked to them as if they were his children. They hadn't been very good and he was sorry for them. He would like to help them to be better. The other side, too, had been doing wrong, and they were having a bad time. They were suffering, and as he went on to tell them in that wonderful voice of his about the women and children, every man in the room, so the governor said, was wondering how much he had in his pocket. And then he told them of how wicked it was for men whose sons had died together in France to be fighting each other here in Canada. Well, you know my governor. As he told me this tale, we just both of us bowed our heads and wept. It's the truth, so help me, just as you are doing now, Pat."

"I am not," cried Patricia indignantly. "And I don't care if I am. He is a dear and those men are just—"

"Hush, dear," said Mrs. Templeton gently. "And did they agree to anything?"

"Alas, not they, for at that moment some old Johnny began asking questions and then that old fire-eater, McGinnis, horned in again. No Arbitration Committee for him—no one could come into his foundry and tell him how to run his business—same old stuff, you know. Well, then, the Methodist Johnny took a hand. What's his name? Haynes, isn't it?"

"Yes, Haynes," said Hugh Maynard.

"Well, Brother Haynes took up the tale. He is an eloquent chap, all right. He took the line 'As you are strong, be pitiful,' but the psychological moment had gone and the line still held strong. Campbell of the woollen mills invited him up to view his $25,000.00 stock 'all dressed up and nowhere to go.' 'Tell me how I can pay increased wages with this stock on my hands.' And echo answered 'How?' Haynes could not. Then my old chief took a hand—the Reverend Murdo Matheson. He is a good old scout, a Padre, you know—regular fire-eater—a rasping voice and grey matter oozing from his pores. My governor says he abandoned the frontal attack and took them on the flank. Opened up with a dose of economics that made them sit up. And when he got through on this line, he made every man feel that it was entirely due to the courtesy and forbearance of the union that he was allowed to carry on business at all. He spiked Brother McGinnis's guns by informing him that if he was harbouring the idea that he owned a foundry all on his own, he was labouring under a hallucination. All he owned was a heap of brick and mortar and some iron and steel junk arranged in some peculiar way. In fact, there was no foundry there till the workmen came in and started the wheels going round. Old McGinnis sat gasping like a chicken with the pip. Then the Padre turned on the 'Liberty of the subject' stop as follows: 'Mr. McGinnis insists upon liberty to run his foundry as he likes; insists upon perfect freedom of action. There is no such thing as perfect freedom of action in modern civilisation. For instance, Mr. McGinnis rushing to catch a train, hurls his Hudson Six gaily down Main Street thirty miles an hour, on the left-hand side of the street. A speed cop sidles up, whispers a sweet something in his ear, hails him ignominiously into court and invites him to contribute to the support of the democracy fifty little iron men as an evidence of his devotion to the sacred principle of personal liberty. In short, there is no such thing as personal liberty in this burg, unless it is too late for the cop to see.' The governor says McGinnis's face afforded a perfect study in emotions. I should have liked to have seen it. The Padre never took his foot off the accelerator. He took them all for an excursion along the 'Responsibility' line: personal responsibility, mutual responsibility, community responsibility and every responsibility known to the modern mind. And then when he had them eating out of his hand, he offered them two alternatives: an Arbitration Committee as formerly proposed, or a Conciliation Board under the Lemieux Act. My governor says it was a great speech. He had 'em all jumping through the hoops."

"What DO you mean, Vic?" lamented Mrs. Templeton. "I have only the very vaguest idea of what you have been saying all this time."

"So sorry, Mrs. Templeton. What I mean is the Padre delivered a most effective speech."

"And did they settle anything?" inquired Patricia.

"I regret to say, Patricia, that your friend Rupert —"

"My friend, indeed!" cried Patricia.

"Who comforts you with bonbons," continued Vic, ignoring her words, "and stays you with joy rides, interposed at this second psychological crisis. He very cleverly moves a vote of thanks, bows out the deputation, thanking them for their touching addresses, and promising consideration. Thereupon, as the door closed, he proceeded to sound the alarm once more, collected the scattered forces, flung the gage of battle in the teeth of the enemy, dared them to do their worst, and there you are."

"And nothing done?" cried Adrien. "What a shame."

"What I cannot understand is," said Hugh, "why the unions do not invoke the Lemieux Act?"

"Aha!" said Vic. "Why? The same question rose to my lips."

"The Lemieux Act?" inquired Mrs. Templeton.

"Yes. You know, Mrs. Templeton, either party in dispute can ask for a Board of Conciliation, not Arbitration, you understand. This Board has power to investigate—bring out all the facts—and failing to effect conciliation, makes public its decision in the case, leaving both parties at the bar of public opinion."

"But I cannot understand why the unions do not ask for this Conciliation Board."

"I fear, Hugh," said Victor in an awed and solemn voice, "that there is an Ethiopian in the coal bin."

"What DOES he mean, Patricia?"

"He means that there is something very dark and mysterious, Mamma."

"So there is," said Hugh. "The unions will take an Arbitration Committee, which the employers decline to give, but they will not ask for a Conciliation Board."

"My governor says it's a bluff," said Vic. "The unions know quite well that McGinnis et hoc genus omne will have nothing to do with an Arbitration Committee. Hence they are all for an Arbitration Committee. On the other hand, neither the unions nor McGinnis are greatly in love with the prying methods of the Conciliation Board, and hence reject the aid of the Lemieux Act."

"But why should they all be dominated by a man like McGinnis?" demanded Adrien. "Why doesn't some employer demand a Conciliation Board? He can get it, you know."

"They naturally stand together," said Hugh.

"But they won't long. Maitland declares that he will take either board, and that if the committee cannot agree which to choose, he will withdraw and make terms on his own. He furthermore gave them warning that if any strike-breakers were employed, of which he had heard rumours, he would have nothing to do with the bunch."

"Strike-breakers?" said Adrien. "That would certainly mean serious trouble."

"Indeed, you are jolly well right," said Vic. "We will all be in it then. Civic guard! Special police! 'Shun! Fix bayonets! Prepare for cavalry! Eh?"

"Oh, how terrible it all is," said Mrs. Templeton.

"Nonsense, Vic," said Hugh. "Don't listen to him, Mrs. Templeton. We will have nothing of that sort."

"Well, it is all very sad," said Mrs. Templeton. "But here is Rupert. He will give us the latest."

But Rupert appeared unwilling to talk about the meeting of the morning. He was quite certain, however, that the strike was about to break. He had inside information that the resources of the unions were almost exhausted. The employers were tightening up all along the line, credits were being refused at the stores, the unions were torn with dissension, the end was at hand.

"It would be a great mercy if it would end soon," said Mrs. Templeton. "It is a sad pity that these poor people are so misguided."

"It is a cruel shame, Mrs. Templeton," said Rupert indignantly. "I have it from scores of them that they didn't want to strike at all. They were getting good wages—the wage scale has gone up steadily during the war to the present extravagant height."

"The cost of living has gone up much more rapidly, I believe," said Adrien. "The men are working ten hours a day, the conditions under which they labour are in some cases deplorable; that McGinnis foundry is a ghastly place, terribly unhealthy; the girls in many of the factories are paid wages so shamefully low that they can hardly maintain themselves in decency, and they are continually being told that they are about to be dismissed. The wrong's not all on one side, by any means. To my mind, men like McGinnis who are unwilling to negotiate are a menace to the country."

"You are quite right, Adrien," replied Hugh. "I consider him a most dangerous man. That sort of pig-headed, bull-headed employer of labour does more to promote strife than a dozen 'walking delegates.' I am not terribly strong for the unions, but the point of vantage is always with the employers. And they have a lot to learn. Oh, you may look at me, Adrien! I am no bolshevist, but I see a lot of these men in our office."

CHAPTER XV
THE STORM

Slowly the evening was deepening into night, but still the glow from the setting sun lingered in the western sky. The brave little songster had gone from the top of the elm tree, but from the shrubbery behind the church a whippoorwill was beginning to tune his pipe.

"Oh, listen to the darling!" cried Patricia. "I haven't heard one for a long, long time."

"There used to be a great many in the shrubbery here, and in the old days the woods nearby were full of them in the evenings," said Mrs. Templeton.

As they sat listening for the whippoorwill's voice, they became aware of other sounds floating up to their ears from the town. The hum of passing motors, the high, shrill laughter of children playing in the streets, the clang of the locomotive bell from the railroad station, all softened by distance. But as they listened there came another sound like nothing they had ever heard in that place before. A strange, confused rumbling, with cries jutting out through the dull, rolling noise. A little later came the faint clash of rhythmic, tumultuous cheering. Patricia's quick ears were the first to catch the sound.

"Hush!" she cried. "What is that noise?"

Again came the rumbling sound, punctuated with quick volleys of cheering. The men glanced at each other. They knew well that sound, a sound they had often heard during the stirring days of the war, in the streets of the great cities across the seas, and in other places, too, where men were wont to crowd. As they listened in tense silence, there came the throbbing of a drum.

"My dear," said Mrs. Templeton faintly to her eldest daughter, "I think I shall go in."

At once Hugh offered her his arm, while Adrien took the other, and together they led her slowly into the house.

Meanwhile the others tumbled into Rupert's car and motored down to the gate, and there waited the approach of what seemed to be a procession of some sort or other.

At the gate Dr. Templeton, returning from his pastor visitations, found them standing.

"Come here, Papa!" cried Patricia. "Let us wait here. There is something coming up the street."

"But what is it?" asked Dr. Templeton. "Does anybody know?"

"I guess it is a strikers' parade, sir. I heard that they were to organise a march-out to-night. It is rather a ridiculous thing."

Through the deepening twilight they could see at the head of the column and immediately before the band, a double platoon of young girls dressed in white, under the command of an officer distinguished from the others by her red sash, all marching with a beautiful precision to the tap of the drum. As the head of the column drew opposite, Patricia touched Vic's arm.

"Vic!" she cried. "Look! Look at that girl! It is Annette!"

"My aunt! So it is!" cried Vic. "Jove! What a picture she makes! What a swing!"

Behind that swinging company of girls came the band, marching to the tapping of the drum only. Then after a space came a figure, pathetic, arresting, moving—a woman, obviously a workman's wife, of middle age, grey, workworn, and carrying a babe of a few months in her arms, marched alone. Plainly dressed, her grey head bare, she walked proudly erect but with evident signs of weariness. The appearance of that lone, weary, grey-haired woman and her helpless babe struck hard upon the heart with its poignant appeal, choking men's throats and bringing hot tears to women's eyes. Following that lonely figure came one who was apparently the officer in command of the column. As he came opposite the gate, his eye fell upon the group there. Swiftly he turned about, and, like a trumpet, his voice rang out in command:

"Ba-t-t-a-a-lion, halt!! R-r-r-i-g-h-t turn!"

Immediately the whole column came to a halt and faced toward the side of the street where stood the group within the shadow of the gate.

"I am going to get Annette," said Patricia to her father, and she darted off, returning almost immediately with the leader of the girls' squad.

"What does this mean, Annette? What are you doing? It is a great lark!" cried Patricia.

"Well, it is not exactly a lark," answered Annette, with a slight laugh. "You see, we girls want to help out the boys. We are strikers, too, you know. They asked us to take part in the parade, and here we are. But it's got away past being a lark," she continued, her voice and face growing stern. "There is a lot of suffering among the workers. I know all my money has gone," she added, after a moment, with a gay laugh.

Meantime, the officer commanding the column had spoken a few words to the leader of the band, and in response, to the surprise and dismay of the venerable Doctor, the band struck up that rollicking air associated with the time-honoured chorus, "For He's a Jolly Good Fellow." Then all stood silent, gazing at the Doctor, who, much embarrassed, could only gaze back in return.

"Papa, dear," said Adrien, who with Hugh Maynard had joined them at the gate, "you will have to speak to them."

"Speak to them, my dear? What in the world could I say? I have nothing to say to them."

"Oh, but you must, Papa! Just thank them."

"And tell them you are all for them, Daddy!" added Patricia impulsively.

Then the old Doctor, buttoning his coat tightly about him and drawing himself erect, said:

"Rupert, please run your car out to the road. Thank you." Mounting the car, he stood waiting quietly till the cheering had died down into silence, his beautiful, noble, saintly face lit with the faint glow that still came from the western sky but more with the inner light that shines from a soul filled with high faith in God and compassion for man.

"Gentlemen—" he began.

"Ladies, too, Papa," said Patricia in a clear undertone.

"Ah!" corrected the Doctor. "Ladies and Gentlemen:" while a laugh ran down the line. "One generally begins a speech with the words 'I am glad to see you here.' These words I cannot say this evening. I regret more deeply than you can understand the occasion of your being here at all. And in this regret I know that you all share. But I am glad that I can say from my heart that I feel honoured by and deeply moved by the compliment you have just paid me through your band. I could wish, indeed, that I was the 'jolly good fellow' you have said, but as I look at you I confess I am anything but 'jolly.' I have been in too many of your homes during the last three weeks to be jolly. The simple truth is, I am deeply saddened and, whatever be the rights or wrongs, and all fair-minded men will agree that there are rights and wrongs on both sides, my heart goes out in sympathy to all who are suffering and anxious and fearful for the future. I will try to do my best to bring about a better understanding."

"We know that, sir," shouted a voice. "Ye done yer best."

"But so far I and those labouring with me have failed. But surely, surely, wise and reasonable men can find before many days a solution for these problems. And now let me beg your leaders to be patient a little longer, to banish angry and suspicious feelings and to be willing to follow the light. I see that many of you are soldiers. To you my heart goes out with a love as true as if you were my own sons, for you were the comrades of my son. Let me appeal to you to preserve unbroken that fine spirit of comradeship that made the Canadian Army what it was. And let me assure you all that, however our weak and erring human hearts may fail and come short, the great heart of the Eternal Father is unchanging in Its love and pity for us all. Meantime, believe me, I shall never cease to labour and pray that very soon peace may come to us again." Then, lifting his hands over them while the men uncovered, he said a brief prayer, closing with the apostolic blessing.

Startled at the burst of cheering which followed shortly after the conclusion of the prayer, the babe broke into loud crying. Vainly the weary mother sought to quiet her child, she herself well-nigh exhausted with her march, being hardly able to stand erect. Swiftly Adrien sprang from the car and ran out to her.

"Let me carry the babe," she cried, taking the child in her arms. "Come into the car with me."

"No," said the woman fiercely. "I will go through with it." But even as she spoke she swayed upon her feet.

With gentle insistence, however, Adrien caught her arm and forced her toward the car.

"I will not leave them," said the woman stubbornly.

"Speak to her, Annette," said Adrien. "She cannot walk."

"Mrs. Egan," said Annette, coming to her, "it will be quite all right to go in the car. It will be all the better. Think of the fine parade it will make."

But, still protesting, the old woman hung back, crying, "Let me go! I will go through!"

"Sure thing!" cried Patricia. "We will take you along. Where's Rupert?"

But Rupert, furious and disgusted, hung back in the shadow.

"Here, Vic!" cried Patricia. "You take the wheel!"

"Delighted, I am sure!" cried Vic, climbing into the seat. "Get in here, Patsy. All set, Colonel," he added, saluting to the officer in command of the parade, and again the column broke into cheering as they moved off to the tap of the drum, Rupert's elegant Hudson Six taking a place immediately following the band.

"All my life I have longed for the spotlight," murmured Vic to his companion, a delighted grin on his face. "But one can have too much of a good thing. And, with Wellington, I am praying that night may come before I reach the haunts of my comrades in arms."

"Why, Vic, do you care?" cried Patricia. "Not I! And I think it was just splendid of Adrien!"

"Oh, topping! But did you see the gentle Rupert's face? Oh, it was simply priceless! Fancy this sacred car leading a strikers' parade." And Vic's body shook with delighted chuckles.

"Don't laugh, Vic!" said Patricia, laying her hand upon his arm. "The lady behind will see you."

"Steady it is," said Vic. "But I feel as if I were the elephant in the circus. I say, can we execute a flank movement, or must we go through to the bitter end?"

"Adrien," said Patricia, "do you think this night air is good for the baby?"

"We shall go on a bit yet," said Adrien. "Mrs. Egan is very tired and I am sure will want to go home presently."

But Mrs. Egan was beginning to recover her strength and, indeed, to enjoy the new distinction of riding in a car, and in this high company.

"No," she said, "I must go through." She had the look and tone of a martyr. "They chose me, you see, and I must go through!"

"Oh, very well," said Adrien cheerfully. "We shall just go along, Vic."

Through the main streets of the town the parade marched and countermarched till, in a sudden, they found themselves in front of the McGinnis foundry. Before the gate in the high board fence which enclosed the property, a small crowd had gathered, which greeted the marching column with uproarious cheers. From the company at the gate a man rushed forward and spoke eagerly to the officer in command.

"By Jove, there's Tony!" said Vic. "And that chap McDonough. What does this mean?"

After a brief conversation with Tony, who apparently was passionately pressing his opinion, the officer shook his head and marched steadily forward. Suddenly Tony, climbing upon the fence, threw up his hand

and, pointing toward the foundry, shouted forth the single word, "Scabs!" Instantly the column halted. Again Tony, in a yell, uttered the same word, "Scabs!" From hundreds of throats there was an answering roar, savage, bloodthirsty as from a pack of wild beasts. Tony waved his hand for silence.

"Scabs!" he cried again. "McGinnis strike-breakers! They came to-night. They are in there!" He swung his arm around and pointed to the foundry. "Shall we give them a welcome? What do you say, boys?" Again and more fiercely than before, more terribly cruel, came the answering roar.

"Here, this is no place for you!" cried Vic. "Let's get out." At his touch the machine leaped forward, clear of the crowd.

"Annette!" cried Adrien, her hand on Vic's shoulder. "Go and get her!"

Halting the car, Vic leaped from the wheel, ran to where the girls' squad was halted and caught Annette by the arm.

"Annette," he said, "get your girls away from here quick! Come with us!"

But Annette laughed scornfully at him.

"Go with you? Not I! But," she added in a breathless undertone, "for God's sake, get your ladies and the baby away. These people won't know who you are. Move quick!"

"Come with us, Annette!" implored Vic. "If you come, the rest will follow."

"Go! Go!" cried Annette, pushing him. Already the crowd were tearing the fence to pieces with their hands, and rocks were beginning to fly.

Failing to move the girl, Vic sprang to the wheel again.

"I will get you away from this, anyway," he said.

"But Annette!" cried Patricia. "We can't leave her!"

But Vic made no reply, and at his touch the machine leaped forward, and none too soon, for already men were crowding about the car on every side.

"We are well out of that!" said Vic coolly. "And now I will take you all home. Hello! They're messing up McGinnis's things a bit," he added, as the sound of crashing glass came to their ears.

Through the quiet streets the car flew like a hunted thing, and in a very few minutes they were at the Rectory door.

"No fuss, now, Patricia," said Adrien, "we must not alarm Mamma. All steady."

"Right you are! Steady it is!" said Patricia springing from the car. Quietly but swiftly they got the woman and the child indoors.

"Hugh! Rupert!" said Adrien, speaking in a quiet voice. "Vic needs you out there. That is a wild car of yours, Rupert," she added with a laugh. "It fairly flies." Gathering in her hands the men's hats and sticks, she hurried them out of the door.

"Cheerio!" cried Vic. "A lovely war is going on down at the McGinnis plant. Get in and let us plan a campaign. First, to Police Headquarters, I suppose." As they flew through the streets Vic gave them in a few words a picture of the scenes he had just witnessed.

They found the Chief of Police in his office. At their first word he was on the move.

"I was afraid of this thing when that fool parade started," he said. "Sergeant, send out the general alarm!"

"How many men have you, Chief?" inquired Hugh.

"About twenty-five, all told. But they are all over the town. How many men are down there?"

"There are five hundred, at least; possibly a thousand, raging like wild bulls of Bashan."

As he spoke, another car came tearing up and Jack Maitland sprang from the wheel.

"Are you in need of help, Chief?" he asked quietly.

"All the good men we can get," said the Chief curtly. "But first we must get the Mayor here. Sergeant, get him on the phone."

"You go for him, Vic," said Jack.

"Righto!" cried Vic. "But count me in on this."

In fifteen minutes Vic was back with the Mayor, helpless with nervous excitement.

"Get your men out, Chief!" he shouted, as he sprang from the car. "Get them out quick, arrest those devils and lock 'em up! We'll show them a thing or two! Hurry up! What are you waiting for?"

"Mr. Mayor," Jack's clear, firm, cool voice arrested the Mayor's attention. "May I suggest that you swear in some special constables? The Chief will need help and some of us here would be glad to assist."

"Yes! Yes! For God's sake, hurry up! Here's the clerk. How do you swear them in, clerk?"

"The Chief of Police has all the necessary authority."

"All right, Chief. Swear them! Swear them! For heaven's sake, swear them! Here, you, Maitland—and you, Maynard—and Stillwell—"

With cool, swift efficiency born of his experience in the war, the Chief went on with his arrangements. In his hands the process of swearing in a number of special constables was speedily accomplished. Meantime many cars and a considerable number of men had gathered about the Police Headquarters.

"What is that light?" cried the Mayor suddenly, pointing in the direction of the foundry. "It's a fire! My God, Chief, do you see that fire? Hurry up! Why don't you hurry up? They will burn the town down."

"All right, Mr. Mayor," said the Chief. "We shall be there in a few minutes now. Captain Maitland," said the Chief, "I will take the men I have with me. Will you swear in all you can get within the next fifteen or twenty minutes, and report to me at the foundry? Sergeant, you come along with me! I'm off!" So saying, the Chief commandeered as many cars as were necessary, packed them with the members of his police force available and with the specials he had secured, and hurried away.

After the Chief had retired, Jack stood up in his car. "Any of you chaps want to get into this?" he said, addressing the crowd. His voice was cheery and cool. At once a dozen voices responded. "Righto!" "Here you are!" "Put me down!" In less than fifteen minutes, he had secured between forty and fifty men.

"I want all these cars," he said. "Get in, men. Hold on!" he shouted at a driver who had thrown in his clutch. "Let no man move without orders! Any man disobeying orders will be arrested at once! Remember that no guns are to be used, no matter what provocation may be given. Even if you are fired on, don't fire in return! Does any man know where we can get anything in the shape of clubs?"

"Hundreds of axe handles in our store," said Rupert.

"Right you are! Drivers, fall in line. Keep close up. Now, Mr. Mayor, if you please."

Armed with axe handles from Stillwell & Son's store, they set off for the scene of action. Arrived at the foundry they found the maddest, wildest confusion raging along the street in front of the foundry, and in the foundry yard which was crowded with men. The board fence along the front of the grounds had been torn down and used as fagots to fire the foundry, which was blazing merrily in a dozen places. Everywhere about the blazing building parties of men like hounds on the trail were hunting down strike-breakers and, on finding them, were brutally battering them into insensibility.

Driving his car through the crowd, Maitland found his way to the Chief. In a few short, sharp sentences, the Chief explained his plan of operations. "Clear the street in front, and hold it so! Then come and assist me in clearing this yard."

"All right, sir!" replied Maitland, touching his hat as to a superior officer, and, wheeling his car, he led his men back to the thronging street.

Meantime, the Fire Department had arrived upon the scene with a couple of engines, a hose reel and other fire-fighting apparatus, the firemen greatly hampered in their operations.

Swinging his car back through the crowd, Maitland made his way to the street, and set to work to clear the space immediately in front of the foundry. Parking his cars at one end of the street, and forming his men up in a single line, he began slowly to press back the crowd. It was slow and difficult work, for the crowd, unable to recognise his ununiformed special constables, resented their attack.

He called Victor to his side. "Get a man with you," he said, "and bring up two cars here."

"Come along, Rupert," cried Victor, seizing Stillwell, and together they darted back to where the cars stood. Mounting one of the cars, Maitland shouted in a loud voice:

"The Chief of Police wants this street cleared. So get back, please! We don't wish to hurt anyone. Now, get back!" And lining up level with the cars, the special constables again began to press forward, using their axe handles as bayonets and seeking to prod their way through.

High up on a telegraph pole, his foot on one of the climbing spikes, was a man directing and encouraging the attack. As he drew near, Maitland discovered this man to be no other than Tony, wildly excited and vastly enjoying himself.

"Come down, Tony!" he said. "Hurry up!"

"Cheerio, Captain!" shouted Tony. "What about Festubert?"

"Come down, Tony," said Maitland, "and be quick about it!"

"Sorry, can't do it, Captain. I am a fixture here."

Like a cat, Maitland swarmed up the pole and coming to a level with Tony, struck him swiftly and unexpectedly a single blow. It caught Tony on the chin. He swung off from the post, hung a moment, then dropped quietly to the ground. As he fell, a woman's shriek rang out from the crowd and tearing her way through the line came Annette, who flung herself upon her brother.

"Here you," said Jack, seizing a couple of men from the crowd, "get this man in my car. Now, Annette," he continued, "don't make a fuss. Tony isn't hurt. We'll send him quietly home. Now then, men, let's have no nonsense," he shouted. "I want this street cleared, and quick!"

As he spoke, a huge man ran out from the crowd and, with an oath, flung himself at Maitland. But before he came within striking distance, an axe handle flashed and the man went down like a log.

"Axe handles!" shouted Maitland. "But steady, men!"

Over the heads of the advancing line, the axe handles swung, men dropping before them at every step. At once the crowd began a hasty retreat, till the pressure upon the back lines made it impossible for those in front to escape. From over the heads of the crowd rocks began to fly. A number of his specials were wounded and for a moment the advance hung fire. Down through the crowd came a fireman, dragging with him a hose preparatory to getting into action.

"Hello, there!" called Maitland. The fireman looked up at him. Jack sprang down to his side. "I want to clear this street," he said. "You can do it for me."

"Well, I can try," said the fireman with a grin, and turning his hose toward the crowd, gave the signal for the water, holding the nozzle at an angle slightly off the perpendicular. In a very few moments the crowd in the rear found themselves under a deluge of falling water, and immediately they took to their heels, followed as rapidly as possible by those in front. Then, levelling his nozzle, the fireman proceeded to wash back from either side of the street those who had sought refuge there, and before many minutes had elapsed, the street was cleared, and in command of Maitland's specials.

Leaving the street under guard, Maitland and his specials went to the help of the Chief, who was hampered more or less by His Worship, the Mayor, and very considerably by Mr. McGinnis, who had meantime arrived, mad with rage and demanding blood, and proceeded to clear up the foundry yard, and rescue the strike-breakers who had taken refuge within the burning building and in holes and corners about the premises. It was no light matter, but under the patient, good-natured but resolute direction of the Chief, they finally completed their job, rounding up the strike-breakers in a corner of the yard and driving off their assailants to a safe distance.

There remained still the most difficult part of their task. The strike-breakers must be got to the Police Headquarters, the nearest available place of safety. For, on the street beyond the water line, the crowd was still waiting in wrathful mood. The foundry was a wreck, but even this did not satisfy the fury of the strikers, which had been excited by the presence of the strike-breakers imported by McGinnis. For the more seriously injured, ambulances were called, and these were safely got off under police guard to the General Hospital.

The Chief entered into consultation with the Mayor:

"The only safe place within reach," he said, "is Police Headquarters. And the shortest and best route is up the hill to the left. But unfortunately, that is where the big crowd is gathered. There are not so many if we take the route to the right, but that is a longer way round."

"Put the men in your cars, Chief," said McGinnis, "and smash your way through. They can't stop you."

"Yes, and kill a dozen or so," said the Chief.

"Why not? Aren't they breaking the law?"

"Oh, well, Mr. McGinnis," said the Chief, "it is easy to kill men. The trouble is they are no use to anybody after they are dead. No, we must have no killing to-night. To-morrow we'd be sorry for it."

"Let us drive up and see them," suggested the Mayor. "Let me talk to the boys. The boys know me."

The Chief did not appear to be greatly in love with the suggestion of the Mayor.

"Well," he said, "it would do no harm to drive up and have a look at them. We'll see how they are fixed, anyway. I think, Mr. McGinnis, you had better remain on guard here. The Mayor and Captain Maitland will come with me."

Commandeering Rupert and his car, the Chief took his party at a moderate pace up the street, at the top of which the crowd stood waiting in compact masses. Into these masses Rupert recklessly drove his car.

"Steady there, Stillwell," warned the Chief. "You'll hurt someone."

"Hurt them?" said Rupert. "What do you want?"

"Certainly not to hurt anyone," replied the Chief quietly. "The function of my police force is the protection of citizens. Halt there!"

The Chief stepped out among the strikers and stood in the glare of the headlights.

"Well, boys," he said pleasantly, "don't you think it is time to get home? I think you have done enough damage to-night already. I am going to give you a chance to get away. We don't want to hurt anyone and we don't want to have any of you down for five years or so."

Then the Mayor spoke up. "Men, this is a most disgraceful thing. Most deplorable. Think of the stain upon the good name of our fair city."

Howls of derision drowned his further speech for a time.

"Now, boys," he continued, "can't we end this thing right here? Why can't you disperse quietly and go to your homes? What do you want here, anyway?"

"Scabs!" yelled a voice, followed by a savage yell from the crowd.

"Men," said the Chief sharply, "you know me. I want this street cleared. I shall return here in five minutes and anyone seeking to stop me will do so at his own risk. I have a hundred men down there and this time they won't give you the soft end of the club."

"We want them sulphurously described scabs," yelled a voice. "We ain't goin' to kill them, Chief. They're lousy. We want to give 'em a bath." And a savage yell of laughter greeted the remark. On every hand the word was taken up: "A bath! A bath! The river! The river!" The savage laughter of the crowd was even more horrible than their rage.

"All right, boys. We are coming back and we are going through. Leave this street clear or take your chances! It's up to you!" So saying, the car was turned about and the party proceeded back to the foundry.

"What are you going to do, Chief?" inquired the Mayor anxiously.

"There are a lot of soldiers in that crowd," said the Chief. "I don't like the looks of them. They are too steady. I hate to smash through them."

Arrived at the foundry, the Chief paced up and down, pondering his problem. He called Maitland to his side.

"How many cars have we here, Maitland?" he inquired.

"Some fifteen, I think. And there are five or six more parked down on the street."

"That would be enough," said the Chief. "I hate the idea of smashing through that crowd. You see, some of those boys went through hell with me and I hate to hurt them."

"Why not try a ruse?" suggested Maitland. "Divide your party. You take five or six cars with constables up the hill to that crowd there. Let me take the strikebreakers and the rest of the cars and make a dash to the right. It's a longer way round but with the streets clear, we can arrive at Headquarters in a very few minutes."

The Chief considered the plan for a few minutes in silence.

"It's a good plan, Maitland," he said at length. "It's a good plan. And we'll put it through. I'll make the feint on the left; you run them through on the right. I believe we can pull it off. Give me a few minutes to engage their attention before you set out."

Everything came off according to plan. As the Chief's detachment of cars approached the solid mass of strikers, they slowly gave back before them.

"Clear the way there!" said the Chief. "We are going through!"

Step by step the crowd gave way, pressed by the approaching cars. Suddenly, at a word of command, the mass opened ranks and the Chief saw before him a barrier across the street, constructed of fencing torn from neighbouring gardens, an upturned delivery wagon, a very ugly and very savage-looking field harrow commandeered from a neighbouring market garden, with wicked-looking, protruding teeth and other debris of varied material, but all helping to produce a most effective barricade. Silently the Chief stood for a few moments, gazing at the obstruction. A curious, ominous growl of laughter ran through the mob. Then came a sharp word of command:

"Unload!"

As with one movement his party of constables were on the ground and lined up in front of their cars, with their clubs and axe handles ready for service. Still the mob waited in ominous silence. The Chief drew his gun and said in a loud, clear voice:

"I am going to clear away this barricade. The first man that offers to prevent me I shall shoot on the spot."

"I wouldn't do that, Chief," said a voice quietly from the rear. "There are others, you know. Listen."

Three shots rang out in rapid succession, and again silence fell.

Meantime from the corner of the barricade a man had been peering into the cars.

"Boys!" he shouted. "They ain't there! There ain't no scabs."

The Chief laughed quietly.

"Who said there were?" he asked.

"Sold, by thunder!" said the man. Then he yelled: "We'll get 'em yet. Come on, boys, to the main street."

Like a deer, he doubled down a side street, followed by the crowd, yelling, cursing, swearing deep oaths.

"Let 'em go," said the Chief. "Maitland's got through by this time." As he spoke, two shots rang out, followed by the crash of glass, and the headlights of the first car went black.

"Just as well you didn't get through, Chief," said the voice of the previous speaker. "Might've got hurt, eh?"

"Give it to him, Chief," said Rupert savagely.

"No use," said the Chief. "Let him go."

Meanwhile, Maitland, with little or no opposition, had got his cars through the crowd, which as a matter of fact were unaware of the identity of the party until after they had broken through.

Their way led by a circuitous route through quiet back streets, approaching Police Headquarters from the rear. A ten-minute run brought them to a short side street which led past the Maitland Mills, at the entrance to which they saw under the glare of the arc lights over the gateway a crowd blocking their way.

"Now, what in thunder is this? Hold up a minute," said Maitland to his driver. "Let me take a look." He ran forward to the main entrance. There he found the gateway, which stood a little above the street level, blocked by a number of his own men, some of whom he recognised as members of his hockey team, and among them, McNish. Out in the street among the crowd stood Simmons, standing on a barrel, lashing himself into a frenzy and demanding blood, fire, revolution, and what not.

"McNish, you here?" said Maitland sharply. "What is it, peace or war? Speak quick!"

"A'm haudden these fules back fra the mill," answered McNish with a scowl. Then, dropping into his book English, he continued bitterly: "They have done enough to-night already. They have wrecked our cause for us!"

"You are dead right, McNish," answered Maitland. "And what do they want here?"

"They are some of McGinnis's men and they are mad at the way you handled them over yonder. They are bound to get in here. They are only waiting for the rest of the crowd. Yon eejit doesn't know what he is saying. They are all half-drunk."

Maitland's mind worked swiftly. "McNish, listen!" he said. "I am in a deuce of a fix. I have the scabs in those cars there with me. The crowd are following me up. What shall I do?"

"My God, man, you're lost. They'll tear ye tae bits."

"McNish, listen. I'll run them into the office by the side gate down the street. Keep them busy here. Let that fool Simmons spout all he wants. He'll help to make a row."

His eyes fell upon a crouching figure at his feet.

"Who is this? It's Sam, by all that's holy! Why, Sam, you are the very chap I want. Listen, boy. Slip around to the side door and open it wide till I bring in some cars. Then shut and bar it quick." Carefully he repeated his instructions. "Can you do it, Sam?"

"I'm awful scared, Captain," replied the boy, his teeth chattering, "but I'll try it."

"Good boy," said Maitland. "Don't fail me, Sam. They might kill me."

"All right, Captain. I'll do it!" And Sam disappeared, crawling under the gate, while Maitland slipped back to his cars and passed the word among the drivers. "Keep close up and stop for nothing!"

They had almost made the entry when some man hanging on the rear of the crowd caught sight of them.

"Scabs! Scabs!" cried the man, dashing after the cars. But Sam was equal to his task, and as the last car passed through the gateway he slammed and bolted the door in their faces.

Disposing of the strike-breakers in the office, Maitland and his guard of specials passed outside to the main gate and took their places beside McNish and his guard. Before them the mob had become a mad, yelling, frenzied thing, bereft of power of thought, swaying under the fury of their passion like tree tops blown by storm, reiterating in hoarse and broken cries the single word "Scabs! Scabs!"

"Keep them going somehow, McNish," said Maitland. "The Chief won't be long now."

McNish climbed up upon the fence and, held in place there by two specials, lifted his hand for silence. But Simmons, who all too obviously had fallen under the spell of the bootleggers, knew too well the peril of his cause. Shrill and savage rose his voice:

"Don't listen to 'im. 'E's a traitor, a blank and double-blank traitor. 'E sold us (h)up, 'e 'as. Don't listen to 'im."

Like a maniac he spat out the words from his foam-flecked lips, waving his arms madly about his head. Relief came from an unexpected source. Sam Wigglesworth, annoyed at Simmons's persistence and observing that McNish, to whom as a labour leader he felt himself bound, regarded the orating and gesticulating Simmons with disfavour, reached down and, pulling a sizable club from beneath the bottom of a fence, took careful aim and, with the accuracy of the baseball pitcher that he was, hurled it at the swaying figure upon the barrel. The club caught Simmons fair in the mouth, who, being, none too firmly set upon his pedestal, itself affording a wobbling foothold, landed spatting and swearing in the arms of his friends below. With the mercurial temper characteristic of a crowd, they burst into a yell of laughter.

"Go to it now, McNish!" said Maitland.

Echoing the laughter, McNish once more held up his hand. "Earth to earth, ashes to ashes," he said in his deepest and most solemn tone. The phenomenal absurdity of a joke from the solemn Scotchman again tickled the uncertain temperament of the crowd into boisterous laughter.

"Men, listen tae me!" cried McNish. "Ye mad a bad mistake the nicht. In fact, ye're a lot of fules. And those who led ye are worse, for they have lost us the strike, if that is any satisfaction tae ye. And now ye want to do another fule thing. Ye're mad just because ye didn't know enough to keep out of the wet."

But at this point, a man fighting his way from the rear of the crowd, once more raised the cry "Scabs!"

"Keep that fool quiet," said McNish sharply.

"Keep quiet yourself, McNish," replied the man, still pushing his way toward the front.

"Heaven help us now," said Maitland. "It's Tony, and drunk at that!"

It was indeed Tony, without hat, coat or vest.

"McNish, we want those scabs," said Tony, in drunken gravity.

"There are nae scabs here. Haud ye're drunken tongue," said McNish savagely.

"McNish," persisted Tony in a grave and perfectly courteous tone, "you're a liar. The scabs are in that office." A roar again swept the crowd.

"Men, listen to me," pleaded McNish. "A'll tell ye about the scabs. They are in the office yonder. But I have Captain Maitland's word o' honour that they will be shipped out of town by the first train."

A savage yell answered him.

"McNish, we'll do the shipping," said Tony, moving still nearer the speaker.

"Officer," said Maitland sharply to a uniformed policeman standing by his side, "arrest that man!" pointing to Tony.

The policeman drew his baton, took two strides forward, seized Tony by the back of the neck and drew him in. An angry yell went up from the mob. Maitland felt a hand upon his arm. Looking down, he saw to his horror and dismay Annette, her face white and stricken with grief and terror.

"Oh, Jack," she pleaded, "don't let Tony be arrested. He broke away from us. Let me take him. He will come with me. Oh, let me take him!"

"Rescue! Rescue!" shouted the crowd, rushing the cordon of police lining the street.

"Kill him! Kill the traitor!" yelled Simmons, struggling through and waving unsteadily the revolver in his hand. "Down with that tyrant, Maitland! Kill him!" he shrieked.

He raised his arm, holding his gun with both hands.

"Look out, Jack," shrieked Annette, flinging herself on him.

Simultaneously with the shot, a woman's scream rang out and Annette fell back into Maitland's arms. A silence deep as death fell upon the mob.

With a groan McNish dropped from the fence beside the girl.

Annette opened her eyes and, looking up into Maitland's face, whispered: "He didn't get you, Jack. I'm so glad."

"Oh, Annette, dear girl! He's killed you!"

"It's—all—right—Jack," she whispered. "I—saved—you."

Meanwhile McNish, with her hand caught in his, was sobbing: "God, have mercy! She's deed! She's deed!"

Annette again opened her eyes. "Poor Malcolm," she whispered. "Dear Malcolm." Then, closing her eyes again, quietly as a tired child, she sank into unconsciousness. The big Scotchman, still kissing her hand, sobbed:

"Puir lassie, puir lassie! Ma God! Ma God! What now? What now?"

"She is dead. The girl is dead." The word passed from lip to lip among the crowd, which still held motionless and silent.

"We'll get her into the office," said Maitland.

"A'll tak her," said McNish, and, stopping down, he lifted her tenderly in his arms, stood for a moment facing the crowd, and then in a voice of unutterable sadness that told of a broken heart, he said: "Ye've killed her. Ye've killed the puir lassie. Are ye content?" And passed in through the gate, holding the motionless form close to his heart.

As he passed with his pathetic burden, the men on guard at the gate bared their heads. Immediately on every hand throughout the crowd men took off their hats and stood silent till he had disappeared from their sight. In the presence of that poignant grief their rage against him ceased, swept out of their hearts by an overwhelming pity.

In one swift instant a door had opened from another and unknown world, and through the open door a Presence, majestic, imperious, had moved in upon them, withering with His icy breath their hot passions, smiting their noisy clamour to guilty silence.

CHAPTER XVI
A GALLANT FIGHT

In the Rectory the night was one long agony of fear and anxiety. Adrien had taken Mrs. Egan and her babe home in a taxi as soon as circumstances would warrant, and then, lest they should alarm their mother, they made pretense of retiring for the night.

After seeing their mother safely bestowed, they slipped downstairs, and, muffling the telephone, sat waiting for news, slipping out now and then to the street, one at a time, to watch the glare of the fire in the sky and to listen for the sounds of rioting from the town.

At length from Victor came news of the tragedy. With whitening face, Adrien took the message. Not for nothing had she walked the wards in France.

"Listen, Victor," she said, speaking in a quick, firm voice. "It is almost impossible to get a nurse in time and quite impossible to get one skilled in this sort of case. Come for me. I shall be ready and shall take charge. Tell Dr. Meredith I am quite free."

"All right. Lose no time."

"Oh, what is it, Adrien?" said Patricia, wringing her hands. "Is it Jack? Or Victor?"

Adrien caught her by the shoulders: "Patricia, I want your help. No talk! Come with me. I will tell you as I dress."

Swiftly, with no hurry or flurry, Adrien changed into her uniform, packed her bag, giving Patricia meantime the story of the tragedy which she had heard over the telephone.

"And to think it might have been Jack," said Patricia, wringing her hands. "Oh, dear, dear Annette. Can't I help in some way, Adrien?"

"Patricia, listen to me, child. The first thing is keep your head. You can help me greatly. You will take charge here and later, perhaps, you can help me in other ways. Meantime you must assume full responsibility for them all here. Much depends on you!"

The girl stood gazing with wide-open blue eyes at her sister. Then quietly she answered:

"I'll do my best, Adrien. There's Vic." She rushed swiftly downstairs. Suddenly she stopped, steadied her pace, and received him with a calm that surprised that young man beyond measure.

"Adrien is quite ready, Vic," she said.

"Topping," said Vic. "What a brick she is! Dr. Meredith didn't know where to turn for a nurse. The hospital is full. Every nurse is engaged. So much sickness, you know, in town. Ah, here she is. You are a lightning-change artist, Adrien."

"How is Annette, Vic? Is she still living?" asked Patricia.

"I don't know," replied Vic, wondering at the change in the girl before him.

"Darling," said Adrien, "I will let you know at once. I hate to leave you."

"Leave me!" cried Patricia. "Nonsense, Adrien, I shall be quite all right. Only," she added, clasping her hands, "let me know when you can."

When the ambulance arrived at the Maitland home, Adrien was at the door. All was in readiness—hot water, bandages, and everything needful to the doctor's hand.

McNish carried Annette up to the room prepared for her, laid her down and stood in dumb grief looking down upon her.

Adrien touched him on the arm.

"Come," she said. And, taking his arm, led him downstairs. "Stay here," she said. "I will bring you word as soon as possible."

An hour later she returned, and found him sitting in the exact position in which she had left him. He apparently had not moved hand or foot. At her entrance he looked up, eager, voiceless.

"She is resting," said Adrien. "The bullet is extracted. It had gone quite through to the outer skin—a clean wound."

"How long," said McNish, passing his tongue over his dry lips, "how long does the doctor say—"

"The doctor says nothing. She asked for you."

McNish started up and went toward the door.

"But you cannot go to her now."

"She asked for me?" said McNish.

"Yes. But she must be kept quite quiet. The very least excitement might hurt her."

"Hurt her?" said McNish, and sat down quietly.

After a moment's silence, he said:

"You will let me see her—once more—before she—she—" He paused, his lips quivering, his great blue eyes pitifully beseeching her.

"Mr. McNish," said Adrien, "she may not die."

"Ma God!" he whispered, falling on his knees and catching her hand in both of his. "Ma God! Dinna lee tae me."

"Believe me, I would not," said Adrien, while the great eyes seemed to drag the truth from her very soul. "The doctor says nothing, but I have seen many cases of bullet wounds, and I have hope."

"Hope," he whispered. "Hope! Ma God! hope!" His hands went to his face and his great frame shook with silent sobbing.

"But you must be very quiet and steady."

Immediately he was on his feet and standing like a soldier at attention.

"Ay, A wull," he whispered eagerly. "Tell me what tae do?"

"First of all," said Adrien, "we must have something to eat."

A shudder passed through him. "Eat?" he said, as if he had never heard the word.

"Yes," said Adrien. "Remember, you promised."

"Ay. A'll eat." Like a man under a mesmeric spell, he went through the motions of eating. His mind was far away, his eyes eager, alert, forever upon her face.

When they had finished their meal, Adrien said:

"Now, Mr. McNish, is there anything I can do for you?"

"A would like to send word to ma mither," he said. "She disna ken onything—aboot—aboot Annette—aboot Annette an' me," a faint touch of red coming slowly up in his grey face.

"I shall get word to her. I know the very man. I shall phone the Reverend Murdo Matheson."

"Ay," said McNish, "he is the man."

"Now, then," said Adrien, placing him in an easy chair, "you must rest there. Remember, I am keeping watch."

With the promise that he would do his best to rest, she left him sitting bolt upright in his chair.

Toward morning, Maitland appeared, weary and haggard. Adrien greeted him with tender solicitude; it was almost maternal in its tone.

"Oh, Adrien," said Maitland, with a great sight of relief, "you don't know how good it is to see you here. It bucks one tremendously to feel that you are on this job."

"I shall get you some breakfast immediately," she answered in a calm, matter-of-fact voice. "You are done out. Your father has come in and has gone to lie down. McNish is in the library."

"And Annette?" said Maitland. He was biting his lips to keep them from quivering. "Is she still—"

"She is resting. The maid is watching beside her. Dear Jack," she uttered with a quick rush of sympathy, "I know how hard this is for you. But I am not without hope for Annette."

A quick light leaped into his eyes. "Hope, did you say? Oh, thank the good Lord." His voice broke and he turned away from her. "You know," he said, coming back, "she gave her life for me. Oh, Adrien, think of it! She threw herself in the way of death for me. She covered me with her own body." He sat down suddenly as if almost in collapse, and buried his head in his arms, struggling for control.

Adrien went to him and put her arm round his shoulder—she might have been his mother. "Dear Jack," she said, "it was a wonderful thing she did. God will surely spare her to you."

He rose wearily from his chair and put his arms around her.

"Oh, Adrien," he said, "it is good to have you here. I do need, we all need you so."

Gently she put his arms away from her. "And now," she said briskly, "I am going to take charge of you, Jack, of you all, and you must obey orders."

"Only give me a chance to do anything for you," he said, "or for anyone you care for."

There was a puzzled expression on Adrien's face as she turned away. But she asked no explanation.

"My first order, then," she said, "is this: you must have your breakfast and then go to bed for an hour or two."

"I shall be glad to breakfast, but I have a lot of things to do."

"Can't they wait? And won't you do them better after a good sleep?"

"Some of them can't wait," he replied. "I have just got Tony to bed. The doctor has sent him to sleep. His father and mother are watching him. Oh, Adrien, that is a sad home. It was a terrible experience for me. Tony I must see when he wakes and the poor old father and mother will be over here early. I must be ready for them."

"Very well, Jack," said Adrien in a prompt, businesslike tone. "You have two clear hours for sleep. You must sleep for the sake of others, you understand. I promise to wake you in good time."

"And what about yourself, Adrien?"

"Oh, this is my job," she said lightly. "I shall be relieved in the afternoon, the doctor has promised."

When the Employers' Defence Committee met next morning there were many haggard faces among its members. In the large hall outside the committee room a considerable number of citizens, young and old, had gathered and with them the Mayor, conversing in voices tinged with various emotions, anxiety, pity, wrath, according to the temper and disposition of each.

In the committee room Mr. Farrington was in the chair. No sooner had the meeting been called to order than Mr. Maitland arose, and, speaking under deep but controlled feeling, he said:

"Gentlemen, I felt sure none of us would wish to transact ordinary business this morning. I was sure, too, that in the very distressing circumstances under which we meet you would feel as I do the need of guidance and help. I therefore took the liberty of inviting the deputation from the Ministerial Association which waited on us the other day to join us in our deliberation. Mr. Haynes is away from town, but Dr. Templeton and Mr. Matheson have kindly consented to be present. They will be here in half an hour's time."

A general and hearty approval of his action was expressed, after which the Chairman invited suggestions as to the course to be pursued. But no one was ready with a suggestion. Somehow the outlook upon life was different this morning, and readjustment of vision appeared to be necessary. No man felt himself qualified to offer advice.

From this dilemma they were relieved by a knock upon the door and the Mayor appeared.

"Gentlemen," he said, "I have no wish to intrude, but a great many of our citizens are in the larger hall. They are anxious to be advised upon the present trying situation. It has been suggested that your committee might join with us in a general public meeting."

After a few moments' consideration, the Mayor's proposition was accepted and the committee adjourned to the larger hall, Mr. Farrington resigning the chair to His Worship, the Mayor.

The Mayor's tongue was not so ready this morning. He explained the circumstances of the meeting and thanked the committee for yielding to his request. He was ready to receive any suggestions as to what the next step should be.

The silence which followed was broken by Mr. McGinnis, who arose and, in a voice much shaken, he inquired:

"Can anyone tell us just what is the last word concerning the young girl this morning?"

Mr. Maitland replied: "Before I left the house, the last report was that she was resting quietly and, while the doctor was not able to offer any hope of her recovery, he ventured to say that he did not quite despair. And that from Dr. Meredith, as we know, means something."

"Thank God for that," said McGinnis, and leaning his head upon his hand, he sat with his eyes fixed upon the floor.

Again the Mayor asked for suggestions, but no one in the audience appeared willing to assume the responsibility of offering guidance.

At length Rupert Stillwell arose. He apologised for speaking in the presence of older men, but something had to be done and he ventured to offer one suggestion at least.

"It occurs to me," he said, "that one thing at least should be immediately done. Those responsible for the disgraceful riot of last evening, and I mean more than the actual ringleaders in the affair, should be brought to justice." He proceeded to elaborate upon the enormity of the crime, the danger to the State of mob rule, the necessity for stern measures to prevent the recurrence of such disorders. He suggested a special citizens' committee for the preservation of public order.

His words appeared to meet the approval of a large number of those present, especially of the younger men.

While he was speaking, the audience appeared to be greatly relieved to see Dr. Templeton and the Reverend Murdo Matheson walk in and quietly take their seats. They remembered, many of them, how at a recent similar

To Him That Hath | 197

gathering these gentlemen had advised a procedure which, if followed, would have undoubtedly prevented the disasters of the previous night.

Giving a brief account of the proceedings of the meeting to the present point, the Mayor suggested that Dr. Templeton might offer them a word of advice.

Courteously thanking the Mayor for his invitation, the Doctor said:

"As I came in this room, I caught the words of my young friend, who suggested a committee for the preservation of public order. May I suggested that the preservation of public order in the community is something that can be entrusted to no committee? It rests with the whole community. We have all made mistakes, we are constantly making mistakes. We have yielded to passion, and always to our sorrow and hurt. We have vainly imagined that by the exercise of force we can settle strife. No question of right or justice is settled by fighting, for, after the fighting is done, the matter in dispute remains to be settled. We have tried that way and to-day we are fronted with disastrous failure. I have come from a home over which the shadow of death hangs low. There a father and mother lie prostrate with sorrow, agonising for the life of their child. But a deeper shadow lies there, a shadow of sin, for the sting of death is sin. A brother torn with self-condemnation, his heart broken with grief for his sister, who loved him better than her own life, lies under that shadow of sin. But, gentlemen, can any of us escape from that shadow? Do we not all share in that sin? For we all have a part in the determining of our environment. Can we not, by God's grace, lift that shadow at least from our lives? Let us turn our faces from the path of strife toward the path of peace, for the pathway of right doing and of brotherly kindness is the only path to peace in this world."

The Chairman then called upon the Reverend Murdo Matheson to express his mind. But at this point, the whole audience were galvanised into an intensity of confused emotion by the entrance of the Executive of the Allied Unions, led by McNish himself. Simmons alone was absent, being at that moment, with some half dozen others, in the care of the police. Silently the Executive Committee walked to the front and found seats, McNish alone remaining standing. Grey, gaunt, hollow-eyed, he met with steady gaze the eyes of the audience, some of them aflame with hostile wrath, for in him they recognised the responsible head of the labour movement that had wrought such disaster and grief in the community.

Without apology or preface McNish began: "I am here seeking peace," he said, in his hoarse, hard, guttural voice. "I have made mistakes. Would I could suffer for them alone, but no, others must suffer with me. I have only condemnation for the outrages of last night. We repudiate them, we lament them. We tried to prevent them, but human passion and circumstances were too strong for us. We would undo the ill—would to God could undo the ill. How gladly would I suffer all that has come to others." His deep, harsh voice shook under the stress of his emotion. He lifted his head: "I cannot deny my cause," he continued, his voice ringing out clear. "Our cause was right, but the spirit was wrong." He paused a few moments, evidently gathering strength to hold his voice steady. "Yes, the spirit was wrong and this day is a black day to me. We come to ask for peace. God knows I have no heart for war."

Again he paused, his strong stern face working strangely under the stress of the emotions which he was fighting to subdue. "We suggest a committee of three, with powers to arbitrate, and we name as our man one who till recently was one of our Union, a man of fair and honest mind, a man without fear and with a heart for his comrades. Our man is Captain Maitland."

His words, and especially the name of the representative of the labour unions produced an overwhelming effect upon the audience. No sooner had he finished than the Reverend Murdo Matheson took the floor. He spoke no economics. He offered no elaborate argument for peace. In plain, simple words he told of experiences through which he had recently passed:

"Like one whom I feel it an honour to call my father," he began, bowing toward Dr. Templeton, "I, too, have made a visit this morning. Not to a home, but to a place the most unlike a home of any spot in this sad world, a jail. Seven of our fellow-citizens are confined there, six of them boys, mere boys, dazed and penetrated with sorrow for their folly—they meant no crime—I am not relieving them of the blame—the other, a man, embittered with a long, hard fight against poverty, injustice and cruel circumstance in another land, with distorted views of life, crazed by drink, committed a crime which this morning fills him with horror and grief. Late last night I was sent to the home of one of my people. There I found an aged lady, carrying with a brave heart the sorrows and burdens of nearly seventy years, waiting in anxiety and grief and fear for her son, who was keeping vigil at what may well be the deathbed of the girl he loves. You have just heard his plea for peace. Some of you are inclined to lay the blame for the ills that have fallen upon us upon certain classes and individuals in this community. They have their blame and they must bear the responsibility. But, gentlemen, a juster estimate of the causes of these ills will convince us that they are the product of our civilisation and for these things we must all accept our share of responsibility. More, we must seek to remove them from among us. They are an affront to our intelligence, an insult to our holy religion, an outrage upon the love of our brother man and our Father, God.

Let us humbly, resolutely seek the better way, the way we have set before us this morning, the way of right doing, of brotherly kindness and of brotherly love which is the way of peace."

It was a subdued company of men that listened to his appeal. In silence they sat looking straight before them with faces grave and frowning, as is the way with men of our race when deeply stirred.

It was a morning of dramatic surprises, but none were so startling, none so dramatic as the speech of McGinnis that followed.

"This is a day for confessions," he said, "and I am here to make one for myself. I have been a fighter, too much of a fighter, all my life, and I have often suffered for it. I suffered a heavy loss last night and to-day I am sick of fighting. But I have found this: that you can't fight men in this world without fighting women and children, too. God knows I have no war with the old, grey-haired lady the Padre has just told us about. I have no war with that broken-hearted father and mother. And I have no war with Annette Perrotte, dear girl, God preserve her." At this point, McGinnis's command quite forsook him. His voice utterly broke down, while the tears ran down his rugged fighting face. "I am done with fighting," he cried. "They have named Captain Maitland. We know him for a straight man and a white man. Let me talk with Captain Jack Maitland, and let us get together with the Padre there," pointing to the Reverend Murdo Matheson, "and in an hour we will settle this matter."

In a tumult of approval the suggestion was accepted. It was considered a perfectly fitting thing, though afterwards men spoke of it with something of wonder, that the Mayor should have called upon the Reverend Doctor to close the meeting with prayer, and that he should do so without making a speech.

That same afternoon the three men met to consider the matter submitted to them. Captain Jack Maitland laid before the committee his figures and his charts setting forth the facts in regard to the cost of living and the wage scale during the past five years. In less than an hour they had agreed upon a settlement. There was to be an increase of wages in keeping with the rise of the cost of living, with the pledge that the wage scale should follow the curb of the cost of living should any change occur within the year. The hours of labour were shortened from ten to nine for a day's work, with the pledge that they should be governed by the effect of the change upon production and general conditions. And further, that a Committee of Reference should be appointed for each shop and craft, to which all differences should be submitted. To this committee also were referred the other demands by the Allied Unions.

It was a simple solution of the difficulty and upon its submission to the public meeting called for its consideration, it was felt that the comment of the irrepressible Victor Forsythe was not entirely unfitting:

"Of course!" said Victor, cheerfully. "It is the only thing. Why didn't the Johnnies think of it before, or why didn't they ask me?"

The committee, however, did more than settle the dispute immediately before them. They laid before the public meeting and obtained its approval for the creation of a General Board of Industry, under whose guidance the whole question of the industrial life of the community should be submitted to intelligent study and control.

CHAPTER XVII
SHALL BE GIVEN

For one long week of seven long days and seven long nights Annette fought out her gallant fight for life, fought and won. Throughout the week at her side Adrien waited day and night, except for a few hours snatched for rest, when Patricia took her place, for there was not a nurse to be had in all that time and Patricia begged for the privilege of sharing her vigil with her.

Every day and in the darkest days all day long, it seemed to Adrien, McNish haunted the Maitland home—for he had abandoned all pretence of work—his gaunt, grey face and hollow eyes imploring a word of hope.

But it was chiefly to Jack throughout that week that Adrien's heart went out in compassionate pity, for in his face there dwelt a misery so complete, so voiceless that no comfort of hers appeared to be able to bring relief. Often through those days did Annette ask to see him, but the old doctor was relentless. There must be absolute quiet and utter absence of all excitement. No visitors were to be permitted, especially no men visitors.

But the day came when the ban was lifted and with smiling face, Adrien came for Jack.

"You have been such a good boy," she cried gaily, "that I am going to give you a great treat. You are to come in with me."

With face all alight Jack followed her into the sick room.

"Here he is, Annette," cried Adrien. "Now, remember, no fussing, no excitement, and just one quarter of an hour—or perhaps a little longer," she added.

For a moment or two Jack stood looking at the girl lying upon the bed.

"Oh, Annette, my dear, dear girl," he cried in a breaking voice as he knelt down by her side and took her hand in his.

So much reached Adrien's ears as she closed the door and passed to her room with step weary and lifeless.

"Why, Adrien," cried her sister, who was waiting to relieve her, "you are like a ghost! You poor dear. You are horribly done out."

"I believe I am, Patricia," said Adrien. "I believe I shall rest awhile." She lay down on the bed, her face turned toward the wall, and so remained till Patricia went softly away, leaving her, as she thought, to sleep.

Downstairs Patricia found Victor Forsythe awaiting her.

"Poor Adrien is really used up," she said. "She has a deathly look in her face. Just the same look as she had that night of the hockey match. Do you remember?"

"The night of the hockey dance? Do I remember? A ghastly night—a horrid night—a night of unspeakable wretchedness."

As Vic was speaking, Patricia kept her eyes steadily upon him with a pondering, puzzled look.

"What is it, Patricia? I know you want to ask me something. Is it about that night?"

"I wonder if you would really mind very much, Vic, if I asked you?"

"Not in the very least. I shall doubtless enjoy it after it's out. Painless dentistry effect. Go to it, Patsy."

"It is very serious, Vic. I always think people in books are so stupid. They come near to the truth and then just miss getting it."

"The truth. Ah! Go on, Pat."

"Well, Vic," said Patricia with an air of one taking a desperate venture, "why did you not give Adrien her note that night? It would have saved her and me such pain. I cried all night long. I had so counted on a dance with Jack—and then never a word from him. But he did send a note. He told me so. I never told Adrien that, for she forbade me, oh, so terribly, never to speak of it again. Why didn't you give her or me the note, Vic?" Patricia's voice was very pathetic and her eyes very gentle but very piercing.

All the laughter died out of Victor's face. "Pat, I lied to you once, only once, and that lie has cost me many an hour's misery. But now I shall tell you the truth and the whole truth." And he proceeded to recount the tribulations which he endured on the night of the hockey dance. "I did it to help you both out, Pat. I thought I could make it easy for you. It was all a sheer guess, but it turned out to be pretty well right."

Patricia nodded her head. "But you received no note?"

"Not a scrap, Patricia, so help me. Not a scrap. Patricia, you believe me?"

The girl looked straight into Vic's honest eyes. "Yes, Vic," she said, "I believe you. But Jack sent a note."

Vic sprang to his feet. "Good-bye, Watson. You shall hear from me within an hour."

"Whatever do you mean? Where are you going?"

"Dear lady, ask no questions. I am about to Sherlock. Farewell."

At the door he overtook Jack. "Aha! The first link in the chain. Hello, old chap, a word with you. May I get into your car?"

"Certainly. Get in."

"Now then, about that note. Nothing like diplomacy. The night of the hockey dance you sent a note to a lady?"

Jack glanced at him in amazement.

"Don't be an ass, Vic. I don't feel like that stuff just now."

"This is serious. Did you send a note by me that night of the hockey dance?"

"By you? No. Who said I did?"

"Aha! The mystery deepens. By whom? Nothing like finesse."

"It is none of your business," said Jack crossly.

"Check," cried Vic.

"What are you talking about, anyway?" inquired Jack.

"A note was sent by you," said Vic impressively, "through some agency at present unknown. So far, so good."

"Unknown? What rubbish. I sent a note by Sam Wigglesworth, who gave it to some of you for Adrien. What about it?"

As they approached the entrance to the Maitland Mills Vic saw a stream of employees issue from the gate.

"Nothing more at present," he said. "This is my corner. Let me out. I am in an awful hurry, Jack."

"Will you tell me, please, what all this means?" said Jack angrily.

"Sorry, old chap. Awfully hurried just now. See you later."

"You are a vast idiot," grumbled Jack, as Vic ran down the street.

He took his place at the corner which commanded the entrance to the Maitland works. "Here I shall wait, abstractedly gazing at the passers-by, until the unhappy Sam makes his appearance," mused Vic to himself. "And by the powers, here Sam is now."

From among the employees as they poured from the gate Victor pounced upon his victim and bore him away down a side street.

"Sam," he said, "it may be you are about to die, so tell me the truth. I hate to take your young life." Sam grinned at his captor, unafraid. "Cast your mind back to the occasion of the hockey dance. You remember that?"

"You bet I do, Mister. I made a dollar that night."

"Ah! A dollar. Yes, you did, for delivering a note given you by Captain Jack Maitland," hissed Vic, gripping his arm.

"Huh-huh," said Sam. "Look out, Mister, that's me."

"Villain!" cried Vic. "Boy, I mean. Now, Sam, did you deliver that note?"

"Of course I did. Didn't Captain Jack give me a dollar for it? I didn't want his dollar."

"The last question, Sam," said Vic solemnly, "to whom did you deliver the note?"

"To that chap, the son of the storekeeper."

"Rupert Stillwell?" suggested Vic.

"Huh-huh, that's his name. That's him now," cried Sam. "In that Hudson car—see—there—quick!"

"Boy," said Vic solemnly, "you have saved your life. Here's a dollar. Now, remember, not a word about this."

"All right, sir," grinned Sam delightedly, as he made off down the street.

"Now then, what?" said Vic to himself. "This thing has got past the joke stage. I must do some thinking. Shall I tell Pat or not? By Jove, by Jove, that's not the question. When that young lady gets those big eyes of hers on me the truth will flow in a limpid stream. I must make sure of my ground. Meantime I shall do the Kamerad act."

That afternoon Annette had another visitor. Her nurse, though somewhat dubious as to the wisdom of this indulgence, could not bring herself to refuse her request that McNish should be allowed to see her.

"But you must be tired. Didn't Jack tire you?" inquired Adrien.

A soft and tender light stole into the girl's dark eyes.

"Ah, Jack. He could not tire me," she murmured. "He makes so much of what I did. How gladly would I do it again. Jack is wonderful to me. Wonderful to me," she repeated softly. Her lip trembled and she lay back upon her pillow and from her closed eyes two tears ran down her cheek.

"Now," said Adrien briskly, "you are too tired. We shall wait till to-morrow."

"No, no, please," cried Annette. "Jack didn't tire me. He comforts me."

"But Malcolm will tire you," said Adrien. "Do you really want to see him?"

A faint colour came up into the beautiful face of her patient.

"Yes, Adrien, I really want to see him. I am sure he will do me good. You will let him come, please?" The dark eyes were shining with another light, more wistful, more tender.

"Is he here, Adrien?"

"Is he here?" echoed Adrien scornfully. "Has he been anywhere else the last seven days?"

"Poor Malcolm," said the girl, the tenderness in her voice becoming protective. "I have been very bad to him, and he loves me so. Oh, he is just mad about me!" A little smile stole round the corners of her mouth.

"Oh, you needn't tell me that, Annette," said Adrien. "It is easy for you to make men mad about you."

"Not many," said the girl, still softly smiling.

McNish went toward the door of the sick room as if approaching a holy shrine, walking softly and reverently.

"Go in, lucky man," said Adrien. "Go in, and thank God for your good fortune."

He paused at the door, turned about and looked at her with grave eyes. "Miss Templeton," he said in slow, reverent tones, "all my life shall I thank God for His great mercy tae me."

"Don't keep her waiting, man," said Adrien, waving him in. Then McNish went in and she closed the door softly upon them.

"There are only a few great moments given to men," she said, "and this is one of them for those two happy people."

In ten days Annette was pronounced quite fit to return to her family. But Patricia resolved that they should have a grand fete in the Maitland home before Annette should leave it. She planned a motor drive in the cool of the day, and in the evening all their special friends who had been brought together through the tragic events of the past weeks should come to bring congratulations and mutual felicitations for the recovery of the patient.

Patricia was arranging the guest list, in collaboration with Mr. Maitland and the assistance of Annette and Victor.

"We will have our boys, of course," she began.

"Old and young, I hope?" suggested Mr. Maitland.

"Of course!" she cried. "Although I don't know any old ones. That will mean all the fathers and Vic, Jack, Hugh and Rupert, and Malcolm—"

"Ah! It has come to Malcolm, then?" murmured Vic. "Certainly, why not? He loves me to call him Malcolm. And then we will have Mr. Matheson. And we must have Mr. McGinnis—they have become such great friends. And I should like to have the Mayor, he is so funny. But perhaps he wouldn't fit. He DOES take up a lot of attention."

"Cut him out!" said Victor with decision.

"And for ladies," continued Patricia, "just the relatives—all the mothers and the sisters. That's enough."

"How lovely!" murmured Vic.

"Oh, if you want any other ladies, Vic," said Patricia severely, "we shall be delighted to invite them for you."

"Me? Other ladies? What could I do with other ladies? Is not my young life one long problem as it is? Ah! Speaking of problems, that reminds me. I have a communication to make to you young lady." Vic's manner suggested a profound and deadly mystery. He led Patricia away from the others. "I have something to tell you, Patricia," he said, abandoning all badinage. "I hate to do it but it is right for you, for myself, for Adrien, and by Jove for poor old Jack, too. Though, perhaps—well, let that go."

"Oh, Vic!" cried Patricia. "It is about the note!"

"Yes, Patricia. That note was given by Jack to Sam Wigglesworth, who gave it to Rupert Stillwell."

"And he forgot?" gasped Patricia.

"Ah—ah—at least, he didn't deliver it. No, Patricia, we are telling the whole truth. He didn't forget. You remember he asked about Jack. There, I have given you all I know. Make of it what you like."

"Shall I tell Adrien?" asked Patricia.

"I think certainly Adrien ought to know."

"Then I'll tell her to-night," said Patricia. "I want it all over before our fete, which is day after to-morrow."

Rupert Stillwell had been in almost daily attendance upon Adrien during the past two weeks, calling for her almost every afternoon with his car. The day following he came for her according to his custom. Upon Adrien's face there dwelt a gentle, tender, happy look as if her heart were singing for very joy. That look upon her face drove from Rupert all the hesitation and fear which had fallen upon him during these days of her ministry to the wounded girl. He took a sudden and desperate resolve that he would put his fate to the test.

Adrien's answer was short and decisive.

"No, Rupert," she said. "I cannot. I thought for a little while, long ago, that perhaps I might, but now I know that I never could have loved you."

"You were thinking of that note of Jack Maitland's which I sent you last night?"

"Oh, no," she said gently. "Not that."

"I felt awfully mean about that, Adrien. I feel mean still. I thought that as you had learned all about it from Victor, it was of no importance."

"Yes," she replied gently, "but I was the best judge of that."

"Adrien, tell me," Rupert's voice shook with the intensity of his passion, "is there no hope?"

"No," she said, "there is no hope, Rupert."

"There is someone else," he said, savagely.

"Yes," she said, happily, "I think so."

"Someone," continued Rupert, his voice trembling with rage, "someone who distributes his affections."

"No," she said, a happy smile in her eyes, "I think not."

"You love him?" he asked.

"Oh, yes," she whispered, with a little catch in her breath, "I love him."

At the door on their return Jack met them. A shadow fell upon his face, but with a quick resolve, he shouted a loud welcome to them.

"Hello, Adrien," he cried, as she came running up the steps. "You apparently have had a lovely drive."

"Oh, wonderful, Jack. A wonderful drive," she replied.

"Yes, you do look happy."

"Oh, so happy. I was never so happy."

"Then," said Jack, dropping his voice, "may I congratulate you?"

"Yes, I think so," she said. "I hope so." And then laughed aloud for very glee.

Jack turned from her with a quick sharp movement, went down the steps and offering his hand to Rupert, said:

"Good luck, old chap. I wish you good luck."

"Eh? What? Oh, all right," said Rupert in a dazed sort of way. But he didn't come into the house.

Never was there such a day in June, never such a fete. The park never looked so lovely and never a party so gay disported themselves in it and gayest of them all was Adrien. All day long it seemed as if her very soul were laughing for joy. And all day long she kept close beside Jack, chaffing him, laughing at him, rallying him on his solemn face and driving him half-mad with her gay witchery.

Then home they all came to supper, where waited them McNish and his mother with Mr. McGinnis, for they had been unable to join in the motor drive.

"Ma certie, lassie! But ye're a sight for sare een. What hae ye bin daein tae her, Mr. Jack," said Mrs. McNish, as she welcomed them at the door.

"The Lord only knows," said Jack.

"But, man, look at her!" exclaimed the old lady.

"I have been, all day long," replied Jack with a gallant attempt at gaiety.

"Oh, Mrs. McNish," cried the girl, rippling with joyous laughter, "he won't even look at me. He just—what do you say—glowers, that's it—glowers at me. And we have had such a wonderful day. Come, Jack, get yourself ready for supper. You have only a few minutes."

She caught her arm through his and laughing shamelessly into his eyes, drew him away.

"I say, Adrien," said Jack, driven finally to desperation and drawing her into the quiet of the library, "I am awfully glad you are so happy and all that, but I don't see the necessity of rubbing it into a fellow. You know how I feel. I am glad for you and—I am glad for Rupert. Or, at least I told him so."

"But, Jack," said the girl, her eyes burning with a deep inner glow, "Rupert has nothing to do with it. Rupert, indeed," and she laughed scornfully. "Oh, Jack, why can't you see?"

"See what?" he said crossly.

"Jack," she said softly, turning toward him and standing very near him, "you remember the note you sent me?"

"Note?"

"The note you sent the night of the hockey dance?"

"Yes," said Jack bitterly, "I remember."

"And you remember, too, how horrid I was to you the next time I saw you? How horrid? Oh, Jack, it broke my heart." Her voice faltered a moment and her shining eyes grew dim. "I was so horrid to you."

"Oh, no," said Jack coolly, "you were kind. You were very kind and sisterly, as I remember."

"Jack," she said and her breath began to come hurriedly, "I got that note yesterday. Only yesterday, Jack."

"Yesterday?"

"Yes, only yesterday. And I read it, Jack," she added with a happy laugh. "And in that note, Jack, you said—do you remember—"

But Jack stood gazing stupidly at her. She pulled the note from her bosom.

"Oh, Jack, you said—"

Still Jack gazed at her.

"Jack, you will kill me. Won't you hurry? Oh, I can't wait a moment longer. You said you were going to tell me something, Jack." She stood radiant, breathless and madly alluring. "And oh, Jack, won't you tell me?"

"Adrien," said Jack, his voice husky and uncontrolled. "Do you mean that you—"

"Oh, Jack, tell me quick," she said, swaying toward him. And while she clung to him taking his kisses on her lips, Jack told her.